Broken Passions

Also by Ger Gallagher

A Life Left Untold

Broken Passions

GER GALLAGHER

POOLBEG

Published 2006
by Poolbeg Press Ltd
123 Grange Hill, Baldoyle
Dublin 13, Ireland
E-mail: poolbeg@poolbeg.com

1 3 5 7 9 10 8 6 4 2

A catalogue record for this book is available from the British Library.

ISBN 1-84223-262-2
ISBN 978-184223-262-0 (From January 2007)

Typeset by Type Design in Garamond 12/15
Printed by Litografia Rosés S.A., Spain

www.poolbeg.com

About the Author

Ger Gallagher lives in Dublin with her husband and two daughters.

Acknowledgements

During the writing of this book I was very fortunate to encounter a number of people who generously gave their time and shared their knowledge about Dublin in the 1920's.

I am indebted to Niamh O'Sullivan, Archivist of Kilmainham Gaol, who was so kind to me when I started out with this book.

A very special thanks must go to Mr Tony Behan for sharing his wealth of information and taking time out to give me a guided tour of the Four Courts; the National Transport Museum, for their e-mails and route maps on tram lines of the period; Ms Alex Ward, from the National Museum, for providing me with notes and drawings of 1920's fashions; Mr Raphael Siev from the Dublin Jewish Museum for assisting me with my queries; my uncle and historian, Mr Fergus Martin, for his great stories of that time.

To the wonderful people at the Tyrone Guthrie Centre, Annaghmakerrig – thank you for your kindness in providing the peace and tranquillity that enabled me to work on this book.

On a more personal note, I would like to thank my

immediate and extended family, who I am blessed with.

My husband Paul, to whom this book is dedicated.

My girls, Jessie and Eve, who I love so much.

Last, but by no means least, a huge thanks to my editor
Gaye Shortland, Paula Campbell and everyone at Poolbeg.

For Paul, my first, my last — my everything.

Chapter 1

Dublin 1921

Anna Barry chose to walk along the grass verge of the Grand Canal. It was usual for her to take the path that ran alongside the row of houses which led to her front door on Portobello Road, but the fashionable new shoes she was wearing had cut into the back of both heels and every step of the journey from the tram had been agony. Hoping no one would notice, she had slipped the stiff black leather shoes off, and put them into the shopping bag that hung from her wrist. The grass was long, almost reaching her ankles and the soft carpet it provided felt like a balm to her throbbing feet. She reached an empty bench and sank down onto it, dropping the bag that contained the shoes and groceries she had bought for the tea on her way home. Anna knew that her father and brother would be sitting at home waiting to be fed, but she allowed herself a few minutes' peace before she went in. The canal water sparkled as rays of mellow evening light shone down from between the trees on the other side of the bank. Anna closed her eyes, enjoying the warmth that spread across her face. May was her favourite month of the year. She loved to see the leaves make a welcome return to the trees, and the evenings begin to grow longer. May had also been the month of her mother's birthday. Anna sighed and shut her eyes more tightly, trying to summon an image of her mother to mind. Sometimes it worked and within seconds her mother would appear – her dark brown eyes creased in the familiar smile that Anna knew so well, her black hair, streaked with strands of silver, neatly pinned back. Sometimes nothing came, just a blank space. The evening sun created an orange glow behind Anna's eyelids, and she could see her mother's face bathed in the soft light.

Another few days and she would have been forty-seven. Anna probably would have bought her a new pair of shoes, or a handbag. It was four years since she had died, but Anna still missed her as if it was yesterday. It was different for her father and brother – they missed her as well, but in a more needy way. They missed the comfort she had provided. The fires set, the shirts pressed, the dinners always ready. The house just wasn't the same without her. Anna had gone some way towards taking over the role of homemaker, trying to keep the place nice and tidy the way her mother had – always having a clean shirt ready for her father and a hot dinner in the evenings. But sometimes it felt so lonely. Anna missed the friend as well as the mother that she had lost. She used to love when her brother and father went off together to the pub; they were the nights that she would sit in with her mother and talk for hours with no interruptions.

A loud shout made Anna jump from her quiet thoughts.

"Anna! Is that you?"

She turned around and saw her brother hanging from the window of his bedroom at the front of the house.

Grabbing her shoes from the bag, she wriggled into them, wincing at the fresh wave of pain that shot through her feet.

"What are you doing there?" shouted Seán, waving at her from the open window.

Anna looked around quickly to see if any of the neighbours could see her brother roaring like a lunatic, but the street was deserted. She looked up at him and brought a finger to her pursed lips, in an attempt to silence him.

Seán shot down the stairs as Anna turned her key in the front door. "Where were you? We're starving."

Anna kicked off the offending shoes once again and put her feet into a pair of comfortable slippers. "I had to lock up this evening. Mr Jacob went home sick. Anyway, if you're starving, why didn't you make yourself some tea?"

Seán took the shopping bag from the floor and stuck his head in to examine the contents.

"There's nothing in the house to eat," he grumbled.

"You could have gone around to the shops and got something," said Anna, pulling the bag from him.

"I haven't a shillin'. I don't get paid for another two days."

"Oh, for heaven's sake! You know Mr Slattery would let you have a few rashers on credit. You're just a lazy lump, waiting for me to come in and make it for you."

Anna brushed by him and walked down to the kitchen where her father was sitting in his chair by the fire, rolling a cigarette.

"Here she is!" he exclaimed, looking up from his tobacco pouch. "We thought you'd got lost."

Anna let the bag fall onto the kitchen table and taking her apron from the hook on the back of the door she put it over her head wearily and tied the strings behind her back.

"Hello, Dada, I'm sorry I'm so late. I had to lock up this evening. Mr Jacob went home sick this afternoon."

"What was wrong with the poor man?"

"He had a pain in his head."

Anna reached for a frying pan and set it on the cooker, took the rashers and eggs from the shopping bag and proceeded to cook the men their evening meal.

"Will you have a bit of fried bread, Dada?" she asked, reaching for the bread knife.

"I will indeed," replied her father, moving from the armchair over to his place at the table.

Seán hovered over Anna's shoulder, picking at bits of bread as she cut the slices.

"Do something useful, Seán!" she said, elbowing him away from her. "Go and set the table!"

Seán grabbed a lump of bread and stuffed it into his mouth. Then muttering to himself, he opened the drawer of the dresser and grabbed a handful of cutlery. He slumped into a chair and dropped the knives and forks down on to the table with a noisy clatter.

As Anna at last carried the plates of food from the dresser to the table, there was a knock at the hall door.

"That'll be Joe," said Seán, jumping up from his chair and rushing to answer the door.

Anna could feel her heart sinking. She had hoped that Joe wouldn't call this evening. They had only recently agreed not to see so much of each other and here he was already, calling on a Wednesday evening. The two young men burst into the kitchen, talking loudly. Anna's father put down his knife and fork and gave them a wink.

"Well, if it isn't my future son-in-law, Joe Maguire!"

Anna's face reddened. "Stop it, Dada!" she hissed.

Joe grinned at Anna and she turned quickly towards the sink to hide her embarrassment.

Joe and Anna had been going together for almost two years, and it seemed that lately Anna's father never missed an opportunity to bring up the subject of marriage. It was beginning to annoy her, especially as her feelings for Joe seemed to lessen a little more every day. Almost everything he did of late seemed to get on her nerves for no good reason. But she knew it wasn't Joe that had changed, it was her. It was gradually beginning to dawn on her that she might not love him any more.

"Hello, Anna."

"Joe, sit down and have some tea. Will you have a fried egg?" Anna went to the dresser to get an extra cup and saucer.

"I won't, thanks. I ate earlier."

Joe's large frame sank on to the kitchen chair, making it creak under his weight.

Mr Barry buttered himself a slice of bread and gave Joe a knowing nod. "Any action tonight, lads?"

"Not tonight," answered Joe quickly. "There is talk of something happening next week though." Joe shot a look towards Anna.

"Eh, Anna, love," said Mr Barry, giving the other two a quick glance. "You wouldn't run up to my bedroom and get the paper? I must have forgotten to bring it down.".

Anna pushed her plate away and looked at the three men scornfully, then stood up slowly and left the room, making sure to close the door behind her.

Mr Barry pulled his chair closer to the table and stared at Joe intently. "So, what's happenin'?"

"I'm waiting for orders, but I'm told that they want to arrange a meeting next week. They're talking about the back room in Lawlor's pub next Thursday."

Seán wiped his hands on his trouser legs. "No problem, Joe, we'll put the word out."

"Well, hold off telling anyone till they confirm it," said Joe. "We don't want people turning up unless it's definitely happening."

"Who's speaking at it?" asked Mr Barry.

Joe opened his mouth to speak but stopped when they heard Anna's footsteps on the floor outside. The door opened and Anna entered carrying her father's newspaper.

"There you are, Dada," she said, handing him the paper.

"You're a little gem," he said, putting the paper on his knee. He leaned back in his chair and looked from Anna to Joe. "Are the lovebirds going courting this evening?"

Anna could feel the blood rushing to her face with annoyance. She gathered the empty plates from the table, clattering them together, and began to scrape them clean over the sink.

Joe got up from the table and took his cup and saucer over to her. "Would you like to go out, Anna?" he asked under his breath.

Anna brushed a strand of hair from across her eyes. "Not really, Joe. I'm exhausted, and I have to get in very early in the morning – Mr Jacob is sick."

"Why don't you go out and enjoy yourselves? A

pair of children like you shouldn't be exhausted!" exclaimed Mr Barry as he rose from the table.

Anna forced a smile. "I know, Dada, but I want to get to bed early tonight." She searched Joe's face and tried to see if he was in any way aware of her complete lack of interest in spending the evening with him. There was something in the way he returned her smile that suggested he did.

Mr Barry walked towards the door. "I'm going inside to sit down." As he passed Seán he hit him playfully across the head with the rolled-up newspaper. "You come in and play a few hands with me, son, and leave these two in peace."

Seán stuffed the last piece of his bread and jam into his mouth and followed his father out of the room.

Joe stood behind Anna and put his arms around her waist. He kissed the back of her neck and pulled her closer. Anna breathed in sharply and pulled away from him.

"What's wrong with you?" he groaned.

"It's nothing."

"Why won't you come out with me?"

He looked at her, waiting for an answer, but Anna was lost for an explanation. She couldn't understand why she didn't want to be with Joe any more. He was the best-looking fellow around for miles. His thick wavy black hair and deep blue eyes had every girl in town competing for his attention. Anna knew he was a genuinely nice person but it made no difference any more, everyone seemed to be in love with Joe, except her.

"I thought we weren't going to see so much of each other," she said in her defence. "Why are you calling on a Wednesday evening when we both agreed?"

Joe threw his head back indignantly. "*You* said we shouldn't be seeing so much of each other. *You* said keep it to weekends, but I agreed nothing. And if I can't call to my girl's house to see her on a Wednesday evening —"

This time Anna cut across him, not wanting her father to hear Joe raising his voice. "Of course you can call to see me, Joe. I'm sorry, it's just that I really am tired tonight."

She moved towards him and put her arms around his neck.

Joe slid his hands around her waist and kissed the crown of her head, then raised her chin gently and kissed her on the mouth. "You know how much I love you, Anna?" he whispered.

"I know." Anna shot a glance towards the door to see if her brother might be spying on them through the glass panel.

Joe pulled her closer. "We'll get married one of these days – just as soon as I have the money to buy us a little house."

Anna felt a flash of panic run through her. "Joe, stop talking about marriage – you know we're far too young!"

"No, we're not – plenty of people get married at our age."

"I'm not getting married anytime soon, and if you had any sense you wouldn't be talking about it! Anyway, Dada would go mad if he knew we were even thinking about it." Anna knew this was a lie. Nothing would please her father more than have his only daughter marry a hero of the irregular forces that were wreaking havoc on the city. Joe Maguire never spoke of his involvement with the Irish Republican Army, but Anna knew exactly what they were up to. Michael Collins had signed the Anglo-Irish treaty with the British government which had caused a deep divide amongst Irish republicans. Those that opposed the treaty were determined to fight it every step of the way. Anna believed that the treaty, although far from perfect, was the only hope of achieving peace in the country. One evening, while playing cards with Joe and her father, she had mistakenly voiced her thoughts about this. Her opinion had been met with a cold glare from both men – and Anna knew immediately that trying to argue with them was pointless. Their political convictions were set in stone, and nothing she could say or do would ever make them change their minds.

Anna kissed the tip of Joe's nose and pulled him towards the door. "Come inside for a while and we'll play cards with the other two, then I'm going to bed."

They walked out of the kitchen and across the hall to what Anna's mother had called the back kitchen. Inside, her father and Seán sat beside an empty fire grate. The evening was mild enough to do without a fire. The last rays of sunshine spilled in through the window that looked out on to the small back garden.

After a few hands of sevens, Anna could feel her eyes getting heavy. Her feet still throbbed from the tight shoes she had worn that day. "I'm off to bed, lads. Goodnight."

"It's only half eight!" exclaimed Seán.

"I don't care. I'm tired and I'm going to bed."

Joe stood up. "I'll see you over the weekend," he said uncertainly.

"Yes," smiled Anna. "Goodnight all."

Mr Barry waited until he heard Anna's footsteps lighten as she ascended the stairs to her bedroom. Then he cleared his throat. "I believe they raided the dairy in Rathfarnham yesterday."

"It was a good job. No one was caught and no one was hurt, and they all got away," said Seán.

"Ah, you'd wonder if it's all worth it." Mr Barry shook his head as he spoke. "Frightening the innocent decent working people. This struggle will turn us all into a pack of criminals."

"There is no choice," Joe broke in quickly. "Until we have a United Ireland and that sham of a treaty is re-negotiated, we'll have to fight them every step of the way."

Joe's voice softened. "I lost my brother in the Easter Rising six years ago. I'm not about to swear an oath of allegiance to the British crown, the very people who murdered him. I'm not giving up now."

"I'm not giving up either, Joe. It just wears me out sometimes, that's all." Mr Barry threw his cards on the table and sat back in his chair. A sombre air descended on the three of them with the mention of Joe's brother.

Joe looked down at the floor and shook his head. "It makes me laugh – hearing them call us the Free State, with our Free State Army. Until they tear up that treaty, there'll never be anything free about our state."

Mr Barry knitted his thick fingers together and sighed loudly. He perked up a moment later as he thought of something that would cheer them up. "Will we go around to Lawlor's for a pint?"

"Good idea, Da." Seán jumped up and gathered the deck of cards together. "Joe, are you coming?"

"Might as well, seeing that your woman upstairs is too tired to entertain me," he said, throwing his eyes up towards the ceiling.

Mr Barry laughed. "Sure she has to get her beauty sleep, son. Keep herself looking gorgeous for you."

The three men filed up to the front door and left the house. Anna sat at her dressing table and heard her brother laugh loudly out on the street. With a crooked finger she pulled back the lace curtain and looked at the three of them as they strolled away from the house. Her heart sank as she thought of what she had been putting off for months – she didn't know which bit was going to be more difficult, breaking it off with Joe or breaking the news to her father and brother.

Anna went to her wardrobe and picked out the clothes she would wear to work the next day, placing them neatly on the end of her bed. Today was the first time that she'd had to run the office on her own – Mr Jacob had never missed a day – and Anna had felt nervous being the only person in charge. Even though she was the office manager and could run the company without any assistance,

Mr Jacob was always a reassuring presence. Anna had left school at the age of sixteen and started in Jacobs' shoe shop on Sackville Street as a junior shop assistant. After only a few months on the shop floor, Mr Jacob spotted her bookkeeping abilities and quickly moved her up to the office. Now, five years on, she was his personal secretary and ran the office like clockwork. Mr Jacob trusted her completely and Anna took pride in the fact that she was the only member of staff that was trusted with a set of keys to the premises. The shop opened at nine thirty every morning, and Anna was always there at nine o'clock sharp to get a head start on the day, and open the shop for the staff. It was hard work but she loved her job and was proud of the fact that she had worked her way up from the shop floor to where she was now.

Anna climbed into bed and as she struggled through her prayers she could feel herself beginning to drift off to sleep.

★ ★ ★

Anna took the tram to work the next morning. She had planned to walk – she could get from her house to Jacob's in twenty-five minutes – but her feet still hurt from the shoes she had worn the day before.

The steep flight of stairs creaked as she walked up to her office at the top of the building. It was a big airy room and Anna's tidy desk was set into an alcove on the wall opposite Mr Jacob's office. It looked more like a room in a house than an office. Beside the door was a brown leather couch and coat-stand, and alongside the entrance to Mr Jacob's office was a fireplace where a fire was lit on the colder winter days. Anna sat at her desk and began work on some import documents she had got a start on the previous evening. Shortly after nine o'clock, Mr Jacob entered the office looking pale and drawn.

"Good morning, Anna," he said as he hung his hat beside the door.

"Mr Jacob! Are you feeling any better?"

"Yes, dear. Thank you."

Anna came out of the small recess which served as her office. "You still look very pale."

"Oh, don't *you* start! I've had Irene nagging me all morning. I'm fine – just a headache, nothing more."

"Well, I'm going to make you a cup of tea," said Anna, moving towards the door.

"That I will allow," Mr Jacobs replied with a weak smile.

When Anna came back with the tea Mr Jacob was sitting behind his desk thumbing through the morning paper. She stood still for a few seconds and observed him through the glass pane in the office door. His tall thin frame was bent over the desk and Anna could see where he had brushed his hair over the bald spot on the crown of his head. He sensed her presence and looked up. Anna quickly moved into his office and handed him the tea.

"Now this will put me right!" he said cheerily.

Anna noticed that his hands shook as he took the cup and saucer from her.

"Can I get you anything else?"

"Nothing, thank you. I'll let you get back to work."

Anna returned his smile as she closed the door of his office. He was the kindest man that she had ever met. He always made her feel like a lady. Even when she worked as an assistant in the shop he had taken care to treat her with the utmost courtesy and respect. Unlike her own father, Mr Jacob was a true gentleman. Anna's father didn't say things like 'utterly' and 'splendid'. He didn't sip his tea noiselessly or crook his little finger as he raised the cup to his lips. Instead he liked to pour his tea into a saucer and drink it, making loud slurping sounds as he did. Over the years Anna had become used to the genteel manners of Mr Jacob and saw how they contrasted sharply with her father's coarse ways. These unkind thoughts about her father sometimes made her feel ashamed of herself, but there were times when she wished her father could be more like Mr Jacob.

Chapter 2

Anna put the dinner on the table for her father and called out loudly for Seán.

Seán appeared at the kitchen door with a towel around his shoulders.

"How many times do I have to call you? Dinner is ready," said Anna.

"Lovely," said Seán, pulling up a chair. "Da, would you trim my hair? It's growing wild."

Mr Barry was a barber. His small shop on Capel St had belonged to his father and when he had died he'd passed the business down to his only son.

"Who are you scrubbing up for, son?"

Seán laughed slyly. "I'm taking Betty Smith to the dance tonight."

"She's a nice girl," Mr Barry said. Then assuming a more serious tone, he added, "Have her home early."

"I will, Da."

Anna shook her head and smiled at her brother's simple ways. He was twenty-three years of age yet took orders from their father as if he was still a boy.

"What about you, Anna, any plans for this evening?"

"I'm going to the pictures with Joe," she said, failing to sound in any way enthusiastic.

"Well, don't get too excited about it," Mr Barry muttered.

"I'm just a bit tired this evening," she said, trying to brighten her tone.

Her father put down his knife and fork and lifted the pork chop from his plate. He held the greasy bone between his fingers and sank his teeth into the meat, a habit that Anna detested.

"Tired again eh," he said. "I think that Jew boy is working you too hard."

"Don't call him that, Dada," said Anna, standing up from the table, "and don't eat with your hands."

Mr Barry stopped chewing his meat and glared at his daughter. Seán lowered his head and stared down at the mound of mashed potato on his plate.

"I'll eat whatever way I bloody well like in my own house," Mr Barry said slowly, pointing the pork chop at Anna.

"Yes, Dada. Sorry."

When Anna had cleared away the dishes, she left the kitchen and went upstairs, cursing herself for snapping at her father. Having to go out with Joe tonight had put her in a bad humour. She had been mean to Seán earlier as well, telling him he looked too scruffy to be going out on a date.

As she changed her clothes she heard a knock at the front door and let her brother answer it. The sound of Joe's voice drifted up the stairs and Anna waited in her bedroom until she heard them go down towards the kitchen. Maybe it's just the time of the month, she thought as she brushed out her hair. She glanced at her reflection in the mirror and was shocked to see how plain she looked. Her fair hair appeared dull, almost brown. Her blue eyes seemed to have changed to a flat grey. That's it, she assured herself, I'm just a bit worn out this week. She pinned her hair back and dabbed a bit of powder across her cheekbones, then she straightened her skirt and went downstairs to meet Joe.

Seán was in the hall, looking neater after his haircut. He held a clothes brush in his hand and was brushing some stray hairs from the shoulders of his jacket.

"You look much better now," Anna said in an attempt to make up for her earlier comments.

Seán grinned and checked his appearance in the hall mirror.

Anna stood behind him and kissed the back of his head. "Sorry I was mean to you."

Seán blushed. "It doesn't matter."

Anna patted his hair down across his forehead like her mother used to do. Seán was two years older than her, but ever since their mother had died Anna had become his big sister.

"Don't stay out too late. You haven't forgotten you're helping with the delivery tomorrow morning?"

"Yes, I know, and don't wait up for me or keep checking my bed every five minutes. I'll be there in the morning no matter what time I get in at," Seán assured her.

He took his coat from the hallstand and opened the front door.

"Don't be late, Seán," Anna said sternly.

"Goodbye," he called as he closed the door behind him.

Seán worked in the post office, but earned extra money every now and then when Jacobs' had a delivery from the docks. Seán would help unload the crates of shoe-boxes from the van and stack them in the basement storeroom of the building. But he had been late for the last two deliveries and Anna had warned him that he was on his last chance.

The men were speaking in hushed tones as she entered the kitchen. Her father stopped talking when he saw her.

"Don't stop on my account," said Anna, glaring over at them.

"Only men's talk, isn't that right, son?" laughed Mr Barry.

"That's right," agreed Joe. "We'd better hurry if we're to make it into town to see a picture."

"I'm ready now."

"Right, we'll be off then. I'll see you on Tuesday, Mr Barry."

"You will indeed. Mind that daughter of mine, she's the only one I've got."

"Of course I will," Joe said with a broad smile. "Goodnight."

Joe linked Anna's arm as they walked along the bank of the canal. As was usual in recent weeks, Anna could think of nothing to say. The conversation that had always flowed so easily between them had dried up and it had become an effort for her to think of the most trivial things to talk to him about. Whenever she was with Joe, all the doubts she had about their relationship rushed into her head and clouded her thoughts for the evening. Thankfully Joe had just been promoted in the printing company he worked for and his news of this compensated for Anna's silence.

"That's great, Joe. You deserve it."

Joe smiled and squeezed her arm. "I'll be earning more money. I'm going to start putting something away every week, so we can get married."

Anna could feel her face getting hot.

"Another year and I'll be able to afford a nice engagement ring and have something to put down on a house of our own."

"Yes," Anna said in a tiny voice.

They stood in line in the foyer of the cinema. When they reached the ticket booth the man behind the glass recognised Joe and the men nodded to each other.

"Evening, Cathal," said Joe digging into his trouser pocket for money. "How are you?"

"I'm grand, Joe."

Joe lowered his voice. "Will we be seeing you on Tuesday?"

"You will indeed," he said and pushed two tickets across the desk towards Joe.

Joe went to put his money down, but the man

behind the booth pushed his hand away.

"No need for that. Enjoy your evening."

Joe smiled and put his money back into his pocket.

"See you next week, Cathal."

Anna took Joe's hand and they walked into the darkened cinema. It was the same everywhere they went. People who recognised Joe treated him with the reverence they usually reserved for the clergy. For those involved in the struggle for independence, people like Joe were heroes, constantly risking their lives for the sake of the country. By day, they lived normal lives, working in offices and factories, but by night they carried out raids on services that would assist in disabling the city leaving the government in disarray. Earlier in the year the Anglo-Irish treaty was signed following a truce in the War of Independence. The treaty established the Free State, granting twenty-six southern counties dominion status within the British commonwealth. It also stated that all members of the Free State government would have to swear an oath of allegiance of the British crown. When the Irish protested that this was unacceptable, Lloyd George, the British Prime Minister, threatened "immediate and terrible war". Those opposing the treaty refused to be a part of the Irish Provisional Government. The split was deeply personal. The protagonists on both sides had been close friends and comrades during the War of Independence and now found themselves on opposing sides of a deep and bitter feud.

Joe's beloved older brother Francis had been shot dead outside the GPO during the 1916 rising. His death had devastated the sixteen-year-old Joe, and he had vowed to continue the fight against the British and avenge the killing of his only brother.

After the picture ended they stepped out into the chilly night air on Sackville Street. Joe pointed to the Hammans' Hotel. "Will we go in for a drink?"

"I'd like to get home, Joe. We have a delivery tomorrow morning and I said I'd be there early for them."

They walked towards home, neither of them saying much.

"What's happening next Tuesday?" Anna asked, knowing that Joe hated any questions about his meetings.

"Nothing much. Just a few of the fellas want to discuss some things."

"What do they talk about?"

Joe stopped walking and turned to face Anna. "Now you know that I'm not able to tell you that."

"Why not? You tell my father and my brother. Why can't you tell me?" She glared at Joe. "Are you afraid I'd go to the police on you? I don't agree with what you are doing, I've made that clear already – and I'm entitled to an opinion. But you and Dada and Seán are treating me like some sort of spy ever since I dared to disagree with the lot of you."

"Anna!" Joe looked stunned.

Her outburst was completely out of character, but she found it hard to resist the urge to start an argument with Joe. "You're always talking in whispers with them whenever I leave the room. Did you ever think of how that makes me feel?"

They had both stopped walking now and Joe looked around to see if anyone was looking at them.

"Well, did you? It makes me feel like an intruder in my own home, Joe. How can you talk about getting married to someone that you won't trust?"

Joe made a whistling sound through his teeth. "Jesus, Anna, what brought this on?"

"I don't know," Anna said, sulking.

Joe took her arm gently and they fell into step again. "Well, seeing as we're on the subject, I might as well tell you now that I won't be able to see you as much over the next few weeks. This meeting on Tuesday is important. There are things about to happen that will take up a lot of my time. Is that enough information for you?"

"Would you tell me more even if I wanted to know?"

Joe breathed out sharply.

Anna could feel her spirits lift. Not having Joe around as much would give her some time to think. "I don't want any more information, Joe. But it would be nice if you trusted me a little bit more every now and again."

"It's not a matter of trust, Anna. The less you know about what I do the better it is for all concerned. I don't want you ever getting into trouble on my account."

They walked towards home. A light mist had descended on the canal, giving a still and gloomy appearance to the night. They reached Anna's house and Joe walked as far as the front door.

"I'll let you get on to bed."

"Sorry I was angry with you," said Anna.

Joe put his arms around her and kissed her goodnight.

Anna closed the front door behind her and walked into the dark hall. When her mother was alive, the hall lamp was always lit until everyone in the house was in bed. Anna had to feel her way along the wall for fear of knocking into something and waking her father. In the darkness, she could hear the loud snores that came from the back kitchen and she crept down the hall quietly. She opened the door and tip-toed into the room. In the armchair by the dying fire was her father, his head drooped to one side in a deep sleep. Anna went over to him and let her hand rest on his arm. Looking into his face she saw the deep lines that ran across his forehead and felt a pang of sympathy as she took hold of his arm and shook it gently. He was fifty years of age but had come to look like an old man since the death of her mother.

"Dada, wake up!"

Mr Barry jumped to life and looked around the room in a daze. "What time is it?"

"It's nearly twelve. You're cold," said Anna, feeling his hands.

"I must have dozed off." Mr Barry stretched his arms above his head and yawned.

"You go on up to bed – I'll clear away here," Anna said taking the cup and plate from the floor beside the chair.

"I must have dozed off," he repeated as he got to his feet. "Good night, love," he said as he left the room.

"Good night, Dada."

Anna pulled the fire-guard over the dying embers and wound the clock on the mantelpiece. Beside the clock Anna's mother smiled at her from the silver picture frame and Anna ran her fingers over her mother's smooth and ageless face. "Goodnight, Mam," she whispered.

On her way to bed she checked Seán's room. He was still out. Anna went back downstairs and lit the gas lamp in the hall, knowing that her brother would definitely crash into something if it was still dark when he came in.

Anna rose early the following morning and washed and dressed herself, before trying to wake Seán. It was always the same on the Saturday mornings that he agreed to help out with a delivery. Seán would go out drinking the night before, and waking him was next to impossible. Anna marched into his bedroom and wrinkled her nose when the stale smell of porter reached her nostrils. With one single movement, she pulled the curtains open and the rings on the curtain rail made a sharp scratching noise as she did so.

"Seán, get up! It smells like a brewery in here. What time did you get in at?" Seán's tousled hair appeared from under the bed covers. He opened his eyes in tiny slits. "Shut the curtains for a minute," he whispered hoarsely.

"No. Get up quickly. I'll go down and make you some breakfast."

Anna left the room and heard the sound of the creaking bed as Seán settled back down to sleep. She swung around and entered the room again, this time taking the warm covers from around her brother and pulling them roughly down to the end of his bed.

Seán sat up looking like a madman. "You mean cow," he moaned, "I'm dying!"

"That's your own doing," Anna chided him. "Now make a move or we'll be late."

Chapter 3

Ben Jacob walked slowly up the steps of his Georgian home on the South Circular Road. He had left the house, and was on the way into the office to oversee the delivery, but the headache that had dogged him for weeks had worsened and he had reluctantly decided to turn back. He was annoyed with himself for turning back, not because he was needed at the office – he could always rely on Anna to do the job every bit as well as he could – it was just that he couldn't bear the thought of his wife fussing over him again. As he approached the last step, a feeling of lightness came over him and he knew that if he didn't get a hold of something he was going to fall. He struggled over to the side of the front door and caught the handrail with both hands. His head was spinning and he felt almost drunk in a nauseous way. The morning paper slipped out from under his arm and he reached up to the door-knocker and hit it against the brass as hard as he could. Within seconds, as if she had anticipated his knock, his wife Irene was standing at the open door, her face aghast as she looked down at her husband slumped against the railings. She took his arm and put it around her shoulders and with all the strength she could muster led him inside, feeling his body getting heavier with every step.

Mary the housemaid appeared at the end of the hall and shrieked, "What's happened to Mr Jacob?"

She ran and took Ben's other arm around her shoulders and together they walked him into the drawing room and lowered him onto the couch.

"Oh, Mrs Jacob, what's wrong with his eyes?" Mary cried.

Irene looked down at her husband and saw that his eyes had begun to flicker open and closed in a frightening way. She turned to Mary and caught her by the arm.

"Go quickly and get a doctor."

Mary backed out of the room, twisting her apron

in her hands. "Yes, Mrs Jacob," she said faintly.

"Quickly!" shouted Irene.

* * *

Anna unlocked the huge back door of the darkened storeroom under the building. It made a thunderous noise as Seán pulled it across its rolling frame.

"Jaysus, my head," he groaned to himself as Anna looked on without a shred of sympathy for her hungover brother.

A shaft of pearly morning light crept across the floor of the dusty cavernous storeroom. Satisfied that she had succeeded in getting Seán to work on time, Anna took the papers from the driver of the van and left them to their unloading. "Right. I'll leave you two to get on with it. Come up when you're finished."

After several hours of paper work Anna checked the clock and wondered why Mr Jacob hadn't arrived into the office yet. He usually signed off the papers and checked the boxes on the Saturday deliveries. It was two o'clock and there was still no sign of him.

Seán stuck his head around her office door. "We're finished."

Anna looked up from her work. "Did you lock the door?"

Seán nodded and moved over to her desk, rubbing his hands together. "Can you pay us now?"

Anna handed over two envelopes and Seán snatched them from her. "Lovely," he said with a smile. "I'm off home now – back to bed for the rest of the day."

Anna gave him a withering look. "Well for some. I'll see you later on."

Seán winked at her as he stuffed the envelopes into his trouser pocket. "Don't work too hard," he said over his shoulder as he left the office and ran down stairs, eager to get home to his bed again.

Anna did some paperwork and waited for another hour in the hope that Mr Jacob might show up, but by three o'clock he had not arrived and was hardly likely to come in so late. Anna had finished her work so she decided to close up the office and go home.

★ ★ ★

Later that evening when the doctor had examined Ben Jacob for the second time that day, he entered the drawing room clutching his bag and went over to where Irene was sitting.

"I'm afraid Mrs Jacob, it's as I suspected earlier,

your husband has suffered a stroke. He seems to be comfortable and for the moment I don't see any need to move him to hospital."

Irene sat by the fire with a frozen look on her doll-like face. "Why is he speaking like that?"

The doctor sat down across from her. "That is what happens. Part of the brain has been damaged and certain things like speech and movement can be affected badly. Sometimes the speech can return but it is too early to tell anything at the moment. There is also a chance that he could suffer another stroke – only time will tell."

Irene looked lost as the tears rolled down her face. "What can I do to help him?"

"The only thing you can do now is to watch him closely. If he shows any signs of having another seizure, get him to the hospital immediately. I will call again to examine him tomorrow morning."

Irene wiped her wet cheeks and stood up. "Thank you, doctor. Mary will show you out."

When the doctor left the room Irene threw herself back into the armchair sobbing loudly. When she was certain that she had no more tears left she went back upstairs to the bedroom. He lay very still in the bed but opened his eyes as she approached. Irene reached down and took her husband's frail hand. He looked up at her and she recognised the fear in his eyes. He tried to say something but only a strangled sound came from the back of his throat.

Irene put her finger to his lips. "The doctor says your speech will come back — it's just a matter of time, my darling."

Ben's head moved around the pillow in jerking movements and Irene ran her hand along his forehead to calm him. After a few minutes he seemed to drift back into a light sleep. Irene crept out of the room and shut the door quietly behind her. It was the first time she had ever seen her husband sick and it frightened her. It was always she who suffered the ailments, and Ben who sat on the side of her bed and brought her tea and pills when she was blinded by migraine, or had simply taken to her bed with fatigue. How on earth, wondered Irene, was she going to find the strength to look after him?

Later that evening, Rabbi Goldstein called and prayed with Ben and Irene. They lit candles in the bedroom and the rabbi sang the Sabbath prayers over the ghostly figure of Ben Jacob.

Chapter 4

Irene watched her husband eat the dinner that Mary had prepared for him. Even though every piece of food had been boiled to a pulp and mashed together with the greatest care to make it easier to eat – Irene could see his face contort in frustration as he tried to swallow it. A trickle of brown gravy ran down his chin and she reached over quickly and wiped it away with her napkin. When he had eaten all he could, Ben dropped his fork beside his plate.

"Well done, darling, you really are improving," Irene said. "Last week you could only manage one or two mouthfuls on your own."

Ben looked at her and frowned. He tried to say something but only a strained cry came from his contorted lips. It was the first week since his stroke that Irene did not have to feed her husband every meal, and she had taken heart that he was on the road to recovery. Having to feed him like a helpless child had seemed such a cruel punishment to a man as proud and independent as Ben. He had been confined to a wheelchair, which was the hardest thing of all. Although his speech had not returned, he did not have to say anything – Irene just had to look into his eyes to know how much he hated the loss of independence. Those eyes, which had once been so bright and animated had become lifeless pools that seemed to reflect the sadness within.

Ben tried to talk again, but the same strange sound emerged. He banged the table with his frail fist in a show of frustration.

Irene reached across and took his hand. "The doctor said this would be a slow process. It has only been six weeks, Ben. We have to be patient. You will get better, it will just take some time." Irene could hear the doubt that crept into her voice as she tried to reassure her husband. The truth was, there really had been very little change in Ben's condition since his stroke. It seemed that their whole world had been turned upside down. Irene kept hoping that one morning her husband would walk down for breakfast and say he felt altogether better, but she was now beginning to realise that that was never going to happen. Learning to feed himself again had been a huge improvement. He had also on one occasion managed to take a few steps from the wheelchair to his bed, but apart from that he was completely dependent on Irene for everything.

After dinner they sat by the fire. The heat had made them silent and sleepy and Irene watched Ben's head slump forward as he nodded off. She stood up and stretched her weary arms – they seemed to ache permanently from lifting her husband from one position to another. She crossed the room and pulled the bell and a few seconds later Mary appeared at the door.

Irene smiled at her. "I'm afraid it's that time of night again."

Mary saw Ben asleep in his chair and moved nimbly across the room. Her tiny frame belied the physical strength she had shown in the past few weeks. Although barely reaching Irene's shoulder in height, Mary had proved herself to be as strong as an ox when it came to manoeuvring Ben from his wheelchair into his bed.

Irene released the brake gently and pushed the

chair into the hall and down to the study where she had made a bedroom for her husband. The two women undressed Ben and pulled his nightshirt on over his bony blue-veined limbs. Then with an arm around each of their shoulders they heaved his body onto the bed.

"Is that all, Mrs Jacob? Will you be needing me for anything else tonight? Maybe you'd like me to make you some hot milk?"

Irene sat on the bed beside her sleeping husband and stroked his forehead. "No, thank you Mary. You can go home now."

Mary crept over to the door and closed it gently behind her.

Irene sat in the darkness and whispered a prayer under her breath. Never in her entire life had she experienced the anxiety and desolation she had felt over the past six weeks. At first she could only focus on her husband's health, but as the weeks had gone by a new worry had emerged, that of the business. It was now clear that Ben would not be returning to work, at least not for the foreseeable future, and Irene was at a loss as to what to do. Anna had been running the company as best she could, working long hours to ensure that Irene had nothing to worry about on that side of things. But Irene knew that Anna was overworked and it could not continue for very much longer. She had visited the office a week ago to sign some papers, and was shocked when she saw how exhausted Anna looked. But what was to be done, wondered Irene as she sat in the dark listening to her husband's peaceful snoring. Their two sons, Peter and Daniel, had spent some of their youth in Dublin but both had left to live in England. Peter was the practical worker of the two of them. As soon as he had finished with school he had gone to England to work alongside his grandfather in the family shoe factory in Leeds. Old Mr Jacob had died shortly afterwards and Granny Jacob had taken over the running of the entire operation and depended heavily on Peter, although she would never admit this to anyone, especially Peter. Granny Jacob doted on him. He was now twenty-five years of age and still living with his grandmother. Irene sometimes wondered if the old woman ever let any girls near her precious grandson. Every time Peter came to visit his parents, Irene always made a point of asking him if he had met a nice girl yet. Peter reacted the same way every time: he blushed and changed the subject. His younger brother Daniel was very different. He had tried working with Peter in the factory but hated every minute of it. In fact, it had caused tension between the two of them and for the first time in their lives the two brothers had bickered constantly. Daniel had no interest and therefore didn't work hard enough, causing Peter to lose his temper on several occasions. When Daniel came home two summers ago and told Irene that he had been accepted to study law in Edinburgh University, she was quite relieved. She couldn't bear the thought of her two sons arguing. They had always got along so well as children, she didn't want anything to ever come between them.

Irene got up from the bed and walked over to the desk, which had been pushed into the corner of the room. On it was a photograph in a silver frame of her two boys, taken five years ago on Peter's twentieth birthday. Irene lifted the frame and ran her fingers over the their smiling faces. They were leaning against the huge trunk of the chestnut-tree in the back garden, both with folded arms and cheeky grins. Peter was heavy set with thick black hair and had the dark features of his father. Daniel looked very different. He was slender and fair-haired and possessed the delicate angles of his mother's face. Irene remembered the moment he was born, she was sure he was a girl. He was far too pretty to be a boy. Even as a toddler, people always mistook him for a girl. His fair hair had begun to recede in the past few years, but to Irene he would always be the most beautiful baby in the world. She kissed each of them and put the photograph back down on the desk. "I miss you, boys," she whispered. Then she went to the side of the bed and, leaning over, gently kissed her husband's forehead. She tiptoed across the room and paused before opening the door, looking back to her frail husband who looked so small in the bed. "I miss you too, my dear," she said softly before leaving the room.

★　★　★

Anna sat in her office surrounded by a mountain of post and papers that had yet to be sorted out. Her stomach began to rumble and she looked up at the wall clock – almost three, and she hadn't eaten since her meagre breakfast that morning. Remembering Mrs Jacob's words, Anna forced herself to put down her pen and break for lunch. Outside the icy rain clattered at the windowpanes and in the distance Anna could hear the carol singers outside the GPO. The shop had been busy doing a brisk Christmas trade and Anna finally felt that she was beginning to get on top of things. For the first few months after Mr Jacob's stroke, she had felt she just could not cope with the amount of work that had been piled on to her, but what she had learned from the experience was that some things could wait until tomorrow. Six months ago, if her desk had looked the way it did now, Anna would have screamed in panic. Now she only looked at the basket nearest to her with the most urgent tasks to be done, and ignored the rest. She had spent the first few weeks of working alone trying to run the company with the same efficiency as she had done when Mr Jacob was there to oversee things. But this soon took its toll and Anna became weak with exhaustion, never leaving the office until her desk was completely cleared of any work. Until the day Irene paid a visit to put her signature to some cheques and papers and was shocked when she saw the pale overworked face of her employee.

Irene made Anna promise that she would only attend to the urgent matters and leave everything else until her husband returned to work.

"You are our only hope of staying in business until Mr Jacob is well enough to get back. If you run yourself into the ground, there will be no one else to take over," she told Anna firmly.

"I really don't want to let you down, Mrs Jacob. And I don't want Mr Jacob worrying about the place, because I *can* take care of it."

"We have no doubt that you can take care of things, Anna. But please try to take care of yourself as well."

Irene scribbled hastily on the mountain of cheques and papers that had been put in a pile for her to sign. As she leaned over the desk her eyes were obscured by the rim of her hat and Anna looked down at the diamond rings that sparkled on her long pale fingers as the pen scratched out her signature on the papers. Mrs Jacob looked a lot younger than her husband. Her face was like fine porcelain and when she smiled only the tiniest wrinkles appeared around her sparkling blue eyes. She had never been anything but polite and friendly towards Anna, yet her fine style and cool elegance always managed to make her feel extremely nervous in her presence.

"Now, Anna, take heed of what I have said and look after yourself. I will not be held responsible for running you into bad health." Mrs Jacob buttoned her coat and pulled on her beige suede gloves.

Anna stood up from her desk and, crossing the room, pulled the door open for her.

"Goodbye, dear," said Mrs Jacob.

"Goodbye, Mrs Jacob, and please give my regards to Mr Jacob – we all miss him."

Irene picked up the back of her dress and gracefully made her way down the narrow wooden staircase.

Chapter 5

Irene hung the last glass angel on the Christmas tree and stood back to admire her work. For the first time in months she had something to look forward to: her boys would be home to spend Christmas with them and Irene had been gripped with excitement all day at the thought of seeing them again.

"There now, how does that look?"

Ben was sitting in his wheelchair with a rug around his legs. "Warry nice!" he shouted, his head rolling with each syllable.

"Yes, it is very nice." She moved over to him and took his hand. "Oh Ben, I am excited about seeing the boys again."

"Ish gooood!" His face contorted as he tried to spit the words out. During the months following his stroke, his speech had come back gradually but only Irene could understand him fully.

"They arrive at four o'clock tomorrow," she said excitedly. "Mary is going to cook a wonderful homecoming dinner. It's going to be a special Christmas this year, darling."

"Mmm," Ben nodded.

Irene stood up and warmed herself by the fire. "Ben, we should agree on something before they arrive tomorrow."

Ben looked at her questioningly.

Irene's back stiffened as she gazed into the leaping flames. "We have to face the fact that you are not going back to work any time soon."

She turned to face him and he threw his hands forward in a gesture for her to stop.

"No, Ben, you must listen to me, because I have thought about nothing else for months and I know what we must do."

Irene could see how difficult this was for him but she knew she had to broach the subject before the arrival of her sons.

"We cannot leave Anna to run the entire business alone. It is too much to expect of anyone, and I'm afraid she'll find it all too exhausting and leave us. We could hire a manager, of course, but dare we put our livelihood into the hands of a complete stranger? Besides, it would be costly. Until you are well enough to return we have only one choice, and that is to ask Daniel to come home and take over."

Ben groaned and ran a quivering hand across his brow.

He was so proud of the fact that Daniel had been accepted to university and he had fully supported his decision to leave the family business. Irene looked at Ben's wrinkled forehead and could read his thoughts.

"I know he has no interest in the business. I don't expect he's going to like the idea any more than you do, but it's the only solution for the moment."

This was putting it mildly. Asking her son to give up his studies and move to Dublin, a place where he knew nobody, was going to be the most difficult thing in the world. Daniel was wilful and could be unreasonably stubborn when faced with anything he didn't want to do. Ben's hands shook as he gripped the arms of his wheelchair and Irene looked away when she saw the tears well up in his eyes.

"We have no choice," she said softly.

★   ★   ★

The boat had been delayed because of fog and Irene fluttered about the house nervously rearranging anything she could lay her hands on. Mary had cooked dinner to serve at seven o'clock, but it was almost half past eight and there was still no sign of them. Ben sat by the fire in the living room and struggled to stay awake.

The sharp rat-a-tat of the door knocker echoed through the silence of the house, making Irene jump, even though she had been expecting it for hours. Her skirt rustled as she hurried down the stairs to the hall where Mary was standing.

"It's them!" Mary cried excitedly.

As she reached the hall door Irene paused and took a deep breath, then nodded at Mary to open the door. Her heart pounded as the two boys were revealed standing before her, their black overcoats sprayed with a fine mist.

Peter stepped in first and put his suitcase on the floor.

"My darling! How I've missed you!" Irene exclaimed, putting her arms around him and hugging him tightly.

"It's good to see you, Mother. Happy Christmas!"

Behind him Daniel put down his case and waited in turn for his mother's embrace.

Irene unlocked Peter and turned to her younger

son. "Daniel, my sweetheart!"

Daniel was smothered as his mother kissed him and threw her arms around his neck. He patted her back gently. "Hello, Mother. It's good to be back."

Mary fussed about how cold they looked and took their coats and gloves from them.

They filed into the living room and Irene looked closely at the boys' faces as they saw their father for the first time since his stroke. She had written to warn them about how the illness had affected him, but it had not been easy to put it into words. The drooping left eyelid and collapsed mouth had made him almost unrecognisable.

Peter was the first to react. He cleared his throat and knelt down beside the wheelchair. "It's so good to see you again, Father," he said, giving him an awkward hug.

Ben remained silent, his mouth fixed in a tight grimace.

Daniel hung back, looking at his father in shock.

"Daniel dear, say hello to your father," whispered Irene, pushing him gently towards the wheelchair.

Daniel bent down slowly and put his arm around Ben's shoulder. "Hello, Father." Daniel looked up at Irene silently, pleading for her to say something.

Irene clapped her hands together. "You two must be starving! Poor Mary has been trying to keep dinner warm all evening. Peter, you take Father into the dining room." Irene pointed to the safety brake. "There, just release that lever and wheel him in." Then she put her arm through Daniel's and led them into the dining room.

The best crystal and silverware had been taken out for the occasion. Six white candles flickered in the silver candelabra, throwing shadows onto the walls. They had been lit by Mary earlier in the evening, in joyful anticipation of the homecoming but they had burned almost halfway down and had left a pool of wax on the white linen tablecloth. Peter positioned his father's wheelchair at the head of the table and sat down opposite his brother. In the centre of the table the overcooked goose lay under a silver dome. Mary shuffled into the room carrying a tray laden with several tureens of vegetables which she placed on the sideboard. With immense pride she carried each tureen to the table, lifting the lids to reveal Brussels sprouts, carrots, parsnips and roast potatoes.

Irene stood and lifted the silver dome. Handing the carving knife to Peter she said, "Please, sweetheart, will you carve?"

Peter stood up and took the knife from her and tried to cut the bird in delicate slices.

"How is Granny Jacob?" Irene inquired, as she

tried to think of the questions her husband would ask.

"Granny is fine, and says that next Christmas you will have to go to her. She says that she is getting too old to travel."

Irene smiled and tried not to betray the thoughts that ran through her head. She had been married to Ben for twenty-seven years yet she still had not completely forgiven her mother-in-law. Granny Jacob had been furious when Ben told her of his intention to marry Irene Goddard, and had threatened to throw him out onto the street without a penny if the marriage went ahead. He was to find a Jewish girl and that was her final word. Ben came close to breaking it off with Irene as a result of the pressure that his mother put him under. In the end Irene reluctantly agreed to convert to Judaism, but she'd never truly embraced the religion despite her mother-in-law's bullying. Irene and Ben had agreed to bring the boys up in the Jewish faith, but since moving to Dublin and out of the watchful eye of Granny Jacob, they had let their religious persuasions lapse, and the boys had grown up with little religious guidance.

Irene now smiled to herself at the thought of Granny Jacob being too old to do anything. There was plenty of life left in the old goat, she mused.

"Next Christmas seems so far away. We'll see how father is then and who knows? Perhaps we could go over to you."

Peter served the slices of goose to each plate. Irene got up and took Ben's knife and fork and began to cut his meat into small cubes. The brothers looked across at each other uneasily.

"Wouldn't it be nice to see your mother again, Ben?" Irene asked brightly.

Ben kept his eyes on his plate and a small sound came from the back of this throat.

Irene sat back down again and turned her attention to Daniel. "What about you, Daniel? Are your studies going well?"

"Very well. I had to lock myself into my room for the month of November to catch up on all my work. It's so easy to fall behind."

"Well, you relax for the next few days and enjoy the rest you've deprived yourself of," said Irene. "Now everyone eat, before it gets cold again."

⋆　⋆　⋆

Anna sat at the kitchen table and looked at the spiced beef that her father was trying his best to carve. There had been no time to put into preparing a special Christmas meal and she felt guilty for not having made more of an effort when she looked at the meagre spread. Her mother had always cooked a spiced beef on Christmas Eve but ever since she died it had never tasted the same. Anna's legs throbbed. She had finished work at lunchtime, but they had been so busy in the days before the Christmas holidays that she'd had to leave the office and work in the shop serving customers like she had done in her early days in Jacob's. Anna had enjoyed meeting her old customers again and working alongside her pal Maureen Dolan. They had both started working in Jacobs' on the same week and Anna had missed Maureen's company when she was moved up to the office. They had rushed about the shop, serving customers and stopping to gossip whenever there was a lull, but Anna had forgotten just how tiring it was.

"Here, Dada, let me cut it," she said, taking the carving knife from her father.

Mr Barry gladly handed the duty over to his more capable daughter.

"Seán, you spoon some of that mash on to the plates," ordered Anna.

Mr Barry sat back in his chair and observed his son and daughter. He reached out and caught both their wrists in a strong grip.

"I don't know what I'd do without both of you,"

he said, choking back his tears.

Christmas had always been a bad time for her father.

Anna put her hand firmly on his shoulder and looked across at Seán. "We're lucky to have each other," she said and quickly resumed the task of putting the meat on to the plates.

Mr Barry nodded solemnly and blessed himself. Then he took up his knife and fork and made a sawing motion as he tucked into his forlorn Christmas Eve dinner.

The sherry trifle was more successful. This was the one thing her mother made that Anna could replicate without much effort. Seán was scraping away the last of his second helping when they heard the front door knocker.

"It's nine o'clock on Christmas Eve! Who is that? Anna groaned, throwing her napkin on to the table.

"Joe," said Seán, putting his dessert spoon down. "I told him to call in if he was passing." He went to get up but Mr Barry held out a hand to stop him rising any further.

"Let Anna open the door for him," he said.

Seán looked across at Anna and shrugged his shoulders as he flopped back into his chair.

Anna looked at her father and wondered what he was up to.

"Well, let the man in!" Mr Barry exclaimed.

Anna stood up and the beginnings of a smile played at the corners of her mouth. Her father had guessed that Joe was calling with her Christmas present and he was probably trying to give them some privacy. Anna was touched by his thoughtfulness and, as she walked past his chair on the way out of the kitchen, she gave his shoulder a gentle squeeze.

She opened the door and Joe stood there smiling at her with a yellow haze of fog and drizzle behind him.

He stepped into the hall and kissed Anna. His mouth was cold and damp and she could taste the bitter stout on his lips.

Anna took his coat and shook off the beads of rain before hanging it on the hallstand. "Come down to the kitchen and warm up," she said, leading the way.

Joe reached out and caught her around the waist. "Come here for a minute," he said, pulling her towards the parlour.

Anna saw the smile on his face and she looked at him suspiciously. "What?"

Joe pulled her gently into the parlour and closed the door. His face was beaming with happiness and Anna was glad that he had called – they needed someone like Joe to lift the gloomy atmosphere in the house tonight.

"Thanks for calling, Joe," she said and kissed him gently.

"I want to ask you something before we go downstairs." He looked over at Anna and held her gaze for a moment without saying anything. Anna waited for him to continue but Joe just stood there. Then he dug into his coat pocket and pulled out a small box.

"What is it, Joe?" she asked.

He fumbled with the top of the box and prised it open, to reveal a small diamond ring. "Will you marry me?"

Anna could feel a sudden rush of blood to her head. For a moment she was speechless and desperately tried to find a way to let him down gently.

But why? she thought then. Perhaps this is just what we need. Joe looked down at her, still holding the ring box in his hand. He looked drunk with happiness as he waited for her answer. He would make a good husband, Anna thought as she met his gaze, and some day a good father. Perhaps all the doubt that had played on her mind recently was because she knew that this day was imminent. After all, she had heard from other brides-to-be that it was only natural to have doubts about the future.

"Oh Joe, I don't know what to say."

"Then say yes," he implored.

Anna put her hand up to her chest and tried to calm the thoughts that were racing through her mind. They would get married and get a house of their own and have children. Wasn't that what she had always wanted?

Joe searched her face for an answer, his happiness hanging by a thread and in his eyes she saw the fire of complete love that burned for her.

"Yes," she said faintly.

He snatched the ring from the box as if his life depended on it, and stuffed it on to her finger, for fear she might change her mind. "It fits!" he said, as if this made all the difference. "That's a sign of good luck."

Anna stared down at the ring, feeling slightly dazed.

"I love you, Anna. We might not get married today or tomorrow, but now we know we belong together."

Anna stepped close to him and ran her hand down the side of his face. "I love you too, Joe. It's the best Christmas present ever."

Joe beamed down at her. "Let's go and tell the others." He pulled away slightly and looked into her eyes. "I can't believe it," he whispered. He drew her towards him again and kissed her very lightly on the mouth as if he was afraid that any sudden movement would make this precious moment slip away. Anna rested her head against his chest and held her hand out to admire the pretty ring on her finger.

"Dada will be delighted," she said.

"He is," Joe replied, breaking out of his dazed state. "I asked his permission yesterday."

When they entered the kitchen there were three bottles of stout already opened on the table.

Mr Barry hovered just inside the door and looked over at his daughter anxiously.

"We're engaged," announced Joe proudly.

"Well, I thought you'd never ask her!" shouted Seán. He rushed over to his sister and hugged her tightly before reaching out to shake Joe's hand. "Brother-in-law!" he said with a grin.

Mr Barry walked over to Anna and blinked hard with watery eyes. With a loud cough he swallowed his tears, his chest puffed out with pride.

"Congratulations, pet. You have a good man in Joe – he'll always look after you."

"Thanks, Dada, I know he will," said Anna.

He shook his head. "It's a pity your mother isn't here to see it," he said, taking a handkerchief from his trouser pocket and wiping his nose.

Seán poured three glasses of stout for the men,

and a small sherry for Anna. "Now raise your glasses. To Joe and Anna!" he said, grinning from ear to ear.

"May you both be very happy," said Mr Barry, stuffing the handkerchief back into his pocket and joining in Seán's gaiety.

Anna's heart thumped loudly as she looked at Joe's beaming smile. *I am engaged to be married*, she thought, *I am engaged to be married*.

Chapter 6

Irene knocked on the door of Daniel's bedroom and entered before he had time to reply. The icy January sunshine poured through the window, giving the room a deceptively warm glow. Daniel threw a handful of socks onto the untidy pile of clothing in the open suitcase on the floor.

Irene looked at the jumble of shirts and trousers and shook her head in amusement. "You know, it will close a lot more easily when the time comes if the garments are folded."

Daniel grinned. "It also closes very easily if it is sat on."

Irene sat down at the edge of the bed and ran her hand along the eiderdown thoughtfully.

"Daniel, I must talk to you. Now."

Daniel looked at her and waited.

Irene sat quite still, trying to think of the right way to break the news to her son.

"Well?" asked Daniel.

She hung her head and sighed. "This is the hardest thing I have ever had to do." Her voice quivered as she continued. "Sweetheart, I know how much your studies mean to you and I would never ask this of you were it not so completely necessary."

Daniels face dropped as he realised what was coming next.

Irene clasped her hands together and looked at him without saying anything.

"You want me to come back," Daniel said stiffly.

"It's the only solution for the moment, until your father recovers or at least until we find a suitable replacement. Anna, the girl who is running the office, is doing the best she can, but it's far too much for her. She can't continue to run the entire business single-handedly. We could hire a manager – at great cost – but we can't risk putting our livelihood into the hands of a stranger, who may turn out to be incompetent – or dishonest."

Daniel looked stricken. "Mother, you know how

unhappy I was working with Peter in Leeds. I'm not cut out for that kind of work, I wasn't even any good at it."

"I know that, Daniel. What I am asking of you is to make a huge sacrifice on our behalf. It is a family business and we cannot run it without someone from the family being here."

"Can't you ask Peter?" he asked desperately.

Irene shook her head. "I wish I could but Granny Jacob needs him in Leeds."

He blinked slowly as he thought of what was being asked of him. "How long do you want me to stay?"

"As long as it takes to find someone trustworthy and competent to take over, and I can't put a time on that. Daniel, I hate asking this of you, but we are desperate." Irene looked at her son's ashen face and it broke her heart to think of what he was going through. "If you could talk to the Dean and explain the situation I'm sure that he will understand. You can always return to Edinburgh when things are sorted out here."

Daniel walked to the window and turned his back on Irene. "Very well," he whispered.

Irene eased herself off the bed without saying anything else and walked quietly from the room.

Daniel remained at the window, trying to absorb

the enormity of his mother's demand and what effect it would have on his life. To leave his studies and come home to run a shoe-shop was like asking him to kill himself. "I'd rather die," he said under his breath, as he blinked back the angry tears that stung his eyes.

*　　*　　*

It was the final night of the boys' holidays and Irene had booked seats at the theatre. Daniel had feigned an upset stomach and stayed in his room all evening. After reading for several hours he undressed and got into bed but nothing could relieve him of his state of agitation. He was to spend the month of January in Edinburgh, before returning to Dublin to take up his position as his father's replacement.

He had fallen into a half sleep when he awoke to the sound of muffled voices in the hall below. They had returned, and he could hear the rustle of coats being discarded and the squeak of the springs on his father's wheelchair. A few minutes later his bedroom door opened.

Irene put her head in and whispered, "Daniel we're home. Are you awake?"

Daniel shut his eyes and steadied his breathing in

the hope that she would think that he was sleeping. He was still far too upset to face his mother.

Later, when the house was quiet and Peter had gone to bed, Daniel heard the sound of his parents' voices coming from the study beneath his room, where his father now slept. At first it was a low mumble. Daniel could tell it was his mother's voice. But several minutes later he could hear the guttural cries of his father, sounding like a wounded animal. He knew they were arguing over his mother's decision to ask him to come home. Daniel knew this was going to be as hard for his father to accept as it was for him. It was a cruel reminder to Ben Jacob that he was never going to get better.

* * *

Anna had washed her hair and taken time to wind it into a soft coil at the back of her neck. Mrs Jacob had requested that she visit their house on the South Circular Road, and Anna wanted to look her very best for them. The green wool dress she had bought especially for the occasion was stylish and elegant without being too fussy. Sitting at her dressing table, she placed her silver hairbrush carefully alongside the matching comb and reached for her hat. With both arms raised, she lowered it on to her head and tilted it forward, careful not to disturb her hairstyle. When she was satisfied that it was at the correct angle, she took the hat-pin from her pursed lips and pressed it gently through the felt.

"My God! Is it royalty you're going to meet this afternoon?" asked Mr Barry as she stepped into the kitchen and picked up her freshly polished boots that stood on some old newspaper beside the back door.

"No, Dada. I just want to look my best," said Anna, tying the boot-laces.

Mr Barry shook his newspaper closed and looked at his daughter.

"You look like a princess," he said, smiling over at her proudly.

Anna was pleased at his approval and returned his smile. "Thanks, Dada. I won't be long," she said as she left.

* * *

The gate squeaked on its hinge as she pushed it open and carefully picked her way along the gravel driveway that led to the Jacob's house.

Mary was standing at the open doorway polishing the front door brasses and smiled cheerfully as Anna walked up the front steps towards her. "You must be Anna. They're expecting you inside." She abandoned the cloudy brasses and threw her cloth on the ground. "Follow me," she said, leading Anna into the house.

Anna smiled anxiously and stepped into the hall.

"Let me help you," Mary said, relieving Anna of her coat.

Irene appeared at the end of the hall. "Anna. I do appreciate your visit," she said, walking towards them. "Mary, we'll take our tea in the conservatory now." Mary's head and shoulders bounced forward in a slight curtsy and she walked away towards the kitchen. Irene gave Anna a sympathetic look and sighed. "Oh dear, Anna! What a time we've all had of it lately! I hope you haven't been overdoing it at work."

"I'm fine, Mrs Jacob. Things are busy, but we're all coping well."

"That's good. I really don't know how we would have coped without you over the past few months. You have been such a great help."

"Not at all, Mrs Jacob," said Anna, trying to brush off the compliment.

Irene took Anna by the arm and led her through the large hall. "Now, the reason I asked you here today is to meet our son Daniel. "He has given up his studies in Edinburgh and kindly agreed to come home and work in the business until Mr Jacob is well enough to take over."

Anna felt a tightness creep across her chest. It was certainly not what she had expected. She'd presumed her visit was to give the Jacobs an update on how the business was doing and perhaps to say hello to Mr Jacob, who she hadn't seen since his stroke. The last thing she had expected was an introduction to her new employer. "Oh really," was all she managed to say.

Irene stopped walking and turned to face Anna. "I'm afraid, Anna, you must prepare yourself for the change you will see in Mr Jacob. The stroke has left him with little power in the left side of his body. He gets somewhat better every day, but I'm afraid his speech is still quite poor. He refuses to speak in front of anyone but me, because of the way he sounds, which makes conversation very difficult."

"I see," said Anna.

Irene smiled. "He really is looking forward to seeing you though. Your visit will certainly cheer him up."

The two women entered the bright conservatory. Ben was sitting motionless in the wheelchair with a plaid rug pulled around his legs. Opposite him was Daniel who looked up from his book and gave Anna a terse smile. Irene led Anna directly to Ben's wheelchair.

"Look who's come to see you, darling," she cooed.

Ben looked up at Anna and his eyes softened. He lifted a shaky hand and Anna took it in hers.

"Hello, Mr Jacob. It's nice to see you again. We've all missed you so much."

Ben's hand slipped out of her grip and fell limply on to his knee. Irene took Anna's arm and led her over to Daniel. He stood up, clutching the book to his chest. As she and Daniel looked at each other, Anna noticed the striking resemblance between mother and son. Daniel eyes possessed the same shade of deep blue as Irene's, although the gaze was not as intense. His thin fair hair was swept back from his forehead, and he sported a neatly-trimmed moustache. There was certainly no denying that he had inherited the handsome face of his mother.

"Daniel, this is Anna, who you have heard all about," Irene said jauntily.

"I'm very pleased to meet you," he said flatly and sat back down. He put the open book on his lap and kept a finger on the page, as if he were about to resume his reading.

Anna felt unprepared for the introduction and tried not to show how nervous she was. Her eyes rested fleetingly on Irene's cream silk dress, and although her own one wasn't nearly as beautiful, Anna was silently thankful that she had seen fit to buy a new one for the occasion.

"Please, sit down," said Irene, pointing to the chair beside hers.

Mary entered the room carrying a large tray with tea and sandwiches.

"Just leave it on the table, Mary. I will pour." Mary bustled out of the room and Irene looked from Anna to Daniel with a nervous smile. "I was just telling Anna how you had to abandon your studies in Edinburgh," she said, attempting to lure her son into conversation.

Daniel looked across at his mother with a bored expression, as if he had heard her say this a thousand times before. "Yes. It's all been a bit sudden."

Irene turned to Anna. "Daniel hasn't had much experience in the business, so I'm afraid it will fall to you to try to train him in, so to speak."

"Of course. I'll do all I can to assist," Anna said meekly.

Irene handed her a cup and saucer. "Thank you, Anna. I know you'll have Daniel running the place in no time." Irene poured the steaming tea into the cup and Anna struggled to keep her hand from shaking. Irene got up to pour Daniel's but turned back to Anna suddenly. "Oh my goodness! How awful of me! I forgot to congratulate you on your recent engagement."

Anna tightened her grip to stop the tea from

spilling over on to the saucer. How on earth had Irene Jacob heard about her engagement? Anna guessed it must have been from one of the girls in the shop. "Thank you, Mrs Jacob."

"When is the big day?"

"Nothing has been set yet. It won't be for another year or two."

"Well it's very exciting, and I wish you the very best."

Anna looked over to Mr Jacob who was gazing over at her. She smiled at him and tried not to show the sadness she felt at seeing him this way. His head swayed as if it was too heavy to hold up and Anna looked away, unable to disguise her pity.

Irene placed a plate bearing several exquisite little sandwiches on an occasional table next to Anna's chair, and performed the same service for Daniel. Then she sat back down again and smoothed out the pleats of her dress. "Daniel will start next Monday. Perhaps you will tell the rest of the shop staff to expect him."

They sat sipping their tea in awkward silence.

"Hasn't the weather been kind to us lately?" Irene said, looking over at her son for a reply. Daniel looked down at his cup and ignored her remark.

"Yes," Anna obliged. "Just February and it's so mild."

"We've been able to take Mr Jacob out to the garden every day this week. It makes such a difference to his health when we can get him out into the fresh air." Irene tried her best to keep the conversation going, but her words rang shrill against the brittle glass and white light of the conservatory. Her energy seemed to ebb and for a few moments she fell silent.

Anna wondered if Daniel was just shy or extremely rude. He had remained determinedly distant since her arrival and had not feigned even the slightest interest in anything that she or his mother had said.

Irene seemed to sense Anna's thoughts and shot a stern glance at her son. "Daniel, are there any questions you might like to ask Anna?"

Daniel put his cup down on the table beside him and appeared to be thinking deeply about something. He cleared his throat and smiled pleasantly. "No, mother. I have no questions."

"Very well then," said Irene, clasping her hands together tightly. "You'll start on Monday morning?"

"Yes," Daniel answered.

Again a silence descended on the three of them. Irene grabbed another plate and insisted that Anna try one of Mary's shortbread biscuits.

The two women chatted awkwardly on about

inconsequential matters until, eventually, Anna wiped some biscuit crumbs from her skirt and stood up slowly. "I must be going. Thank you for inviting me over. It was so nice to see Mr Jacob again."

Ben uttered a few incoherent sounds and Anna walked over to where he sat and took his hand again.

"Goodbye, Mr Jacob. I hope we will see you back at work soon."

His sad brown eyes met Anna's and she gave his long bony hand a gentle squeeze. When she turned around, Irene was waiting by the door to see her out. Anna looked across at Daniel, which prompted him to stand.

"It was very nice to meet you. Goodbye," he said, and shook Anna's hand limply.

"I'll show you out," said Irene.

Anna gladly left the oppressive conservatory and followed her down the hall.

At the front door Irene helped Anna on with her coat. "I'm sure the two of you will get along very well. Daniel is a bit apprehensive – it's such a big change for him. But I know he'll be back to his old self again once he's had a few weeks to adjust."

"Yes. It must be very difficult for him," Anna said, trying to sound genuinely sympathetic.

She walked away from the house, feeling slightly numb with shock. The last thing she had expected was for one of their sons to come home to run the shop. She had resigned herself to the fact that Mr Jacob was never coming back, but now she felt close to tears as she thought of her beloved employer reduced to a withering wreck in a wheelchair. Anna's sombre thoughts soon dissipated when she thought of Daniel Jacob and his arrogant air of detachment. They had only spent an hour in one another's company and already he had managed to irk her. Anna wondered how on earth she was going to work with him.

* * *

Anna put her father's dinner on the table before him.

"Put a bit of dinner by for Seán – he's not coming home this evening," said Mr Barry.

"Where is he?"

Seán always came home on a Saturday evening to spruce himself up for the night ahead.

"He was going straight out from work. He didn't say where."

Anna sat down and blessed herself before she began to eat.

"Did you go over to see Mr Jacob?" her father asked.

"I did. He's not looking well at all. The poor man, it was sad to see him like that. He can't even speak."

"Why did they want you over? Was it just a social call?"

"No. They wanted me to meet their son Daniel. He's taking over the business until Mr Jacob gets better. But judging by the way he looked today, I don't think he'll ever be back."

"Poor devil. What's the son like?"

Anna chose her words carefully, knowing her father needed little encouragement to criticise the Jacobs. "He seems a bit quiet. I don't think he's too impressed with his new job."

"What's wrong? You seem a bit downhearted after your visit." Mr Barry's eyes narrowed as he looked across at his daughter.

"Nothing, Dada," said Anna quickly. "It'll be a big change, that's all."

"Well, he better treat you right!" Mr Barry waved his knife around in the air. "Them bloody Jew-boys have been working you like a dog."

"Please don't use that word, Dada," said Anna, bowing her head. "I don't like it."

"Well, all I'm saying is that you've been worked to the bone in that place, and this new fella better appreciate you."

"I'm sure he will, Dada," said Anna, reaching for

the milk jug.

Anna watched her father pour the tea from his cup into the saucer. He brought it up slowly to his mouth and slurped it back in noisy gulps.

"By the way, Joe won't be coming around tonight," he said.

Anna looked up in surprise. "Why not?"

"He called into the shop earlier and told me to tell you he couldn't make it."

"Did he say why?"

Mr Barry looked irate. "No, he didn't say why. He only said to give you that message."

"Is he with Seán?" Anna could see that her questions were annoying her father.

"How would I know where he is?"

Anna stared across at her father and raised her eyebrows but he turned his face away and reached for another slice of bread.

★　★　★

The dull thudding noise woke Anna from her sleep. At first she thought it must have been a dream but as she wakened fully she heard it again downstairs. It grew louder and more persistent. Anna sat up and listened in the darkness. This time she jumped when it happened again. It was the front door being hammered on from outside. Anna slipped out of her bed and tip-toed out to the landing.

Mr Barry came out of his bedroom, tying the cord of his dressing-gown. "What in God's name is that?"

"Someone is trying to break down the front door," Anna said in a terrified whisper as she peered down the stairs.

The banging started again and they heard a muffled voice outside. Mr Barry rushed past Anna and ran down the stairs. He opened the door of the parlour and came back out swinging a poker in his hand. He raised it in the air as he opened the front door slowly. In the half light Anna saw the figure of a man as he hurled himself head first into the hallway and fell on the floor at her father's feet. Standing at the top of the stairs, Anna screamed.

Mr Barry jumped back against the wall in fright.

"Be quiet," said the figure in a hoarse whisper. "It's me, Joe. Shut the door!"

Mr Barry dropped the poker and slammed the door shut, then hurried over to light the gas lamp on the wall behind him. "What's happened to you, Joe?"

Joe lay face down on the floor and raised his head slightly. "Seán's behind me. Please God let him be behind me!"

Anna saw the blood trickling down the side of Joe's face and put her hand to her mouth. "Joe, what's going on? Who did that to you?" she said, running down the stairs.

Joe rolled over onto to his back and tried to sit up, but he fell back onto the floor.

Mr Barry bent down and pulled him into a sitting position, then put his head under Joe's arm and pulled him up. Joe looked around the hall in a daze. "Get the other arm, Anna, we'll move him into the parlour."

Anna took a hold of the other arm and buckled under the weight of Joe's heavy frame. With tiny steps they led him into the parlour and across it until they reached the couch and let Joe collapse onto it in a heap.

"I'll get something to clean that up," Anna said, pointing to the deep cut on the side of his head. She rushed out of the room, leaving the two men alone.

Joe put his hand up to his temple to search for the cut and winced when his fingers located it. "Where the hell is Seán?" he groaned. Mr Barry went to light a lamp but Joe stopped him. "Don't turn on any more lights," he ordered.

Mr Barry checked that Anna was safely out of earshot, then he turned to Joe. "What happened?"

Joe let his head flop back onto the arm of the

couch. "Someone tipped them off."

Mr Barry exhaled loudly.

"We were loading up the artillery, when half the Free State Army appeared from out of nowhere."

"Jesus!" Mr Barry said under his breath.

"The first truck was loaded and gone but they fired on the second one. I think Bertie Slattery was shot." Joe raised himself up with one elbow. "Seán was behind me when we made a run for it, but when I rounded the corner at Gardiner Street I lost him."

Mr Barry clenched his jaw and gave Joe a worried look.

Anna came back into the room, carrying a basin of warm water and a towel which she set down on the table beside the couch. She knelt down beside Joe and began to dab gently at his wound. Her father paced the floor behind her. The water in the white tin basin turned pink as Anna rinsed the blood from the towel. "Dada, turn on a light."

"No," both men said in unison.

Anna raised her head and frowned. "I'm sure you have a good reason for sitting in the dark but I won't ask," she said sharply. "Joe, where is Seán? I thought you said he was behind you."

Mr Barry looked across at Joe uneasily.

Anna jumped up suddenly.

Joe reached for her hand and pulled her back

towards him. "He was with me. I don't know what happened to him."

Anna pulled her hand free and stepped back. "Where were you tonight? Tell me, Joe," she demanded. Joe let his head fall back once again and stared up at the ceiling. Anna looked at her father accusingly. "You knew they were up to something tonight! Why didn't you stop them?"

"It's not my place to stop them," he answered in a measured tone.

"Seán is your son! You should have talked some sense into him."

"Anna, stop," Joe snapped. "Seán is an adult – your father is not responsible for his actions."

Anna looked across the room at Joe. "He worships you. He would do anything to gain your respect. You should know better than to put him in danger!"

Mr Barry stepped up to Anna and pointed a finger at her. "There's a war going on, and your brother and your fiancé are fighting it." He looked at his daughter and shook his head. "For God's sake, Anna, what side are you on at all?"

Then the three of them stiffened as they heard the sound of heavy footfalls slapping against the pavement outside. A key rattled frantically in the front-door lock. Anna ran into the hall and collided with her brother as he collapsed panting onto the floor. Mr Barry ran out and fell to his knees beside Seán. "Are you hurt son?"

Seán rose up on to his knees. "I'm alright, Da. Is Joe here?"

"He is. He got hit on the head – he's inside on the couch."

Seán threw his head back with relief. "Thanks be to God!"

He entered the parlour wild-eyed and grinned over at Joe.

Joe sat up, holding the towel to his head. "Where did you go? One minute you were behind me and the next you were gone."

"I had a bloody Free Stater stuck to the back of me, so I thought I'd give him a run for his money. I gave him the slip down a laneway behind the Custom House."

"Are you sure you lost him?" asked Joe, making his way across the room to look out a crack in the curtains.

"Of course I lost him. You hardly think I'd lead them back here."

Joe took the towel from his head and threw it into the basin.

"You should rest for a while. It could start to bleed again," said Anna.

Seán went over and looked at the cut on Joe's head. "It looks deep enough. What was it? A rifle butt?" Joe glared at Seán and ignored the question.

Anna stood in the middle of the room and knew that her presence was no longer required. Without saying anything, she left the three of them alone and closed the door behind her.

Chapter 7

Daniel sat behind his father's desk and flicked through the morning newspaper. He gazed down at the calendar and realised that it had been a month since he had started work at the shoe shop, yet it felt more like an eternity. Anna and the rest of the staff had tried their best to help him settle in, but he had not been able to muster up any enthusiasm for the job. Each day he tried to kill the interminable boredom by thumbing through the newspapers or spending long hours poring over his law books. He was determined to prove to his mother that the staff at Jacob's were quite capable of running the company without him. If he could make her see just how useless he was, then perhaps she would release him from this impossible situation and let him return to Edinburgh.

Anna tapped on the glass pane of his office door. Daniel folded the newspaper slowly and indicated for her to enter.

"I'm sorry to disturb you," she said.

Daniel sat up in his chair and rearranged some pens on his desk. "Come in, Miss Barry."

Anna stepped over the threshold into the office but stayed close to the door. "There is a delivery on Saturday morning. Will you be coming in to oversee it?"

Daniel smiled lazily and shrugged his shoulders. "What is there to oversee?"

"Usually Mr Jacob comes in to supervise the unloading. There's some paperwork to be completed and, well, that's it really."

Again Daniel smiled at Anna. "Can you manage it alone or do you need me there?"

"I can manage it by myself. I just thought that you might want to be there."

Daniel threw his hands into the air. "Well, there's no need for me to be there if you can do it alone. I'd probably just get in the way."

"Well," said Anna brusquely, turning to leave, "I

just thought I'd let you know."

Daniel leaned forward. "My mother looks after the extra hours, I presume?"

Anna blushed. Somehow it seemed inappropriate that he should be asking about her wages. "Oh yes, of course," she answered quickly. "Would you like a cup of tea?" she added.

"That would be very nice, thank you."

Anna left the office and ran her hand across the back of her clammy neck. How she wished Mr Jacob were back again! Daniel's lofty manner made him difficult to approach and Anna felt foolish every time she knocked on his office door as her queries were usually met with a vacant stare. He insisted on calling her Miss Barry, even though he knew that his father had called her by her first name. Anna could not bring herself to address him as Mr Jacob which had contributed to the impersonal relationship that had developed between them. He was polite at all times, but Anna couldn't help feeling like a nuisance every time she disturbed him with a query.

★ ★ ★

The drawings for the winter collection had arrived in the post and Anna opened them with a long sigh. This was the one thing she had nothing to do with.

The sketches arrived from Leeds twice yearly, and after passing them around the shop staff for opinions, Mr Jacob made the final decisions. Choosing the wrong design could mean a stockroom full of unsold shoes and Anna did not have the confidence to assume this particular responsibility. The office had been so busy all week that the sketches had remained untouched on her desk. By Friday afternoon, she knew she would have to talk to Daniel and try to get him involved in the ordering. Apart from not wanting the responsibility, she was just too busy to take on anything else. Daniel's head was bent over a book when she entered his office.

Anna waited, clutching the bundle of sketches to her chest.

Daniel closed over the book and stood up. "Miss Barry, I was just about to leave. What can I do for you?"

Anna glanced up at the wall clock. It was only half past three on Friday afternoon – she would be lucky to finish up by seven. "These are the design sketches from Leeds," she said, dropping the papers down on to Daniel's desk.

Daniel stared at them blankly and lifted his gaze to Anna. "What am I supposed to do with them?"

Anna rolled the sketches open and began to explain. "If you can look over the designs and mark the ones that you want for next winter."

"Me?" Daniel exclaimed loudly.

"Yes," Anna said, trying to be as patient as she could. "I can't make that decision."

"Why not? You know more about these things than I do."

"That's not the point. I am not prepared to take on such a huge responsibility. I was asked to assist you in running this office, and it is you who should decide these things."

Anna could hear her heart beating loudly. She did not know where those words had come from.

They stood in silence, both looking down at the sketches.

She took a deep breath, forcing herself to seize the opportunity and say what had been on her mind for months. "I can't do everything," she said quietly.

Daniel looked up at her in shock.

"Perhaps if you took the sketches home and looked over them with Mr Jacob." Her voice trembled as she spoke so brazenly to him. Anna would never have spoken to Mr Jacob like this, but months of being overworked had left her feeling cranky and exhausted. She was immediately angry with herself for her silly outburst and her eyes moistened with the threat of tears. She quickly blinked them away and went to gather up the sketches.

"If you don't want to do them, then I suppose I could find the time to look over them next week," she blurted, not meeting his gaze.

Daniel looked down at the designs in confusion and put a hand on Anna's arm to stop her from taking them away. "I'll take them home with me this evening."

Anna looked up at him. "Are you sure?"

"Yes, I'll show them to father and see what he wants to do," he mumbled.

Anna stepped back from the desk feeling ashamed of herself. She could think of nothing to say that would smooth over the sharpness of her earlier words.

Daniel began to fumble with the papers, rolling them into a messy bundle.

Anna was back at her desk when Daniel came out of his office a few minutes later. He took his overcoat from the stand by the door and threw it over one arm. Under the other arm the rolled-up design papers were crushed carelessly against his side. Anna felt his eyes on her, but she kept her head down and didn't dare to look up.

She heard him hesitate at the door, probably waiting for her to lift her head but she pretended to be oblivious to his presence.

"Goodbye," he said.

To her immense relief he had left the room by the time she raised her head.

★   ★   ★

Daniel moved into the living room after dinner and warmed his hands by the fire. His mother entered the room and joined him by the fireplace. She arched her back and massaged the base of her spine with both hands before lowering herself gently into an armchair.

"Mother, you will break your back one of these evenings. Why don't you let me put Father to bed?"

Irene waved her hand, dismissing Daniel's suggestion. "Mary and I can manage quite well. It's what he's used to. It would only make him feel more of an invalid if you were to start helping." Irene smiled across at her son. "He was in such good form this evening. I'm so glad you brought home those designs and asked for his opinion – it gave him a real sense of purpose. Did you see the way he moved his arms about as he pointed to the sketches he wanted? He even insisted on moving himself from the wheelchair to the bed tonight. Thank you, Daniel, it was a marvellous idea."

Daniel shifted his weight from one foot to the other, feeling fraudulent with such undeserved praise. "Actually it wasn't my idea. Anna suggested it."

"Well it doesn't matter who thought of it. It worked!" Irene said happily.

"I'm afraid I might have upset her today," said Daniel.

Irene sat forward in her chair. "How?"

"My lack of interest in the business has resulted in her having to take on quite a lot. I didn't realise it until now, but the poor girl seems completely overworked. I feel rather bad about it."

"Oh darling! We all feel bad about what you've had to sacrifice to be here. It must be difficult for you to step into a job you know nothing about."

Daniel stared into the fire. "I feel so useless!" He spat the words out angrily.

"Daniel, you are anything but useless. Your father and I would be lost without you!"

"Looking at poor Father this evening made me realise just how useless I am," he went on, ignoring her words. "He would give anything to be back at work again. It took all his strength just to point at the shoes on the paper." Daniel sighed loudly. "I've been no help at all – I've done nothing but mope around feeling sorry for myself."

Irene stretched across and took his hand. "We really appreciate what you've done for us."

Daniel looked down at her and tried to smile.

"It means so much to your father that you have taken over. I hope Anna is being helpful?"

Daniel felt a fresh wave of annoyance as he thought of how his selfish behaviour must look to a hardworking girl like Anna.

"Yes, Mother, she's being too good to me. I'll have to try harder from now on – it isn't fair that everything has been left to her. There is a delivery tomorrow morning – perhaps I should go in and give a hand."

"Good," Irene beamed at him. "Now let me get you a drink before you turn in for the night."

Irene walked over to the drinks cabinet with a contented sense of achievement. It was the first time since Daniel had returned home that he had spoken to her without his usual air of resentment.

"She's a nice girl, isn't she?" Daniel said, breaking the silence.

Irene turned around in surprise and looked at Daniel. "Anna?"

"Yes," Daniel answered quickly, immediately regretting this remark when he saw the glassy smile that spread across his mother's face.

"She's a lovely girl," said Irene, handing him the brandy glass. "She's also engaged to be married." A note of caution had crept into her voice.

Daniel took a sip and blushed. "I wasn't suggesting … "

"She's a very attractive girl but she is spoken for."

Daniel cradled the glass in the palm of his hand and smiled wryly. "Thank you for the warning, Mother."

"I had a letter from Granny today – she was asking if you have met any nice Jewish girls in Edinburgh."

Daniels smile faded and he looked across at his mother with disdain. "I've met plenty of nice girls, but it never crossed my mind to inquire what their religious persuasions might be."

"Anyone special?"

"Not really."

Irene knew not to press him any further on the subject. Daniel had always been open about any romances in the past and Irene didn't want to spoil that confidence by prying. Peter on the other hand was her dark horse. Irene had no idea whether he was romantically involved with anyone. Ever since he had broken off his engagement last year, he had remained guarded about divulging any information about his love life, and any attempt to find out was always met with a flinty silence.

"Hasn't Granny Jacob picked out any nice girl yet? I thought by now she would have them lining up to meet you."

A hint of mischief crossed over Irene's face and Daniel knew he was being teased.

"Luckily I'm far enough away from Leeds and Granny's meddling. She has poor old Peter browbeaten into meeting every eligible Jewish girl in England."

Irene was glad of the part Granny Jacob had played in Peter breaking off his engagement. The girl had been totally unsuitable, seven years his senior, and they had all heaved a sigh of relief on hearing that his marriage plans had been cancelled. But she also remembered how forceful her mother-in-law could be and worried that she might bully Peter into making the wrong decision.

Daniel looked over at his mother and could tell what she was thinking. "Don't worry, he's wise enough to know his own mind on these matters."

"I hope so. I couldn't stand the thought of Granny arranging a marriage for him."

"Peter is shrewd enough. He appears to go along with everything Granny says, but in the end he does exactly what he wants. Unlike me, he can do no wrong in her eyes."

"Daniel, that's not true. Granny adores both of you."

"We never stopped arguing when I lived with her

in Leeds. She told me I was a thorn in her side!"

"It was only because she couldn't understand why you didn't want to join the business."

"She thinks I'm lazy, she told me so."

Irene gave a sudden laugh. "Did she really say that to you?"

"Yes," said Daniel indignantly.

"Sorry for laughing, dear, but you have to admit the woman does know how to speak her mind."

"Yes, I'll give her that. She certainly holds nothing back when it comes to airing her views. I mean, just because I didn't want to haul boxes of shoes up and down the factory stairs, or learn how to work the machinery didn't mean I was lazy. I just wasn't interested."

Irene surprised herself with how quickly she jumped to her mother-in-law's defence.

"I understand, dear, but in her eyes, everyone must start at the bottom and work their way up. It's how your father started, and his father before him. You must remember, your grandparents had nothing when they arrived in England. Old Mr Jacob made the shoes himself in the back room of their house. They built that business up from nothing. Granny Jacob comes from a generation that can't understand why their grandchildren would pass up such an opportunity."

Daniel put his empty brandy glass on the mantelpiece and stretched his arms over his head. "I suppose you're right. Perhaps one day I'll make her proud of me."

"She's proud of you already." Irene stood up and kissed Daniel on the cheek. "Goodnight, my dear."

★   ★   ★

Anna stifled a yawn as she stood outside the entrance to the storeroom. Saturday morning had not quite shaken off the gloomy dawn. It was still grey and misty and she rubbed her hands together against the cold.

"You go on in! We'll sort this out and let you know when we're finished!" shouted Seán over the engine of the reversing truck.

Anna didn't argue. She was chilly and wanted to get inside and warm up. She nodded her head in agreement and took the papers from the truck driver before walking up the narrow laneway that led on to Sackville Street where the entrance to the shop was. Once inside the porch, Anna pushed open the shop door and the bell overhead gave a tinkle as she stepped in. The staff were busy, bustling around carrying boxes of shoes for the waiting customers. Anna stood at the door and looked around, surveying the faces of the people, checking to see if any of them seemed dissatisfied with the service they were getting. Two middle-aged women struggled with shoehorns as they tried to lever their feet into new stiff leather boots. Everything seemed to be under control and Anna turned and left the capable staff to get on with their work. Outside in the porch was another front door that opened onto a small hall which led to a flight of stairs. Anna opened this door and began to take the stairs up to her office. As she approached the small landing she heard a cough. Anna stood still and listened, afraid to open the door to her office.

"Hello?" she called out.

Footsteps sounded behind the door and Anna put her hand on the banisters ready to turn and run.

The door opened slowly and Daniel stuck his head out. "Good morning."

Anna put her hand up to her chest and breathed out slowly. "I didn't expect to see you here. You startled me!"

Daniel opened the door fully and smiled at her. "Sorry, I didn't mean to."

"How long have you been here?" Anna asked, trying to hide her surprise at seeing him.

"Just a few minutes. I decided to come in and help out with this delivery. If you can show me how it's done, then perhaps I can look after it next time and give you a morning off."

Anna followed him into the office.

Daniel turned to face her. "Look, I know I haven't exactly been much help to you since I started working here. You might have guessed by now that this was not something I wanted."

Anna felt her pulse racing. After weeks of barely speaking to her, having him address her with such familiarity was unnerving.

"I thought that by now my mother would have found someone to take over my father's position, but it appears that she is in no hurry to get rid of me. I apologise for my lack of cooperation."

Anna's tongue seemed to be stuck to the roof of her mouth. She stared at Daniel for a few seconds before saying, "There is no need to apologise."

"Yes, there is. And if you could agree to accept my apology and treat this as my first day of work, it would mean a great deal to me."

Anna looked away in embarrassment and smiled shyly.

Daniel took this to be an acceptance of his remorse. "Shall we get to work?" he asked.

Anna looked down and gasped when she saw the shipping documents crumpled into a ball in her hand. "Oh dear," she groaned, "look what I've done with the papers."

Daniel looked down at them and grinned. "I hope my turning over a new leaf is a good idea. You seem to run the place so well by yourself, I'll probably end up being more of a nuisance to you."

Anna put the papers on her desk and smoothed them out with the flat of her hand.

She turned to Daniel and smiled warmly. "Believe me, I could really do with some help."

They worked together for the morning. Anna showed Daniel around the office as if it really was his first day. She showed him the simple everyday tasks, like how to place an order or find a file, and Daniel listened eagerly. Later, when they had got down to their own individual tasks, they heard the sound of heavy boots on the stairway below.

Daniel raised his head.

"It's the men," explained Anna from her desk. "They must be finished unloading."

Seán and the driver arrived at the office door and knocked.

"Come in!" called Anna.

The men stepped inside and nodded at Daniel when he appeared from his office.

"This is Mr Jacob," said Anna. "Mr Jacob, this is my brother Seán and Mr Byrne who drives the truck."

Daniel walked awkwardly towards the men. "I'm pleased to meet you."

Both men looked at him blankly. Seán mumbled a barely audible greeting under his breath, and Mr Byrne the driver rocked back on his heels and grunted.

Anna pulled two envelopes from her desk drawer and handed one to each of them. "Thanks, lads."

Mr Byrne stuffed his into his shirt pocket and pulled on his cap. He looked over at Daniel and nodded. "Goodbye, Anna," he said as he left the office.

Seán hung back at the door.

"Thanks, Seán," said Anna. "I'll see you later."

"Will I wait for you?" Seán asked.

"No. I've a bit more to do. You go on."

Seán tipped his cap to Daniel and left the office. They trundled down the stairs and the door out on to the street closed with a loud bang as they left the building.

Daniel stood at the filing cabinet in the corner and looked across at Anna. He studied her profile as she leaned over an accounts ledger, her head tilted to one side as she concentrated on the lines of numbers in front of her. Her thick fair hair had been pinned back tightly that morning with a silver comb, but the tiny wisps that had come loose created a delicate frame around her face. He noticed she wrote with her left hand, holding the pen crooked in towards her body. Anna moved her head and Daniel jumped away from the cabinet and hurried back into his office. He threw the files he was holding on to his desk and waited a few minutes to steal a glance at her again when she had turned her head back towards the ledger.

Anna finished her work by lunchtime and tidied the files and papers from her desk. When she was ready to leave she knocked on Daniel's door and opened it. Daniel stood up from his desk.

"I'm leaving now, Mr Jacob."

Daniel's forehead creased into a mass of wrinkles. "Do you mind if I call you Anna?"

Anna looked surprised at his question. "No, of course not," she answered.

"Then I insist that you call me Daniel."

"Alright, Daniel. I'll see you on Monday," said Anna, backing out of the office.

Chapter 8

Seán sat in the kitchen polishing his shoes and raised his head as he heard a knock on the front door. He waited for a few seconds, listening out for his father's footsteps on the stairs, but no sound came. He put the shoes down on the newspaper and walked up the chilly hall to answer the door.

Joe was standing outside blowing his thumb-nails against the cold wind that blew into the hall off the canal. "What took you so long? I'm paralysed with the cold."

"Sorry, Joe, I thought Da was getting it. Come in."

Joe stepped into the hall and looked towards the

stairs. "Who's here?"

"Da is. I think he must be asleep. Anna's not in from work yet."

Joe lowered his voice. "Good. I want to talk to you."

Joe walked by Seán and down towards the kitchen.

Seán's eyes lit up with curiosity as he scurried after him. "What is it?" he asked, like an excited child.

When they got into the kitchen Joe closed the door and waited for a few seconds before he said anything.

Seán jumped from one foot to the other. "Have you a job for me?"

Joe nodded towards the chairs. "Sit down and listen."

When they had taken a seat across from each other at the table Joe began. "We've had a tip-off. They're going to raid Tracy's warehouse tomorrow. The ammunition has to be moved."

"Jesus! How did they find out about it?"

Joe looked solemnly at Seán. "Someone is informing Dublin Castle." He sat back in his chair and exhaled loudly. "That's another day's work. Right now we have to move quickly. There's a truck organised to clear the place this evening, but the problem is finding somewhere safe enough to store the stuff."

Seán found it difficult to hide the immense pride he felt by being deemed worthy of receiving such confidential information. "Anything I can do to help, Joe, just say the word."

Joe sat quietly tapping his thumb against his chin, his brow deeply furrowed as he thought. He sighed loudly. "I've tried to think of somewhere safe, but the bastards have everywhere under surveillance. You're the only one I can think of that can help."

Seán sat back in his chair with a look of genuine surprise.

"Me?" he asked incredulously. Seán had been waiting for the chance to show his loyalty to the anti-Treaty forces, always making himself available for whatever task was required of him in the hope that he would be noticed and plucked from the ranks of obscurity for better things. But so far, his missions had only involved cycling around Dublin delivering dispatches to higher-ranking officers. He could feel the blood pulse through his veins at being asked to do something of any significance.

Joe leaned forward. "We need you to take them."

Seán looked around the kitchen in bewilderment. "Sure, but where could I put them?"

"Not here. There are four cases of them. We need somewhere they'll go unnoticed. Can you get a hold of the keys to Anna's work place?"

The colour drained from Seán's face while Joe stared at him waiting for an answer.

"I wouldn't involve you unless I had to, Seán. This is an emergency – we need to act quickly. I'll make sure the boss gets to hear about this. "

Seán ran his hands through his hair. "I suppose I could try to take the keys out of her bag later. I'll have to wait until she's in bed." The fleeting sense of pride had turned to a knot in his stomach as he thought of the risk he'd be taking.

"They're being moved from Tracy's at midnight tonight … " The two men jumped as they heard the sound of Anna's key rattling in the front door. Joe raised a finger to stop Seán speaking. "Listen to me. I don't care how long you have to wait, just make sure she doesn't catch you. As soon as you have the keys, come straight to Lawlor's. Knock five times on the side door. I'll be waiting in the bar for you."

Anna pushed open the kitchen door and smiled across at Joe. Seán stared down at his hands nervously.

"Did I interrupt something?" Anna asked, looking at her brother.

Seán pushed himself away from the table and stood up. "Nothing at all," he said, smiling sheepishly. "What's for the tea?"

Anna threw her eyes up to heaven and put her bags on the table. "Do you ever have anything else to say?"

"I'll be off," said Joe, giving Anna a kiss on the cheek.

"Will you not stay for tea?" she asked half-heartedly.

"No. I've got to get home. I'll see you tomorrow night?"

Anna looked at Joe and then at her brother. "I hope the two of you aren't up to anything."

"Would you give over, Anna? I just called for a chat with Seán. I'll see you tomorrow."

Anna shrugged her shoulders. "Fine," she said and turned to unpack the meat and bread from the bags.

Joe nodded across at Seán. "I'll be seeing you."

"I'll walk up to the door with you," said Seán.

Joe held up a hand to stop him. "Don't bother," he said and walked out of the room.

Seán stood with his mouth open, trying to take in what Joe had asked him to do. He felt his sister's eyes on the back of his head and turned around. He rounded his shoulders and tried to brazen out her knowing stare, but Anna always got the better of him.

"Don't go getting yourself into trouble," she warned.

"Give over!" he shouted in a rush of bravado. "It's none of your business, woman!" He opened the kitchen door and went to leave.

"Where are you going?" demanded Anna.

"Out for smokes."

"No, you are not. Sit down. Your tea will be ready in a few minutes."

Seán kept his hand on the kitchen door, not knowing which side to shut it from.

"Well, what are you standing there for? Set the table and call Dada," Anna said as she reached for her apron.

Seán left the kitchen, and Anna turned to the cooker and put the frying pan down over the heat. She felt guilty at the relief that rushed through her when Joe had said he'd have to rush off. Getting engaged had not chased away the doubts and uncertainties that had lurked at the back of her mind for so long. It had only confirmed to Anna that her feelings for Joe had changed, and she knew that there was no denying it any more. Every time she thought about telling him, it made her feel sick.

* * *

Anna sat by the fire in her dressing-gown and tied her damp hair into rags. It was the way she had styled her hair since she was a child. Her mother would first brush out her long golden hair by the fireside until it was almost dry, then she would wrap it in what they had always called rags – long pieces of cotton that bound around the sections of hair to give it a strong curl the following day.

Her father had spent the evening shining and sharpening his blades and scissors for the barbershop and now he packed them into a small battered leather case and shut the lid. "That's it for me. I'm off to bed," he said yawning. He smoked the last of his cigarette and threw the butt into the fireplace.

Anna struggled with the pieces of hair at the back of her head while Seán sat across from her, shaking his leg impatiently. After she'd made two unsuccessful attempts at reaching the long tresses, he jumped up from the chair. "Here, do you want me to do those bits?"

Anna looked over at her father. He returned her wide-eyed stare and they both started to laugh.

"Well, you've been fiddling with them for ages. It's getting on my nerves," Seán said, aware that they were making fun of him.

Anna felt a pang of pity for her brother and stopped laughing. "Hold this." She turned her back to him and guided his hand to the piece of hair.

"Now, wrap it around tightly," she instructed, giving him the rag. Seán began to wind the rag around the hair as quickly as he could, as if his life depended on it, anything to get her up to bed and out of the way. Mr Barry looked on with amusement. "By God, maybe you should come and work with me in the shop! You could start a new fashion," he said, winking at Anna.

When Seán had finished, Anna ran her hand along the finished sections of hair at the back of her head. They were loose and probably would not curl as well as the ones she had done, but not wanting to hurt her brother's feelings she decided to wait until she was in her bedroom to do them again herself.

"Thanks, Seán, goodnight. Put the fireguard up before you go to bed."

Upstairs, Anna unravelled the rags from the back of hair and redid the sections again in the privacy of her bedroom. Her clothes for the following morning were neatly pressed and hanging on the back of her wardrobe door. She pulled back her bedcovers and removed the hot jar that had been warming the sheets, placing it on the floor. Inside her cosy bed she pressed her cold feet against the warm spot of the heated sheets and looked forward to a good night's sleep. Before turning out the gas lamp by her bed she looked around the room for her handbag. It was not under the chair where she always left it. Looking around the room she tried to remember if she had brought it into the kitchen with her earlier, but she was sure she had left it under her bedroom chair. Swinging her legs over the side of the bed, she put her feet into her slippers and went out into the chilly landing, sighing loudly. She heard Seán at the kitchen door below and leaned over the banisters.

"Seán?" she whispered loudly.

"What?" he answered, his exasperation floating upwards in the darkness.

"Did I leave my bag down there?"

"Yes. It's in the kitchen."

"Will you bring it up?"

Anna stood in silence and waited for an answer.

"I'm making a cup of tea. I'll bring it up when I'm going to bed."

"Well, don't forget. Goodnight." Anna shivered and hurried back to the warmth of her room.

Once in bed, the familiar thoughts that had begun to come to her nightly returned, first with pleasure but followed as always with a wave of guilt. Daniel Jacob's face appeared before her eyes and she replayed every little encounter that had occurred that day, no matter how trivial. A look, a slight brush against his shirt sleeve, the way she had caught him looking at her as she placed a cup of tea on his desk.

There was no denying it, no matter how wrong it was, she found Daniel attractive. It wasn't just physical attraction – there had been none of that in the first few weeks of working with him. It was a deeper feeling. A feeling she knew that both of them shared, an energy that played between the two of them whenever they were together. Like the way things used to be when she first met Joe. As she drifted deeper into her thoughts she felt a presence in the room and heard Seán put her handbag on the floor.

Then, a little later, through the mist of her half-sleep she heard the click of the front door being closed downstairs.

★ ★ ★

The following morning, just as Anna was about to leave the house, Seán came charging down the stairs. His hair had not been brushed and the top buttons of his shirt were still undone.

"Why didn't you call me?" he said as he brushed past Anna.

"I thought you'd left. What are you doing here at this time?"

"I slept it out." Seán grabbed the comb from the hall table and dragged it roughly through his tangled hair.

Anna stood beside him at the mirror. "It's no wonder you couldn't get up, wandering out at all hours of the night."

Seán stopped combing his hair and looked at Anna's reflection in the mirror. "What are you talking about?"

"I heard you going out last night. It must have been after eleven."

Seán threw the comb down on the table and buttoned his shirt. "I didn't go anywhere last night."

Anna kept her eyes on him through the mirror. "Yes, you did. I heard the front door close after you."

"Well, if you had stayed awake you would have heard the door open ten minutes later. I walked down to the end of the road and back again, if you must know."

Anna kept staring, and waited for him to continue.

"I had a headache. I walked up the road for some air, but it was bloody freezing so I came back."

Anna had not stayed awake long enough to hear him come back so she could not accuse him of anything. She lifted her hat from the hall table and noticed that the keys to Jacob's were lying underneath it. "What are my keys doing here?"

Seán glanced down at them quickly. "They fell out of your bag last night. When I found them later,

I thought the noise would wake you if I went into your room so I just left them there."

"Seán," she cried, losing her patience, "I could have gone without them!"

"But you didn't," he said, grinning at her. "I put them under your hat so you'd find them."

"And what if I decided to wear a different hat?" Without waiting for his answer, she stuck a pin into the side of her hat and stuffed the keys into her handbag. "Hurry up and get to work, Seán, or you'll be sacked!"

The front door closed and Seán heard the click of his sister's heels on the pavement outside. He stopped fumbling with his shirt buttons and leaned in towards the mirror. His eyes were puffy from lack of sleep. It had been after four in the morning by the time they had hidden the crates in Jacob's storeroom and Seán was still exhausted. "Christ," he muttered to his reflection.

Chapter 9

Mrs Maguire smiled sweetly at Anna and Joe as she led them into the dainty parlour of her home on Grand Canal Street. Mr Maguire was sitting smoking a pipe, which he lit every evening on hearing the Angelus bells ring. "Anna," he said, standing to greet her. "Lovely to see you."

"Hello, Mr Maguire. Thank you for inviting me."

Joe's mother pointed to a seat by the window. "Please sit down."

Anna sat in the chair by the window and Joe sat beside his mother on the couch.

"We haven't seen you since Joe told us the good

news," said Mr Maguire. "We're very happy for you both. Anna, you know you are very welcome in this family." He stood beside his wife and waved his pipe in the air as he spoke.

Mrs Maguire looked down at the carpet, the smile still frozen on her face. It had been six years almost to the day since she had lost her eldest son Francis in the Easter Rising. He was nineteen years old and although Anna hadn't known the Maguire family back then, she remembered hearing how Mrs Maguire had stayed in bed for almost a year after his death. Anna didn't visit Joe's family very often but, when she did, she was always struck by the heavy silence that pervaded the pristine house. There was never any noise, not even a clang of a pot or pan from the kitchen when Mrs Maguire was cooking. Even Joe, who was normally so good-humoured and boisterous, seemed to take on the same silence when he was at home. Every time Anna visited his parents she was struck by how solemn Joe became in their presence.

"Have you set a date yet?" Mr Maguire asked in a stage whisper.

"Not yet," said Anna, jumping in before Joe could get a chance to say anything.

"How is your father Anna?" Mrs Maguire asked.

"He's very well. Delighted with the news."

"We'll have to meet up with him very soon and celebrate," Mr Maguire said, clenching his pipe between his teeth.

The four of them sat without saying anything for a few seconds. Anna looked across at Joe but he was staring down at his knees and seemed completely detached from their little group.

Mrs Maguire stood up quickly, as if she couldn't bear to sit still for a moment longer. "Will you come into the kitchen for some tea?" she said and led the way out into the hall.

★　★　★

Anna pushed the mound of ham around her plate – she had eaten as much as her stomach would hold and yet the plate still appeared full. Mrs Maguire had given Anna as much food as Joe and her husband but, due to her own birdlike appetite, had only allowed herself a thin slice of ham. Her knife and fork lay neatly together on her empty plate while Anna struggled to eat a little more.

Joe's father was talking about a house his nephew had bought in Malahide. "Lovely spot, by the sea. Nice place to rear children."

Mrs Maguire reached over and placed her hand on Anna's forearm. "Have you tried on any wedding dresses yet?" she asked with a smile.

"Not yet. It's a bit early, maybe next year."

Anna could feel her face getting hot. All this talk about weddings and houses and children was making her feel uneasy. She wished Joe would finish his dinner and suggest a walk, or anything to get her out of the house. He had arranged this tea with his parents without even asking her about it, and Anna felt like a hypocrite accepting their hospitality when all she could really think about was how she was going to break off her engagement to their son.

There was a special cake in honour of their engagement, served with tea in Mrs Maguire's best china cups in the front room.

"Anna, please tell your father that we will be happy to share the cost of the wedding breakfast," said Mr Maguire.

Anna placed her cup back on her saucer. "That's very generous of you, I'll certainly tell him," she said faintly.

"Joe is our only boy. Indeed, our only child. His will be the only wedding we will have in this family. I'd like to contribute." Mr Maguire glanced over at his wife for her reaction but she gazed out the window impassively.

Anna looked at Joe and hoped he would read the message of desperation in her eyes.

Joe leaned across and took the cup from her hand. "It's time Anna was getting home."

Anna stood up a little too quickly. "Yes. That was lovely, thank you very much."

After their goodbyes, the Maguires stood at the garden gate and watched as Joe and Anna walked down the road.

"They really like you, Anna," said Joe as they turned the corner.

Anna smiled up at him, and they walked on in silence for several minutes.

"They never got over Francis, did they?" said Anna.

Joe stared down at the footpath. "No. None of us did."

"Do you find it hard, being the only son now?"

Joe had rarely ever talked about his brother and Anna could see he was uncomfortable with her questions.

"Yes," he said quickly. He took her hand in his and kissed it.

Anna looked down at the ink stains on his fingertips, indelible prints from the plates at work.

"Don't be talking about sad things," he said, letting his face relax into a smile. They kissed behind the trunk of an oak tree and continued the walk to Anna's house. When they got to her front door,

Anna glanced down at Joe's pocket-watch – it was only nine o'clock. The strain of lying to his parents all evening had worn her out but it was too early to send him home again.

"Come in for a while," she said, turning her key in the door.

In the back kitchen Mr Barry had dozed off in his armchair. He jumped when he heard the two of them walk into the room.

"My God, I must have drifted off. How are you, Joe?" He stood up from the chair. "Here, sit down."

"No," said Joe, "sit back down yourself."

Mr Barry pulled a handkerchief from his trouser pocket and wiped his mouth. "No, you sit down. I'm off to bed." He turned to Anna. "Did you have a nice time?"

"We did, Dada. Will you have a cup of tea?"

Mr Barry picked up the crumpled Sunday newspaper and folded it under his arm. "No, thanks, love," he said, kissing her forehead. "Goodnight."

"Goodnight, Mr Barry," said Joe.

"You make yourself comfortable there, Joe," he said, pointing towards his chair. "Anna, make him a cup of tea."

"Yes, Dada," said Anna. "Goodnight."

Anna shovelled more coal onto the fire and stoked it until an orange flame flickered through the dirty smoke. "I'll go and make the tea," she said, getting to her feet.

Joe reached out and grabbed her arm, pulling her down onto his knee. "I don't want any tea," he said, kissing her neck.

Anna reluctantly put her arms around him. Joe pulled her closer and they kissed slowly, Anna all the time listening out for the sound of footsteps in the hall. Joe moved his hand close to her breast but she pulled away from him quickly. He sat back in the chair and gave a low frustrated groan. Anna rested her head on his chest.

"I wish we could get married tomorrow and move into a little place of our own," he said wistfully.

Anna sat still and didn't respond.

"Do you?" he asked.

Anna shifted her weight on his knee. "I don't know."

Joe craned his head down to look at her face. "What do you mean, you don't know?"

Anna sat up and pushed herself away from him. "I don't know, Joe. All the talk of marriage this evening made me nervous."

"We're engaged to be married. Why on earth would it make you nervous to talk about it?"

Anna looked down at the ring on her finger and felt a rush of guilt.

Joe took his arms from around her waist and Anna could feel the warmth that was between them begin to evaporate.

"What's bothering you?" Joe asked with a slight edge of annoyance to his voice.

Anna felt a lump in her throat and struggled to force it back down. "I don't know if I want to get married, Joe."

Anna stood up and began to stoke the smoking coals that had failed to ignite.

Joe's fingers gripped the arms of the chair and he stared over at her. "How long have you felt like this?"

"Just recently. Every time you talk about getting married I get anxious. I can't explain it, Joe."

Joe leaned forward and tried to catch her eye but Anna kneeled down in front of the fire and continued to stoke the coals.

"It's just nerves, Anna, that's all." He moved from the chair and crouched down behind her. "What if we just tied the knot sooner?" He put his arms around her waist and pulled her towards him, until her back was leaning into his chest. "If your father would let us move in here until we find a place of our own, we could get married immediately." His excitement rose and he gripped her tightly but loosened his hold as he felt her body grow rigid.

Anna shook her head. "No, Joe."

Joe jumped to his feet and folded his arms across his chest. "What are you trying to tell me, Anna?"

Anna took a deep breath and was hit with the sudden realisation of what was about to happen. Joe looked down at her, his eyes opened wide in confusion. She buried her face in her hands and tried to stop herself from crying. "Oh, Joe! I don't know what to say. Getting engaged was wrong of me, I shouldn't have agreed to it. I just thought these doubts would pass in time, but they haven't."

Joe rocked gently on his feet, as if he had been punched. He opened his mouth to speak, but no words came. Anna stood up and went towards him but Joe raised his hand to stop her coming any nearer.

"Are you breaking off our engagement?" he asked incredulously.

"Joe, it's just that – "

"Yes or no? Are you breaking it off with me?" he asked again.

Anna stood still and waited for an answer to come to her.

Joe ran his hands through his hair impatiently. "Why did you wait till now?" Anna looked down at the floor in shame. "Jesus, Anna, we've just had tea with my parents and talked about getting married all evening. Couldn't you have spared me that?"

The tears streamed down her cheeks as his crushed expression reminded her of how cruel she had been. She was filled with disgust at herself for not facing up to it sooner. "Joe!" she gasped. "I didn't want to hurt you!"

They stood facing each other for a few seconds until Joe broke the silence. "I love you, Anna," he said in a strained voice.

Anna couldn't bear to see the pain this was causing him and she bit her lip to stop herself from saying anything she might regret. Part of her wanted to run into his arms and push the feelings that had been nagging her away again, but she knew now they would only resurface.

"Do you love me, Anna?" Joe wrung his hands together waiting for an answer.

Anna looked about the room like a trapped animal. "I do love you, Joe – but not enough to marry you." She could hardly believe what she was saying. In one swift motion she twisted the ring off her finger and handed it over to him. "You should take this back."

Joe took a step backwards and stared at the ring in disbelief. He stretched out his hand mechanically and Anna placed the ring in the centre of his palm.

"I'm sorry, Joe."

Joe stood rooted to the spot and looked from the

ring to Anna and back to the ring again. "What am I supposed to do with this?"

"I can't keep it," she said softly.

Joe gulped back his tears and closed his fist around the sparkling diamond. The sound of Seán's key turning in the front door made them both start. The door closed with a loud bang and they could hear Seán's footsteps in the hall outside.

Joe moved towards Anna with a sense of urgency. "Please, Anna. Don't do this. Think about it for a little while."

Anna could feel her heart pounding as Seán's footsteps got closer. "It's not fair on you, Joe – we should just finish it now."

Joe pressed the ring into her hand and closed her fingers around it. "Please, Anna. Please think about it, at least for a little while. I'll wait, I won't rush you." He talked quickly, aware of the few seconds they had left alone.

The door opened slowly and Seán stuck his head around it. He caught Anna's eye and grinned. "Is it safe to come in?" he asked, keeping his body outside the room.

They both stared over at him and Seán walked in slowly. "What's wrong?" he asked.

"Nothing. I'm leaving now," Joe said without taking his eyes off Anna.

"Don't leave on my account," said Seán, sensing the tension.

Anna ignored her brother's remark. "I'll see you out," she said, brushing past Seán.

Joe followed, nodding curtly at Seán as he left the room.

At the front door they stood in the darkness of the hallway as Joe pulled on his coat.

He turned to face Anna before opening the door. "I'll leave you alone to think about it," he said softly. "Let me know when you're ready to see me again." A cold rush of air blew into the hallway as he went out into the night. Anna stood with her back against the door after he had gone, turning the ring over and over in the palm of her hand.

Seán appeared at the end of the hall. "What are you doing standing there? Is something wrong?"

Anna slipped the ring into her cardigan pocket. "Nothing's wrong. Go to bed," she snapped.

She tried to get by Seán, but he stood at the foot of the stairs and blocked her way.

"Why did Joe leave like that?"

"Like what?"

"Without a word of goodbye. Did you have a fight?"

Anna pushed Seán out of her way. "Mind your own business," she said and ran upstairs to her room.

Chapter 10

Anna looked up from her desk and saw that it was already six o'clock. She had meant to file a basket of documents during the afternoon but they still sat in a pile on her desk untouched. The week had dragged by and she had found it hard to concentrate on anything – even the smallest of tasks had proved too much for her.

"Anna," said Daniel, walking out of his office with a handful of shipping papers, "I can look after this evening's delivery."

Anna snapped out of her reverie and looked at him blankly.

Daniel waved the papers. "I have everything under control."

Anna's hand shot up to her mouth. She had forgotten about the delivery. "Oh no! It completely slipped my mind." She pushed her chair out from behind her desk and held her hand out for the papers.

Daniel raised his hand, holding the papers out of her reach. "I got a call earlier from Leeds. There is only a small consignment and I can handle it myself. I insist that you go home immediately."

Anna looked flustered. "But – "

"No buts," Daniel interrupted. "What is the point of my working here if I can't shoulder some of the responsibilities?"

Daniel took Anna's coat from the coatstand and helped her into it.

Anna smiled weakly and slipped her arms into the sleeves. "I really should stay, just in case."

Daniel shook his head in disagreement. "Trust me. I think I am capable of supervising a delivery of shoes." He pulled his father's keys out from his trouser pocket. "Now what I *do* need is for you to tell me which key opens the storeroom. My father has more keys on this chain than a jailer."

Anna stood close to him as he held the keys up for her to see. Examining each one closely, she went through the bunch and stopped at the short fat key that opened the lock to the storeroom. "This one," she said.

Daniel looked down at her as she held up the key, and his heart somersaulted inside his chest when he noticed that she was not wearing her engagement ring. His outstretched arm seemed to lose its strength. He was standing close enough to smell the sweet scent of her cologne and it made him feel light-headed.

"Thank you," he said, looking slightly confused, and took the key.

"Are you sure you don't want me to stay?" Anna asked from the doorway.

"Absolutely," said Daniel. He turned and walked quickly back into his office and sank down into his chair feeling giddy. Had she simply forgotten to put on the ring this morning, or was there a possibility that the engagement was off? Chewing on his thumbnail anxiously, he tried to think of the last time he had seen it on her. He had seen it last week. He remembered, as they said goodbye to each other on Friday evening, the little diamond twinkling as she pulled on her gloves before she left, reminding him that she belonged to someone else.

★   ★   ★

The only sound that came from around the table was the scraping of knives and forks on the dinner plates. Anna could sense the questions that were not being asked yet. More than once, she had seen her brother glance across at her father in an air of anticipation. She had also seen her father scrutinising her fingers, searching for the missing ring.

Mr Barry threw his cutlery carelessly across his plate when he was finished and cleared his throat. "Why aren't you wearing your engagement ring, Anna?"

Anna stopped cutting her meat and looked up at him. She knew by his solemn expression that Seán had been telling tales. "I broke off the engagement. We're not getting married," she said, and hung her head as she waited for his reaction. This was what she had really dreaded all along. She looked across at Seán, but his eyes were fixed firmly on his father. Mr Barry looked shocked. He stared at Anna, waiting for an explanation, his mouth hanging slightly open. Anna couldn't bear the tension any longer and stood up from the table to take her plate over to the sink.

"You broke it off with him?" he asked, his voice thin and strained.

"Yes, Dada," Anna said, busily scraping the food on her plate into the bin. When she turned back around she was confronted with the stony faces of both men. Mr Barry ran his hand over his chin roughly – it was something he always did when he was angry. Anna thought of how nervous her mother used to get when she saw him doing this, for it was usually a warning of what was about to come next. The pit of Anna's stomach burned as the memory flashed through her mind for the first time in years.

Seán looked up at Anna and looked away again, in a silent gesture that told her he had joined forces with his father on this occasion. Anna rubbed her moist hands along the front of her skirt. "I know you are both very fond of Joe, but I can't marry him just because of that. You'll both have to try to understand."

The two men sat in silence as if they had just received news of a death. Then Mr Barry banged his fist onto the kitchen table, making the cutlery bounce off his plate on to the floor. Both Anna and Seán jumped in fright.

Anna rushed across to her father, but once she was beside him she was at a loss as to what to do. "Dada, this is the hardest thing I've ever had to do – please don't make it any worse for me!" she cried.

Mr Barry rose up from the table and looked at Anna in disgust. "What's wrong with you? Joe Maguire is a good man, the best there is, and you've sent him packing." He shook his finger in Anna's face as he spoke.

Anna's tears were uncontrollable as she received the full rigour of her father's anger. Mr Barry looked on in stony disapproval as his daughter broke down in tears. He turned to leave the room and looked back at Anna. "I feel like I have lost a son," he said quietly. Anna and Seán watched as their father walked slowly out of the kitchen. Anna pulled a handkerchief out of her pocket and wiped the tears from her eyes. She looked across at Seán who was still sitting at the table with his head in his hands and waited for him to say something.

"He was like a brother to me," he whispered.

Anna wiped her face and swallowed hard. "He can still be like a brother to you. That's not going to change."

Seán pushed himself away from the table and looked at her with contempt. "You're a bitch!" he spat, and left the room, slamming the door behind him.

Anna pulled out a chair and sank into it. They had taken the news badly, but she had always known that they would. Her relationship with Joe had become more important to them than it had been for her, and that had been the reason she had taken so long to make a decision. Their loss was greater than hers.

After a few minutes had passed, she tucked her handkerchief into her shirt sleeve, picked up her father's cutlery from the kitchen floor and proceeded to clear away the dinner plates.

Anna went to bed without saying goodnight to her father. In the evening she had taken her sewing basket into the kitchen and had mended a tear in one of Seán's work shirts, then she gathered up her things and went straight to her room. Lying in bed, she thought of how angry her father had been, and the contemptuous way that Seán had looked at her. It had been a week since she had broken it off with Joe and even with her father's angry reaction, she had no feelings of regret or remorse. In fact, deep inside Anna felt only relief that this burden she had been carrying for so long had been lifted. She had shattered the hopes of her father and brother and broken Joe's heart, but on the other hand she was free from the lies and insincerity, released from the existence she had felt duty bound to live.

★   ★   ★

The gusts of wind threatened to blow Anna's delicate umbrella inside out as she battled her way through Sackville Street. The spring shower had turned into a torrential downpour and she hurried to get to the door of Jacob's and out of the windswept street. Once inside, she shook the pool of water from the umbrella and left it at the foot of the stairs to dry off. The familiar smell of her cosy office at the top of the building welcomed her as she entered the room. Years of dusty timber floorboards and files that held papers yellowed with age had fused and settled in the air like a fine comforting mist. Anna saw Daniel through the window of his office. He was clutching a bundle of dockets in his hand, looking completely flustered. It was a quarter past eight in the morning and he looked as if his day's work was already underway. Anna smiled as she thought of the surly, rude man that had replaced his father only months earlier, and wondered what had happened to cause his sudden change of heart?

Then he saw her and came out to greet her. "Good morning, did you get caught in the rain?"

"Yes," Anna said, as she took off her coat. "How did the delivery go?"

Daniel waved the bunch of delivery dockets and smiled. "No problems so far – now I just have to sort out these."

"I'll do them," Anna offered.

"No, I might as well learn how to sort them out myself," he said, turning back to his office. Then he remembered what he had come out to say. "Anna, why are there so many laced boots down in the storeroom? There must be almost eighty boxes of them."

"They just don't sell very well. Mr Jacob liked to order them every winter for the older customers, but even they don't seem to want them any more." Anna tried to suppress a smile. For the past three years she had tried to persuade Mr Jacob that the heavy ankle-laced boots were no longer fashionable, but he had insisted on including them in his winter order despite the amount already in storage.

"Well, they're just taking up space down there. What do you suggest we do?"

Anna had mentioned selling them at a discount last winter but Mr Jacob wouldn't hear of it. "We need to sell them at a discount. It's the only way we'll get rid of them." Anna felt underhand, giving her new boss this advice when she knew that Mr Jacob would disagree, but she was just being practical. "Do you want to discuss it with your father? I can give you the figures."

Daniel screwed up his face for a few seconds. "No," he said decisively. "You put a price on them and get them moved on to the shop floor."

"I have never decided on prices before. Shouldn't you do that, or talk to your father about it?" Anna felt oddly uncomfortable with this responsibility.

"Anna, you know more about this business than anyone else working here. We can't go bothering my father with every trivial detail, that's why I'm here. I trust you, and I trust that whatever price you decide will be the right one."

Anna tried to contain her intense gratitude and desperately wanted to prove that she was capable of such a task. "I'll get to work on it straight away," she said, trying to control the beaming pride that threatened to burst forth at any second.

"Good," he said briskly and disappeared back into his office.

★ ★ ★

Mr Barry stood at the window of the barbershop and stared out onto Capel Street. The morning had been busy and kept him from his thoughts, but now the shop was empty, giving him more time to brood over his daughter's broken engagement. He washed his combs and lined them up on the counter by the window. Every morning since Anna had delivered the news, he had woken with a heavy feeling that hung over him all day like a black cloud. Losing Joe Maguire as a future son-in-law was more than just a disappointment, it felt like a bereavement. Not since Pauline, his wife of twenty-one years had passed away, had he felt so down-hearted. It annoyed him that Anna seemed so unaffected at the break-up – not once had he seen her upset or tearful since she had broken it off with Joe, apart from the terrible occasion when she had broken the news to him and Seán. He, on the other hand, could think of nothing else since she'd delivered the devastating blow. It wasn't only the glory of having Joe marry into the family that he was being deprived of – he had also grown to love the boy as if he were one of his own. Ever since his brother, Francis Maguire, had been killed in the GPO, Joe had held a special place in Mr Barry's affections.

The shiny steel combs lay in a neat row on the towel and Mr Barry slowly gathered them together and returned them to the jar behind the counter where they were kept, ready for the next customer. The bell over the door rang as somebody entered the shop. Mr Barry turned and saw Joe standing at the counter, his face set in a distant stare.

"Joe, I haven't seen you in ages," Mr Barry said solemnly.

Joe nodded and thrust his hands deep into his trouser pockets. "You heard then?"

Mr Barry looked down and kicked at something on the floor. "Yes," he said softly. "I'm very disappointed, Joe. I can't understand it."

Joe shifted from one foot to the other. "I was just wondering if maybe you'd talk to her. See if she might change her mind."

Mr Barry looked up in surprise. "Would you not be better doing that yourself, son?"

"I don't want to put her under pressure. I told her I'd leave her be for a while, until she has a think about it. But if you talk to her, she might see things differently."

It was pitiful to see a mighty man like Joe Maguire reduced to this and Mr Barry felt a flash of anger towards his daughter.

Joe wiped his nose with the back of his hand and continued. "Don't tell her I asked you to do this … " He broke off and took a deep breath.

Mr Barry came out from behind the counter and put his hand on Joe's back. "Don't worry. I'll try to talk some sense into her." Then, noticing the shadow of growth around Joe's chin, he gently pushed him towards the barber's chair. "Sit down and I'll give you a quick shave. You'll feel better after it."

Joe nodded and, pulling a handkerchief from his pocket, blew his nose loudly. He allowed himself to be steered towards the chair and sank into it willingly.

Mr Barry took out a fresh white towel and shook it ceremoniously before placing it around Joe's neck. He took the soap dish in one hand, and with the brush in the other hand he applied the white lather onto Joe's chin and cheeks, and began to scrape silently with the razor. Joe's eyes were closed and Mr Barry could see the dark shadows that had formed underneath them.

In a hushed voice he reassured Joe. "Don't worry, son, I'll talk to her."

★   ★   ★

Anna had got used to eating dinner in the monastic silence. The symphony of knives and forks clattering against the plates was the only sound to come from the kitchen when she was there. Recently, her father and brother had begun to communicate in stilted observations and replies, a secret language that excluded her. Joe had stayed away, much to Anna's relief.

"Are you going out tonight?" Mr Barry asked Seán, as he shovelled a mound of mashed potato into his mouth.

"Yep," answered Seán. "I'm taking Sadie Burns dancing."

Anna had to stop herself from jumping in with a comment. Half of Dublin knew that Sadie Burns was as easy as they come and Anna couldn't believe her brother was stepping out with her. She looked over at her father, but her disapproval was met with a cold stare.

"That's nice," said Mr Barry, not taking his eyes from Anna.

Seán looked up at the clock and stood up. "I'd better get ready."

"I ironed a shirt for you. It's hanging in your wardrobe," said Anna.

Seán mumbled a half-hearted thanks before leaving the kitchen.

Anna got up from the table and stretched over to take her father's plate but Mr Barry pushed it out of her reach. "Sit down," he ordered.

Anna felt the blood rush to her face and slowly eased herself back down on to her chair.

Mr Barry laid his arms on the table and leaned across until his face was only inches away from hers.

Anna could guess what he wanted to talk about — she had been expecting it.

"I saw Joe today."

"Did you?" she whispered.

Mr Barry looked up from under his eyebrows and waited a few seconds before continuing. "What are you doing, Anna? The man is destroyed."

Anna swallowed noisily and wished she could get up and run away from this conversation. "I didn't mean to hurt him, Dada."

Mr Barry's eyes narrowed. "Well, you have. He's very hurt." He reached across and put his hand on hers in a reassuring gesture. "Go back to him, Anna. You won't find another man as good as him."

Anna felt her heart sink. She pulled her hand out from under her father's grasp and stood up. "You can't ask me to do that."

"Why not?" Mr Barry snapped.

"Because I don't love him. Can you not understand that?"

"No, I can't." Mr Barry pushed his chair out from under him and stood up. "I can't understand how you would give up the chance of marrying a grand lad like Joe. He loves you, Anna. Isn't that enough for you?"

Anna stood by the table and closed her eyes. "It's not enough, Dada. I can't marry a man I don't love."

Mr Barry swung his heavy bulk around to the door, then back to Anna again. "I'm asking you to reconsider. Give it some time, go and have a think about what you're doing. Will you do that, Anna?" He walked over to the door and stood there waiting for an answer.

Anna wrung her hands together, trying to find the courage to be truthful and end any hope her father was still harbouring, but instead she answered, "Yes, Dada, I'll think about it." Mr Barry stood still and tried to read his daughter's face, but Anna stared ahead blankly. He put his hand on the doorknob. "Good girl," he said quietly, before leaving the room.

Anna collapsed back on to her chair and looked up at her mother, who smiled down from the picture frame on the mantelpiece. "What else could I say?" she whispered. She knew it was wrong to agree to think about it, but her father's refusal to accept her decision left her no choice. Anna hoped that by agreeing to think about it, it might give him some time to resign himself to the fact that her marriage to Joe was never going to happen.

Chapter 11

A second knock sounded on the front door.

"Answer the door, Anna!" Seán shouted from his armchair in the back kitchen.

Anna dried her hands and flung the towel across the back of a chair. "For heaven's sake, Seán, what's wrong with your legs?" she shouted as she hurried up the hall.

At the foot of the stairs she met her father coming down from his bedroom.

"I'll get it," Anna mumbled and walked past him. It had been four days since their confrontation and Anna had tried to avoid being alone with him.

Mr Barry said nothing and remained in the hall to see who was calling. Anna opened the door and took a step back when she saw Joe standing there.

"Come in," she said.

Joe stepped in and took off his hat. "Hello, Anna, Mr Barry," he said sheepishly.

Mr Barry almost tripped over himself rushing to greet Joe. "How are you, Joe? Come in, come in," he fussed. Joe took off his coat and Mr Barry grabbed it from him and bundled it into Anna's arms. "Come on down to the kitchen," he said, taking Joe by the arm and leading him down the hall. "Anna, put on the kettle and make us a cup of tea," he ordered without looking back.

Anna flung the coat onto the hallstand and followed them down to the kitchen.

Seán's eyes instantly lit up at the sight of Joe. "Joe, it's good to see you. I wasn't expecting you tonight."

Inside the kitchen Anna looked over at Joe but he immediately looked away, indicating that this visit was not for the purpose of seeing her. Feeling slightly relieved, Anna placed the teapot and cups in the middle of the table for the men to help themselves.

Joe sat down and laced his fingers through each other. "I've a bit of news," he said flatly.

Anna went to leave the room but Joe turned to

her. "You might as well stay, Anna. You'll hear about it tomorrow anyway."

Mr Barry and Seán looked at each other nervously. It had always been an unspoken rule in their family that politics was never discussed around the women. Mr Barry had always been careful to hide any illegal activities that he was involved in from his daughter. Seán looked over at Joe pleadingly. Having his sister in the room would curtail his bravado and lessen his feelings of importance at being privy to inside information.

Anna hovered at the door for a second before deciding to stay.

"The anti-Treaty forces are moving into the Four Courts as we speak. The plan is to occupy the buildings until the Treaty is re-negotiated. "

Seán made a fist and punched the air defiantly. Joe looked from father to son.

"This is it. Either they listen to us now, or it's war," he said with an air of finality.

Seán jumped up excitedly. "Are we going over to the Four Courts now?"

Joe's expression remained calm. "No, Seán. We're not needed tonight."

Seán looked crushed. "Why? I'm ready to join the fight."

"They need men like us on the ground. There'll

be other things to be done, and don't worry, Seán, you'll be called on soon. If things get dirty, we'll all be needed." Joe stood up. "I have to go now."

"Thanks for coming around, Joe. If there's anything we can do just let us know," Mr Barry said, then looking over at Anna he added, "See him up to the door."

Anna nodded obediently and left the room followed by Joe. At the front door she took his coat from the stand and handed it to him. Joe clutched it to his chest and stood looking down at her, his face illuminated by the orange glow of the street light that poured through the fanlight of the front door. He turned to leave but stopped, and turned to face her again.

Anna lowered her head and waited for him to leave.

"Have you thought any more about it?" he whispered.

Anna's arms hung by her side like weights – she clenched her fists as she heard his question. "Nothing has changed, Joe," she whispered. "I still feel the same way."

Joe remained perfectly still and exhaled loudly. A few seconds passed as they stood on either side of the thick wall of silence between them in the hallway.

"I'm sorry, Joe," Anna said finally.

Joe turned to go and Anna retreated back down the hall into the darkness. When she reached the kitchen, she heard the front door slam loudly.

Seán was pacing the floor, talking in sudden bursts about what was to come. "I'm ready," he said, smashing his fist into the palm of his hand. "By God, I'm ready!"

Mr Barry patted his son on the back. "Good lad," he said proudly.

Anna stood at the door and looked at them scornfully.

"Ready for what?" she asked.

They stopped talking and looked at her.

"Ready to get shot dead, like Francis Maguire?"

A flash of anger crossed over Seán's face and he looked for his father's reaction.

Mr Barry shook his head in disgust.

Seán raised his finger and pointed at Anna. "What if I am? I'm proud to fight for my country."

"And what good are you to the country if you're dead?" Anna folded her arms and cocked her head to one side, waiting for his reply.

Seán's face was red with anger. He moved closer to Anna in a threatening manner. "If it wasn't for the people who died fighting for this country we'd still be licking the boots of the English. Just like you are!"

Anna gave an indignant laugh. "What do you

mean by that?"

"You know well what I mean!" Seán shouted. "Running around taking orders from that English Jewboy!"

Anna looked over at her father. "Are you going to let him talk to me like that?"

"You might as well be one of them yourself, for all you care about this country!" Seán was inches away from her and she could feel his hot breath as he shouted into her face.

"It's you lot who don't care about the country – ruining any chance of peace we might have!" Anna shouted back.

"Enough!" barked Mr Barry. "Seán, leave us alone. I want to talk to Anna."

Seán's bulky frame pushed by his sister roughly as he left the room. Anna lost her balance and held on to the dresser to stop herself from falling.

"Don't push me, Seán!" she shouted after him.

They listened to Seán's footsteps stamping up the stairs and the creak of the floorboards as he walked across his bedroom overhead. Mr Barry shook his head slowly and looked over at his daughter.

Anna threw her hands up in the air. "Are you going to let him get involved? He'll surely be killed. He's acting like a fool. Why don't you put your foot down and stop him?"

Mr Barry rubbed his chin and took a few steps towards Anna. "Don't call your brother a fool," he said quietly.

A wave of fear rippled through her body and she knew she had gone too far.

"Seán's a good boy. A good son. He's ready to fight for a cause he believes in, and if that seems foolish to you then you have no place in this house."

Anna could feel her mouth drying up. "I didn't mean it, Dada," she pleaded. "I just don't want him getting hurt." Unlike Seán, Anna's father could control his rage. He harnessed it inwards, sometimes appearing unnaturally calm in fraught situations.

"Go upstairs and apologise to him," he ordered.

It was unreasonable, Anna knew, but she also knew that any further arguing would lead to more trouble. Without uttering another word she turned to leave, but Mr Barry caught her by the arm.

"Did you talk to Joe?"

"About what?"

"You know what." His grip tightened and pinched the skin under her blouse but Anna refused to flinch.

Too scared to repeat the words she had said to Joe earlier in the hall she replied, "Not yet."

Mr Barry released his grip. "Well, don't wait too long. Now go and say sorry to Seán."

* * *

Anna sat at her desk and glanced over at Daniel's empty office. It was almost lunchtime and he had not shown up for work – she had become used to his company over the past few months and it felt oddly silent without him. Just before one o'clock she heard the door downstairs bang, followed by the thump of hurried footsteps on the stairs. Daniel walked briskly into the office and shook his coat off. Anna looked up from her work and saw the dark shadows that had appeared under his eyes. He looked as if he'd had no sleep at all.

"Did you see what's going on in the Four Courts?" he asked as he tried to secure his coat on a wall hook.

"Yes," answered Anna, trying not to sound too well informed. "The irregular forces have occupied it."

Daniel let out a sigh of exasperation. "Silly fools. I suppose they think it's going to help matters."

"Yes, I suppose they do," said Anna, anxious to change the subject.

"After years of fighting, they've come so close to getting almost everything they wanted, and they're still not happy. It's only a matter of time before the

British hand over the rest of the country, but if these boys continue to wage war they'll ruin it for everyone that wants a peaceful existence." Daniel stopped and smiled wearily when he saw the baffled look on Anna's face at his outburst. He rubbed his eyes like a child. "Sorry, I haven't had much sleep. Father had another mild stroke last night and we had to rush him to hospital. I've been up with him all night."

"I'm so sorry, Daniel!" said Anna with genuine concern.

"He seems quite comfortable now. He was sleeping when I left." Daniel opened his mouth and yawned loudly.

"Why did you come in? You should go home and get some rest."

Daniel dismissed her suggestion with a wave of his hand. "I don't want to go home. I do need to eat something though." He stopped talking and looked at Anna pensively.

Anna waited for him to continue.

"Would you have lunch with me?"

"Me?" Anna felt a surge of heat working its way upwards to her face.

Daniel gave her a boyish smile. "Yes."

"Eh," was the only sound that Anna could utter.

"If you have other plans please say so. I was going to have lunch in the Gresham, but I hate eating alone." Daniel waited for an answer.

Anna took a deep breath. "Yes, I'd love to," she blurted.

"Good," said Daniel. "Let's go now. I could eat a horse."

* * *

In the dining room of the Gresham Hotel Anna looked about nervously to see if she recognised anyone. Her father, Seán and Joe did not have friends who dined out in fancy hotels very often, but still she continued to glance cautiously around the dining room. Being seen with any man other than Joe Maguire would be certain to cause chins to wag. When the waiter came to take their order Anna smiled at him nervously, "I'll have the fish, please."

Daniel handed the waiter his menu without looking at it. "The beef, thank you." Then he leaned over towards Anna. "Wouldn't you prefer to have the beef? It's always very good here."

The waiter stared into the distance and pretended not to notice Anna blushing.

"It's Friday, Daniel. I'll have the fish," she said quietly.

The waiter picked up Anna's menu and left the table.

"I'm so sorry," Daniel apologised.

"It's alright," Anna said, playing with the corner of her napkin.

"Are you very religious?" Daniel asked.

Anna was taken aback by his candour. "I … I suppose I am." It was a question Anna had never been asked. "And you?"

Daniel shrugged his shoulders. "Not very. To me, being Jewish means belonging to a social grouping more than a religion. Perhaps it comes from being the product of a mixed marriage. My mother was a Protestant before she converted, I think she still is at heart. On the other hand my brother Peter and grandmother are devout Jews, so maybe it's just me. I often think the world would be a better place if there was no religion at all."

Anna's eyes widened. "You don't mean that?"

Daniel was amused by her dismay. "I know it sounds shocking, but I wonder if it isn't true. Most conflict in the world comes down to what God you believe in. Wouldn't it be better if we didn't have those religious barriers?"

The waiter arrived carrying the plates of food.

"I won't bore you with my radical ideas any more," Daniel said with a light laugh. He picked up his cutlery and attacked his steak with great speed. "I must say," he said between mouthfuls, "selling those boots off was a great idea. We need to get the remainder of them onto the shop floor and be rid of them completely before the summer comes. Well done!"

"The credit goes to you. It was your idea," Anna said, not wanting to take any undue praise.

"Nonsense!" Daniel said waving his fork. "You priced them wisely and we still made a profit. I would have sold them off at a ridiculously low price and lost money."

Anna accepted the compliment and changed the subject. "How long will your father be in hospital?"

Daniel's shoulders sagged at the mention of his father. "I doubt very much that he will come home from hospital again."

Anna stared down at her plate. "Poor Mr Jacob."

The mention of Mr Jacob's name dispelled the gaiety from their conversation.

"Do you think I could visit him?" Anna asked.

Daniel looked up brightly at this suggestion. "I think he would love that, Anna. He was always so fond of you, it would certainly do him good to have a visit from you."

Anna shifted in her chair and tried to think of something to say. "Does this mean you will have to stay in Dublin ?"

Daniel wiped his mouth with his napkin and

threw it down on the table. "Yes, it does. I'll have to make some tough decisions soon."

Anna looked at him sympathetically. "Do you miss being in college?"

"There are times that I wish I was back there. I hated coming home, I think I made that quite clear when I first started working in the shop."

Anna smiled, remembering his first few weeks, and said nothing.

"It's funny how time can change things. Staying doesn't seem like such a bad prospect now."

When they had finished their coffee, the waiter appeared with a leather folder and opened it discreetly for Daniel to sign. Mr Jacob had always kept an account at the Gresham Hotel so all that was required was a signature. Anna glanced about the room as Daniel scribbled his name on the bill.

"Thank you," she said as they stood up.

"Thank *you*," said Daniel. "I would have had such a miserable lunch without your company."

★　★　★

The following evening when she had finished work, Anna made her way up Sackville Street towards the Adelaide Hospital. In a paper bag were the grapes which she had bought earlier in the day for Mr Jacob. Crossing O'Connell Bridge, Anna looked up the River Liffey to her right and saw groups of men in uniform, members of the Free State army patrolling the streets outside the Four Courts. Ever since the occupation, there had been an air of excited expectation on the city streets. People gathered around the area every day and exchanged heated views on how the stand-off would be dealt with by the government.

On reaching the hospital, Anna climbed the two flights of stairs and followed Daniel's directions to Mr Jacob's ward. There were six beds on each side of the room – Anna looked around and recognised the silhouette of Irene Jacob sitting by the window at the end of the ward. Beside her was a stout elderly woman dressed entirely in black.

"Anna, over here!" Irene said, waving.

Anna walked over and stood at the foot of the bed.

"Daniel said that you might visit this evening. You are so kind!" Irene exclaimed.

The older woman looked at Anna, starting at her ankles, and slowly moved her gaze upwards until she reached her face. Anna waited nervously for an introduction.

"This is Mrs Jacob. Daniel's grandmother."

The old woman's mouth widened to give a terse

smile. "Pleased to meet you," she said in a distinctive northern English Yiddish accent.

Irene patted her husband's wrist. "Look who it is, darling. Anna is here to see you."

Anna and the older Mrs Jacob turned their heads towards the gaunt face that lay staring back at them in the narrow hospital cot. Anna felt a lump in her throat as she saw how thin he had become.

"Hello, Mr Jacob," she managed to say without letting her emotions get the better of her.

Irene looked at her mother-in-law and gave a sympathetic smile. "Ben is terribly fond of Anna," she explained.

Anna felt awkward trying to talk to Mr Jacob with his wife and mother looking on. She remembered the bag of grapes, and set them down on the locker beside the bed. "I didn't know if he could eat or not, it's just some grapes," she said, pointing towards the bag.

"Thank you, Anna," Irene said. Then, fanning her face with her hand, she said, "Isn't it hot in here. Granny? Why don't you take off your coat?"

The older woman shook her head. "I'm fine as I am."

Irene seemed jittery in her mother-in-law's presence. Her hands flapped about as she spoke and her face looked hot and flushed, unlike her usual pale alabaster complexion.

"Anna, do take your coat off – otherwise you'll get cold when you go back outside."

Anna obeyed Irene even though taking off her coat indicated that she would be staying longer than she intended.

Irene pointed towards a stool in the corner and looked about the ward for assistance. "There is never a nurse around when you actually need one," she said tetchily.

Anna walked over to the corner and carried the stool across the ward to the opposite side of the bed. As Anna sat down she realised that the stool was considerably lower than the chairs the other two women occupied. As she looked across at both Mrs Jacobs, she felt as if she had shrunk all of a sudden. The older Mrs Jacob sat rigidly with her hands in her lap. Her austere gaze made Anna nervous. Anna averted her eyes and stared down at her coat which was bundled up in her lap.

Irene leaned towards Mrs Jacob and said in a hushed voice, "Anna is engaged to be married."

Anna could feel the blood rush to her face.

"When is the big day then?" asked the old Mrs Jacob. Her look had softened and she seemed genuinely interested.

Anna twisted her coat button until she felt it

loosen. Both women smiled over, waiting for her answer.

"Actually, the engagement is off," she said quickly.

Irene looked dismayed. "Oh dear. I'm so sorry."

Anna squeezed the palms of her hands together. "We decided not to get married . . ." Her voice trailed off as she saw the shocked expression spread across Irene's face.

A heavy silence descended with her announcement. Anna stared down at the floor and tried to think of an excuse to leave.

Mrs Jacob's large black bonnet wobbled as she nodded her head sagely. "Best to find these things out before it's too late."

Irene glanced at her mother-in-law, as if she was worried that the old woman would say the wrong thing. Then she turned her gaze to Anna. The news of the broken engagement seemed to unsettle her, and Anna felt a shift in her attitude.

"Daniel tells me that you are terribly busy."

"Yes, we are," Anna answered brightly, glad to evade any further questions about her personal life.

Irene cast her eyes downwards to Anna's ring finger. "You've been a great help to him. He's even talking about staying in the business permanently." This was said slowly, as if his mother was only just realising why her son might have had such a change

159

of heart.

"That's news to me," said Mrs Jacob indignantly. "He never said anything to me about staying."

Irene fixed her eyes on Anna and gave a faint smile. "He only mentioned it recently," she said, brushing off her mother-in-law's consternation at not being informed of her grandson's plans.

The palms of Anna's hands felt moist and sticky and she longed for some cold fresh air. She looked down at Mr Jacob, his eyes were closed now, the eyelids flickering slightly. "He's fallen asleep," she said. "I'd better go." She got up quickly.

Both women remained seated.

"Thank you for visiting, Anna," said Irene. "It was very nice to see you again."

Anna pulled on her coat and left the buttons undone.

"Goodbye, Mrs Jacob," she said to Irene. She turned to face the grandmother who was looking at her closely, her black beady eyes taking in every move she made. "It was very nice to meet you, Mrs Jacob."

"Likewise," said the old woman sharply.

Anna felt their eyes bore into the back of her neck as she walked towards the door and out of the ward.

Irene stood up and began to smooth the blankets on her husband's bed.

"A nice girl," she muttered to herself.

"A pretty one," the old woman said with a weary sigh.

Chapter 12

Irene took her hat off and placed it on the hall table. Then she slowly pulled her gloves from each hand and removed her coat. She stopped before the mirror above the table and fixed a few strands of hair into place. She allowed her eyes to close for a few seconds and felt a wave of exhaustion sweep through her. The daily hospital visits were beginning to wear her down – how she wished that Ben could get better again and things could return to normal! But she was slowly coming to realise that her life would never be the same again. She pressed the back of her hand to her mouth and stifled the tears that threatened to break through her stiff composure. Once again she checked her appearance in the mirror before entering the living room.

Inside she found Daniel sitting in his father's chair by the fire. He turned his head from the book he was reading and frowned when he saw how tired his mother looked. "Mother, you look exhausted. Come and sit by the fire."

Irene collapsed gladly into the wing-backed armchair.

"Mary has gone for the evening. She left some dinner in the oven – let me get it for you," said Daniel, standing up.

Irene smiled up at him. "I ate earlier with Granny. But I would love a cup of tea if you could manage it."

"Where is Granny?"

Irene shoulders drooped forward. "She insisted on staying at the hospital. Your father is sleeping, he doesn't even know she is there, but you know Granny, she wouldn't listen to me."

Daniel could see the strain across his mother's face and felt sorry for her. His father's crippling strokes had drained her of all her energy, and his grandmother's unexpected visit was more than she could cope with. He had never understood how his strong confident mother transformed into such a meek obsequious creature on the rare occasions that she had any dealings with his grandmother. His brother also seemed to bend at the knee to please her. Daniel on the other hand had always stood up to the old woman, and as a result had earned her respect.

"You relax. I'll make us some tea," he said. He threw another log on the fire and went out to the kitchen.

Irene closed her eyes and listened to the comforting hiss and crackle of the dry timber. She woke a few minutes later with a jolt when Daniel came back into the room carrying the tea tray. "My goodness, I must be tired, I think I drifted off to sleep for a few minutes."

Daniel set the tray down on a table beside Irene's chair. He poured the steaming tea into a cup and handed it to her. He took a plate of neatly cut chicken sandwiches and held them out for her to take one. "Mary must have made these for you as well."

"Thank you, dear," said Irene, taking one.

The two of them sat quietly, each enjoying the peaceful silence.

Irene was the first one to move. She put down her teacup and looked over at Daniel. She went to say something, but hesitated for a second.

Daniel sensed her anxiety and sat forward in his chair.

"Anna came into the hospital this evening," she said.

Daniel sat back and smiled. "Did she?"

Irene turned her head towards the fire and said nothing.

"Was Father pleased to see her?"

"He was asleep for most of the time," she replied despondently. She straightened her back and cleared her throat. "She is very pretty."

Daniel looked at his mother in surprise. "Yes, I suppose she is."

"Have you been spending time with her?" Irene asked.

The heat from the fire had become oppressive and Daniel ran a finger along the inside of his tightening shirt collar. "Why on earth do you want to know?"

"You had lunch together the other day in the Gresham."

"Yes, I told you so."

"You never told me that she is no longer engaged to be married."

Daniel forced a laugh and tried to hide his embarrassment. "Well, now you know. She is no longer engaged to be married!" It was what he had hoped for. Every day Daniel had glanced down at Anna's ringless finger but hadn't dared to ask any questions.

Irene sat back into her chair and allowed Daniel's evident agitation to pass before she spoke. "Anna's a nice girl," she said, trying to sound reasonable.

Daniel nodded his head in agreement.

"But not suitable," she said, her mouth twisting into a half smile.

Daniel sighed loudly and looked at his mother resentfully. "Have I ever met *anyone* suitable enough for you, mother?"

Irene's eyes opened wide. "Of course you have. There was Marjorie – she was a lovely girl."

Daniel slapped his hands down onto his lap. "Marjorie was rich and Jewish, Mother. She certainly was not lovely!"

"You were made for each other – I'll never understand why you didn't marry her," Irene said, a note of indignation creeping into her voice. "Her parents are still very upset about it."

"I didn't marry her because I didn't love her, and no amount of interfering from you or Granny could change that. In fact I came to loathe the poor girl."

Irene went to say something but Daniel stood up and spoke over her. "Mother, stay out of my personal life. I came, I stayed, and I'm doing what I was asked to do. Can't you just be happy with that?"

Irene stretched out and took his hand in hers. "I

only want what's best for you."

Daniel pulled his hand away and bent down, kissing her fleetingly on the crown of her head. "Goodnight, Mother," he said, and left the room before Irene could say another word.

★　★　★

Seán threw open the front door and pushed his bicycle into the hall. He let the door close behind him and leaned the bicycle against the wall.

"No, you don't!" Anna shouted.

Seán took off his coat, ignoring her.

"You take that bike through to the back yard. You're not leaving it there."

Seán bent down and took off his bicycle clips, deaf to his sister's orders.

Anna put her hands on her hips and marched down the stairs towards Seán. "Did you hear me? Move that thing."

Seán straightened up slowly. Although his attitude towards her had improved slightly in recent days, there was still a hint of resentment that lurked behind his eyes when he looked at her. "Leave it," he called over his shoulder as he walked down the hall, "I'm going out again."

Down in the kitchen Seán took a towel and lifted

his dinner plate from the hot oven. Anna followed her brother into the kitchen and watched him manoeuvre the plate precariously onto the table.

"Where were you? I had the dinner ready hours ago."

Seán sat down and began to pile the food onto his fork.

"Up at the Four Courts," he answered without looking up.

Anna waited until her anger had passed before sitting down beside him. She knew that if she was to get through to Seán she would have to remain calm. There had been too much bickering lately and she did not want this to end in another row.

"Seán, what are you doing up there? You'll end up in trouble, you know that."

Seán chewed his food and kept his head down.

"Don't get involved, Seán, please!"

Seán swung around quickly. "I am involved, and I'm proud of it. Those men up there are sacrificing their time for a cause they believe in. They're sitting in that building day in day out, not seeing their families or eating properly."

Anna could see where the conversation was heading and she tried to steer it back on course. "I know it takes courage to do what they are doing, but I don't want to see you getting hurt or arrested. Is that so wrong?"

Seán pushed his plate away and glanced sideways at Anna. "You don't understand," he mumbled.

"There's nothing to understand. I just want you to stay out of trouble," Anna said, losing her patience. This was all it took to spark another argument.

Seán lit a cigarette and blew the smoke out his nostrils with a loud sigh. "Maybe you don't care what's happening to this country, but I do, and I'm prepared to do something about it." He drew on his cigarette and in a more conciliatory tone he added, "Some of the women are making sandwiches for the men in the Courts. Will you make a few and I'll bring them up later?"

"No," snapped Anna.

Seán looked at her, his mouth gaping in disbelief. "What?"

Anna raised her chin in defiance. "No, I will not make sandwiches. I told you, Seán, you're to stay away from the Four Courts, and stay away from Joe Maguire or you'll end up in trouble!"

"You're doing a very good job of staying away from him yourself," Seán said slyly.

"It's finished between us. Why can't you just accept that?"

"Fine," said Seán, raising his voice. "Do what you want, but don't start telling me how to live my life. I admire Joe and I'm honoured to be a friend of his."

"You mightn't be too honoured to be sharing a prison cell with him," Anna retorted hotly.

"Oh, listen to you! I think you've been working with them Brits so long that you're turning into one of them."

Anna gave Seán a cold stare while she tried to think of a worthy reply to his cutting comment. Seán stubbed his cigarette into the ashtray and twisted it aggressively until it was extinguished. "Will you make the sandwiches or not?"

"No," Anna said resolutely.

Seán leapt to his feet. "You fuckin' – "

The door opened and both of them turned towards it, startled at the sudden movement. Mr Barry's heavy bulk filled the doorframe. He stood without moving and looked into the kitchen.

"Don't let me hear you using that language to your sister," he said in a barely audible voice.

Seán stared over at Anna, shifting his weight from one leg to the other as if he was going to make a run at her. Mr Barry stood away from the door and indicated to Seán to leave the room. Seán gave Anna a stare full of hatred and stamped out of the kitchen and up the stairs. Mr Barry stepped out of the kitchen and went to close the door behind him but stopped and turned back.

"Anna," he said, "you will make those sandwiches. If I have to hold the knife in your hand to butter the bread, you'll make them." With this said, he turned to leave, closing the door soundlessly behind him.

* * *

Anna dug the hard knob of butter into the bread, almost bending the knife as she did so. A hole appeared in the slice of bread, but she didn't care what the sandwiches looked like. They're only for a crowd of savage rebels, she thought as she slapped the thick slices of cheese between each piece of bread. When two fat columns of sandwiches were piled in the middle of the table, Anna washed her hands at the sink and removed the apron she was wearing. She bent down to the lower press in the dresser to search for some paper to wrap them in, but straightened up again. Let him wrap them himself, she thought, and walked out of the kitchen.

Seán was standing in the hall with his coat on. "Are they ready yet?" he asked impatiently.

Without looking at him, Anna turned and began to take the stairs to her bedroom.

"They're on the table," she answered. "You can wrap them yourself."

A few minutes later Anna heard the front door

slam and the sound of Seán's bicycle as he pushed it out onto the footpath. She wanted to run out after him and give him a good thumping. It wasn't often that her father took Seán's side in an argument and Anna was still smarting from the humiliation of defeat.

She stayed in her bedroom for most of the evening, only venturing down to the kitchen after she heard her father going to bed. In the quiet kitchen she rinsed out some stockings and hung them beside the fire to dry. The table was in the exact same state she had left it hours earlier, breadcrusts and crumbs scattered around the block of cheese. Anna shook her head and reached for her apron, knowing that if she didn't clean it up, it would be there to greet her in the morning.

Back in her room, Anna set out her clothes for the following day. It had always been important to her to look neat and well groomed, but ever since Daniel had joined the company she took a little more time every evening planning what she would wear the following day. She had even worn her navy and cream silk dress to work, a dress which was kept wrapped in paper and stored at the back of her wardrobe for special occasions. Anna chose a plain white blouse with a lace collar and a purple skirt that looked flattering on her neat waist. She folded her gloves and placed them in her handbag, then looked inside her purse to make sure she had her tram fare. Her bag felt lighter than usual. She checked to see what was missing and, rummaging through the contents, she realised it was her shop keys. She went to her dressing table and lifted her hairbrushes but the keys were not there. Anna stood in her nightgown and looked down at the floor to see if they had fallen out of her bag, but they were not anywhere to be seen. She felt inside the pockets of the skirt she had worn that day but they were empty. A slight sense of panic began to grow and Anna pulled back her bedcovers to see if they might have found their way under the blankets, but there was no reassuring clink of metal. Feeling her way out into the dark landing Anna tiptoed down the stairs into the hall where her coat was hanging. "Please God let them be here," she muttered as she thrust her hands into the corners of the empty pockets.

"Who's that?" Her father stood at the top of the stairs wearing his long johns and white flannel long-sleeved nightshirt. From where Anna stood he looked like a ghost.

"It's me, Dada," Anna whispered. "I can't find the shop keys."

Mr Barry stood at the top of the stairs in silence. "Sorry, Dada, did I wake you?" Anna moved towards the stairs.

"You did. Go back to bed and we'll find them in the morning."

Anna began to climb the stairs towards him. "I can't understand it. I was sure they were in my handbag."

"They're probably downstairs somewhere. You'll find them in the morning." He put his arm around Anna and steered her towards her bedroom. "It's late. Go back to bed and get some sleep. You've got an early start."

Anna leaned in towards her father and felt her panic subside – he showed a tenderness towards her that had been absent since she'd broken it off with Joe, and she wanted the moment between them to last. Being back in her father's favour made missing keys seem like a trivial matter.

When they reached her bedroom door, he kissed her forehead and hugged her. "You're a good girl for making the sandwiches this evening."

Anna smiled up at him. "Thanks, Dada. Goodnight."

★ ★ ★

Entering the kitchen the following morning Anna found Seán draining the last drop of tea from his mug.

"Morning," he grunted.

The atmosphere of the previous evening's argument still hung in the air between them. Anna did not reply to his half-hearted greeting and set about shifting objects on the dresser to look for her keys.

Seán watched her silently as she stood with her back to him, breathing loudly through her nose. He waited until she slammed a bowl down and exclaimed, "Damn it!" before he asked, "What are you looking for?"

Anna turned around and looked at him, but Seán immediately shifted his eyes to the floor.

"My keys," she wailed. "The shop keys! I've lost them!"

Seán's mouth twisted into a cruel smile and he crooked his thumb, pointing it behind him towards the mantelpiece. "They're up there," he said.

Anna rushed towards the empty fireplace, careful not to get ashes on the end of her skirt. The set of keys were sitting exactly where Seán had pointed. She grabbed them in a panic and looked at them to make sure they were hers, then turned to Seán.

"How did you know they were there?" she asked incredulously.

"I put them there," he answered without looking around.

"When did you find them? I looked everywhere last night."

"I only found them when I came in last night. They were on the floor under the table. They must have fallen out of your bag."

Seán kept his back to her while he spoke and Anna could sense that he had enjoyed her few seconds of frantic searching. His careless attitude annoyed her, but the relief of having the shop keys back in her possession, coupled with the fact that she was late for work, prevented her from saying anything.

Chapter 13

The morning sunshine spilled in through the window, spreading fingers of light across the office floor. Anna squinted at the face of the clock, but the reflection of the sun made it difficult for her to see the exact time. She knew it was after eleven, and Daniel had not yet appeared. All morning she had listened out for his footsteps, putting her pen down every time she thought she heard a noise outside on the stairs. Anna worried that something might have happened to Daniel, and every few minutes she got up from her desk and walked to the window to look down on to the street. On her third trip to the window her heart gave a flutter, as she spotted Daniel in the distance, walking down the street towards the shop. His face was set in a frown, and he seemed to be muttering to himself as he hurried through the crowds. Anna settled back into her chair and assumed a position of deep concentration as she heard him close the door to the street. Her pulse quickened with every footstep on the stairs that brought him closer.

Daniel entered the office with a thunderous look on his face. He threw his coat on the leather couch that was set against the wall, and his face softened slightly when he looked over at Anna. "Good morning," he said quietly, and walked straight into his office, closing the door behind him.

Anna sank back into her chair and stared after him, not bothering to hide her disappointment. It was usual, upon his arrival to the office, for both of them to have a cup of tea together and chat about what was to be done that day. Through the glass pane of his office door Anna could see him pacing the room, looking agitated. He looked out at her but she quickly turned away.

By late afternoon Daniel had still not left his desk. Anna closed the order book that lay untouched in front of her and smoothed back some strands of hair that had come loose around her forehead. She stood up and looked in at Daniel, who was reading a book at his desk. She tapped gently on the glass, and waited until he raised his head and beckoned to her to enter. She opened the door and stepped slowly into the room.

"Can I get you anything?" she asked.

Daniel looked at her and smiled weakly. "No, thank you, Anna."

Anna hesitated at the door for a second, not knowing whether to leave or try to engage him in conversation. "Is there anything wrong?"

Daniel put his head into his hands and pressed his forehead down hard on them. "My father had another bad turn yesterday," he said with a deep sigh.

Anna closed the door behind her and moved across to his desk. "Oh Daniel, I'm so sorry!"

Daniel stared absently at the open book before him. "Mother can't manage him at home, and the doctors at the hospital don't seem to be able to do any more for him. It's just a matter of time I suppose." He spoke mechanically, without any emotion. "My granny has decided to stay a while, and her meddling has turned my mother into a nervous wreck." He shrugged his shoulders and looked up at Anna. "I know it sounds selfish, but sometimes I wish I could banish the whole lot of them from my life."

Anna moved around the desk to his side. "You don't mean that. You're just tired and upset."

"Yes, I suppose I am," he said wearily.

"Poor Mr Jacob! I miss him so much, I wish there was some way to make him better."

Daniel turned to her with a sympathetic look. "Of course you must miss him. Sometimes I forget that you knew each other." Daniel took Anna's hand and squeezed it gently. "It's such a relief to have you to talk to, Anna. I really appreciate your concern."

Anna felt a rush of excitement at his touch – and allowed her hand rest in his for a few seconds, before drawing it gently away and letting it drop back down to her side. Daniel stood up from his desk.

"Why don't we finish up early this evening and go for a stroll?"

Anna looked at him in surprise.

"Will you go for a walk with me? Please say you will. I need to get some air and clear my head before I go back to the hospital."

The prospect of a stroll seemed to lighten his sombre mood and Anna was relieved to see him smile again.

"Yes," she replied bashfully, trying to contain her delight.

They walked out into the bright afternoon sunlight of Sackville Street and set out in the direction of O'Connell Bridge. Anna was conscious of every step they took together. They were close enough for Daniel to brush against her every now and again, and as they approached Grafton Street he slipped his arm gently through hers. At first Anna froze and he looked at her quizzically.

"Am I being impertinent?" he asked.

"No, not at all," she said, trying to hide her terror at the possibility of being seen by anyone.

They walked slowly up towards St Stephen's Green. Anna tried not to show her anxiety and prayed that they would not meet anyone she knew. They entered the archway into the green and continued their stroll towards the duck pond. On reaching the pond, Daniel spied a park bench bathed in sunshine and walked towards it.

"Let's sit here for a while."

As she sat down on the bench, Anna took the opportunity to slip her arm free of Daniel's. They were quiet for the first few minutes, each enjoying the intimacy of the moment. They looked over and smiled at some children playing nearby. Although neither of them spoke, there was an energy that seemed to dance between the two of them. The silence was comfortable, not tense or awkward like the long silences had been with Joe. After a few minutes, Daniel turned to her.

"Tell me about the chap you were engaged to."

The word 'chap' made Anna want to laugh. Daniel spoke with an English accent and sometimes said things like "My word!", or "Heavens above!", that made him sound as if he was speaking a different language.

"His name is Joe, he's a printer, we were going together for two years, and it's finished now," Anna said in one long breath.

"I bet his heart is broken."

Anna looked down at the ground and said nothing.

"I'm sure it wasn't an easy thing to do. I had to break it off with a girl in England last year – we weren't engaged but it was a pretty awful thing to have to do."

"It was very difficult," Anna said quietly. Mentioning Joe's name to Daniel felt like a betrayal and she kept her answers short.

"Have you seen him since you broke it off?" asked Daniel.

"Yes. He is very friendly with my brother and father."

Daniel grimaced. "That must be awkward."

"Yes, yes, it is," Anna answered, looking around the park for something that might help her to change the subject, but Daniel broke in again with another question.

"How do your brother and father feel about it?"

Anna pressed her back against the bench. She could feel perspiration begin to gather at the back of her neck. "They'll get used to it in time," she answered quickly.

"Will you come out with me some evening?" Daniel turned his head to see her reaction.

Anna felt light-headed. "Yes," she answered. Tiny beads of sweat had formed a line above her upper lip and she shivered, even though she felt extremely hot.

"You look flushed, let's move out of the sun," Daniel said, taking her arm.

Anna stood up and felt dizzy. Spots swam in front of her eyes and for a second she thought she might faint.

"Are you alright?" Daniel put his arm around her waist and felt her body become limp.

Anna waited for her head to stop spinning before she spoke, conscious of his arm pressed hard against her back.

"Anna! Are you unwell?"

Slowly she disengaged herself from Daniel's grip and stood up straight. Her head had stopped spinning but she was shivering uncontrollably.

"You look very pale," he said.

"I'm fine now. I don't know what happened, maybe I sat in the sun for too long."

"It's hardly very strong sun. Do you think you might be coming down with something?"

"No," Anna answered definitely. "No, I really feel fine now."

She took her handbag from the bench and tried to stop her teeth from chattering. Her blood seemed to have turned to ice in her veins. "I really should be going now."

"Let me get you a cab."

"No. There's no need, really. Thank you, Daniel."

"I insist on getting you a cab." Daniel examined Anna's pale face closely. "I think you may have caught a chill."

Anna politely dismissed his concern. "Nonsense. I feel fine now. I can get a tram home."

She began to walk away.

Daniel stood by the bench and watched her.

When she had taken a few paces and realised he wasn't following, she turned to him. "Are you staying here?"

Daniel threw his hands up. "Why won't you let me get you a cab?"

"Because I don't need one."

Daniel's face broke into a smile and he walked towards her. "Well, I will see you to your tram."

"There's really no need.

Daniel stopped and stared at her. "If you won't let

me call you a cab then I am walking you to your tram whether you like it or not," he said firmly.

*   *   *

That night Anna woke in a sweat. A blinding headache threatened to crack her skull and her throat felt swollen and raw. Too weak to move, she lay in the same position for hours. When she woke the following morning she felt no better. The bedclothes were damp beneath her back and she could hardly lift her head from the pillow. Her father put his head around the door and gave her a puzzled look.

"Anna, why are you still in bed? It's after nine o' clock."

Anna went to speak but could hardly force the words from her stinging throat. "Oh Dada, I'm too sick to get up," she said, in a raspy whisper.

Mr Barry put his hand on her forehead. "You're burning up, child. You won't be going anywhere today. Stay still and I'll get a damp cloth for your head."

He brought a glass of water for Anna to sip and a cloth soaked in cold water to put on her forehead. Anna had never felt so sick before. She lay back and let her father cool her with the cloth.

"I'll get Seán to call into the shop and tell them you're sick," he said reassuringly. "You get as much rest as you can. I'll come home at lunch-time and see if you can eat something."

Anna stared up at her father. Her eyes felt too heavy to keep open. Normally she would be frantic at the thought of missing work, but she felt too weak to care.

"Can I get you anything else?" her father asked.

Anna pointed to her wardrobe. "Can you hand me out a fresh nightgown? There's one on the top shelf."

Mr Barry opened the wardrobe door and pulled the white cotton garment down. He put it beside Anna on the bed.

"Thank you," she whispered.

A few minutes later Anna heard her father's footsteps as he crept down the stairs – she closed her eyes and drifted back into a deep sleep.

When she opened her eyes again, her father was standing by her bed looking down at her. His voice seemed far away, even though she knew he was right beside her. He was asking her something but she couldn't make out his exact words – she wanted to sit up and try to hear what he was saying, but her limbs were too heavy to move. All she wanted was to drift back to sleep.

When she woke again the room was dark. She sat up slowly, the damp nightgown cold against her back. She shivered and looked around in confusion. The house was still, and she had no idea how long she had slept. Her head felt clearer but her throat felt as if it had been cut into shreds. She threw the covers off and stood up, but a rush of dizziness sent her falling backwards onto the bed. A few minutes passed before she tried to stand again, slowly this time. On her bed was the fresh nightgown that her father had given to her earlier. Anna pulled the stale-smelling damp gown over her head and put on the clean one. She reached over for her dressing-gown which was hanging on a hook on the bedroom door, and slipped it around her shoulders. Her feet felt heavy and sore as she stepped into her slippers. As she made her way downstairs, she could see a light coming from the kitchen and was glad to see that someone was there. Mr Barry looked up from his newspaper as Anna put her head around the door.

"Well, well, the dead has risen!" he exclaimed, putting his paper to one side. "Come over here and sit by the fire."

Anna walked slowly, not trusting her legs to carry her. Mr Barry jumped up from his chair and guided her into it, to sit by the warmth of the fire.

"What time is it?" she asked.

"Just after nine," her father answered, as he poured a cup of tea for her.

Anna looked at him in astonishment.

"That's right. You've been asleep all day." He handed her the cup and saucer. "I think it must be your tonsils at you. I can see that your glands are swollen."

Anna put her hand to her neck and felt the clammy tender skin. As a child she had suffered repeatedly from throat infections but they had lessened as she got older – it had been years since she had had any illness at all.

"Seán didn't have time to call into the shop, so I called over myself and spoke to the young Jacob fella. He said not to worry about coming back until you are fully better."

Anna stared into her steaming tea-cup and smiled dreamily, the mention of Daniel making her feel suddenly brighter.

Her father chuckled. "By God, he speaks like the King of England!" When he saw that Anna didn't find his remark very funny he continued, "He happened to be in the shop when I called in. Nice enough fella. I told him you'd be a few days getting over it, and he said he was very sorry to hear you were sick."

"A few days!" Anna exclaimed. "I'll be fine tomorrow."

Mr Barry shook his head. "You have a fever, and you'll not be going anywhere until that breaks."

Anna put her cup back onto the saucer and opened her mouth to speak, but Mr Barry continued, "It's Tuesday today. I doubt very much that you'll be back at work until next week."

Sinking back into the chair, Anna's head felt light again, and what little strength she'd had a moment earlier had drained from her body.

"Now drink up that tea and I'll help you up to bed again."

*   *   *

Wednesday was no different. Anna slept all day and only got up in the evening to drink a cup of tea. Thursday brought a little improvement. She managed to gather the strength to have a bath, and when her father and Seán came home, she sat in the kitchen for an hour and tried to eat some bread. By Saturday, her fever had passed, and the swelling in her throat had gone down. Anna washed her hair, and put on an old dress as she knew she would not be leaving the house. In the evening, her father pulled a stool out to the front door to read his paper in the last rays of the setting sun. Inside, Anna sat in the parlour mending a collar on her father's shirt.

Outside, she heard voices, and the legs of the stool scraping against the ground as her father stood up. Anna put the shirt down and listened to the voices through the open window.

Her father's laugh filled the hall outside, as the voices drew closer. The parlour door opened and Mr Barry stepped in, his face beaming. "Would you look who's come to see you," he said loudly.

Anna swung her legs from the couch onto the floor and sat up rigidly. Joe stuck his head around the door and grinned. He stepped forward into the room, and produced a bunch of flowers from behind his back. Anna looked up at him and felt the energy drain away from her.

Mr Barry gave Joe a gentle nudge towards Anna. "Come in and sit down, will you?"

Joe stood beside the couch and held out the flowers to Anna. "I heard you weren't well," he said.

Anna took the flowers and tried to hide her annoyance at this unexpected visit. "Thanks, Joe," she said matter-of-factly, "I'm much better now."

"Sit down, Joe. I'll put the kettle on and make us a cup of tea," boomed Mr Barry from the doorway.

Joe went to sit down on the couch beside Anna, but she jumped up quickly.

"No. We'll all go down to the kitchen – I need to put these in water or they'll wilt," she blurted out.

Before her father could say anything, Anna swept out of the room clutching the bunch of flowers.

Down in the kitchen they drank their tea and relied on Mr Barry to lead the conversation. Anna could think of nothing to say. She didn't want to raise Joe's hopes or lead him on by sounding in any way enthusiastic, and any thing she thought of saying sounded trite. Just when it seemed that her father's talk had run its course and they were left to sit in silence, Anna heard Seán's key in the front door. For the first time in months, she was delighted to hear her brother come bounding down to the kitchen. Seán burst in and stopped in his tracks when he saw Joe sitting at the table. His face widened into a warm smile. "Joe!" he said with surprise. "How are you?"

"Grand, Seán. How's it going yourself?"

"Never better," answered Seán. He crossed the kitchen to the sink and ran his hands under the tap. "I thought you were going down to Cork today."

"I'm going tomorrow." A hint of secrecy had crept into Joe's voice.

Seán dried his hands on a dishcloth, but kept his eyes firmly on Joe. "Tomorrow. How long for?"

"A week or two."

Seán turned the cloth over in his hands. Joe fell silent and didn't offer any explanation as to the nature of his trip.

"Now that you're home," Mr Barry said to Seán, "you wouldn't mind helping me with this tree in the back yard? I'm trying to saw a branch off, but I need you to hold the ladder for me."

Seán made a face and threw the cloth into the sink. "Can it wait till after tea? I'm starving, Da," he moaned.

Joe looked up at Mr Barry. "I'll give you a hand," he offered.

"Indeed you will not. Seán, come on out now, it won't take a minute." Mr Barry stood up and cast a warning glance in Seán's direction. "You have another cup of tea, Joe," he said as he left the room, followed by a sulking Seán.

Anna clenched her jaw anxiously as they were left alone together. They both sat in the thick silence until Joe spoke.

"That was an awful dose you had."

"Yes," Anna replied. "Thanks for the flowers." Then a thought occurred to her. "How did you know that I was sick?"

"I met Seán up at the Four Courts yesterday and he told me."

Anna looked up from her tea-cup at the mention of the Four Courts. "What was he doing up there?" she asked crossly.

Joe shifted in his chair and looked down at the

table. "You know I can't tell you that, Anna," he said quietly.

"Please, Joe, tell him not to get involved. You're the only person he'll listen to. He worships you – in fact I wonder if he'd be involved at all if it weren't for you."

Joe exhaled loudly and looked at Anna. "I can't tell him what to do. He has a mind of his own."

"Not where you're concerned, Joe. You know he'd do anything to impress you – that's why you have to tell him to stay out of trouble. He won't listen to me," Anna pleaded.

Joe kept his eyes down and remained silent.

"If anything happened to him my father would lose his reason. Please, Joe, tell me you'll talk some sense into him?"

"Anna," Joe said in exasperation, "the man is fighting for a cause, like the rest of us. I can't tell him to go away just because he's your brother."

"Yes, you can," Anna said, becoming excited. "You both know you're fighting a losing battle. No one up in the Four Courts stands a chance. He only wants to please you, Joe. If you joined the British army tomorrow he'd be right behind you."

Joe shook his head. "You've no respect for him, Anna. You shouldn't speak about him like that, like he's some kind of simple fool."

Anna stood up and glared down at Joe. "Don't pretend you don't know what I'm talking about. You know he'd follow you to the ends of the earth. I love my brother and I don't want to see him arrested, or killed trying to keep up with you."

Joe hung his head for a few moments, until her words had settled between them.

Anna spoke again. "Will you have a word with him?" she asked quietly.

Joe stood up and looked at her coldly. "No, Anna, I won't. He's a grown man, he can make his own decisions."

They stared at each other, both knowing that any fragile remnants of fondness between them had just fallen away.

"Well, be it on your head if any harm comes to him," said Anna.

Joe stared over her shoulder at the vase of flowers on the windowsill that stood mocking him, as if they had been placed there to remind him of how futile this visit had been.

Anna bent down and took her handbag from the kitchen floor and reached inside it.

"I want to give this back to you," she said, handing Joe the engagement ring. He took it from her without looking at it and stuffed it into his trouser pocket.

"I'll be off then," he said gruffly. "I'll see myself out."

Chapter 14

Anna sat behind her desk and slowly rotated her neck from left to right, trying to relieve the stiffness that had set in during the afternoon. Her first day back at work had been busy, but she was glad to be back in the office again. Daniel had kept the place going without her – and had even cleared some of the paperwork on her desk before she returned. To Anna's slight annoyance, the place had run very smoothly without her. Daniel had been down in the stockroom all afternoon sorting out the weekend's delivery, but he would not allow Anna to help out. The chilly stockroom was no place to be after a bout of illness, he said, and he insisted that Anna stay upstairs in the warm office.

At six o' clock, Anna heard the sound of the bolt on the shop door. The staff would leave shortly afterwards by the back door. Outside, in the laneway, she heard the heavy thud of the stockroom door as it rolled into the locking position against the wall.

Daniel walked into the office a few minutes later and Anna knew immediately by the way he looked over at her that something was wrong. He leaned against the doorframe for a few seconds and stared down at his feet with an expression of mild confusion.

"Daniel?"

He dug into his trouser pocket and took out a handkerchief, and began to wipe the dirt from his hands. "Unbelievable," he muttered.

Anna stood up, curious to know what he was talking about.

Daniel looked behind him as if he expected someone to be there. "Anna, I'd like to talk to you before you leave this evening. But please wait until everyone has left the building. I'm going to wash my hands." He left the office and went downstairs to the staff toilet.

Anna sank into her chair and pressed a hand to her forehead. She quickly tried to think of anything she might have done, or neglected to do, that could have her in trouble. Perhaps he had found some stock that she had forgotten to record. She tiptoed down the stairs to see if all the staff had gone. Reaching the porch, Anna pressed against the glass shop door but it was locked. The place was in darkness, the lights had been turned off. On her way back up the stairs she heard Daniel coming out of the toilet on the first landing. He waited until she reached him.

"Is everyone gone?" he asked.

"Yes."

Anna went to continue her climb upstairs but Daniel stood in front of her. "Can you come with me, down to the stockroom?"

Anna hesitated for a moment.

"Stay there," he said. "I'll get your coat."

Anna waited on the stairs until Daniel returned carrying her coat. He placed it around her shoulders and kept his hands resting there, as he guided her down the stairs. Anna walked slowly, feeling a sharp thrill of excitement at his touch.

They left by the front door and walked around to the laneway which led to the back of the building, the only access to the basement stockroom. Daniel put his key into the padlock and it snapped open. Then, with his face twisted with effort, he mustered up his strength and rolled the heavy door open, just enough for their bodies to fit through. Daniel entered but Anna hung back when she saw that the door was only pushed back a few feet.

"We won't be able to see anything," she said. "You need to open it fully for enough light to get in."

Daniel stepped back into the doorway. From his inside pocket he produced two candles and a box of matches. He put out his hand and pulled Anna in beside him. Then, putting his shoulder to the door, he rolled it back against the wall – leaving them in complete darkness. He struck a match against the door and lit one of the candles. He handed it to Anna and lit another one for himself. Then he caught her firmly by the wrist and began to walk around columns of shoe-boxes, taking care not to trip over anything. The storeroom was an enormous cavern, divided into three parts by bare concrete walls. Mr Jacob had always talked about putting in a lift that would service the shop, but he had never got around to doing anything about it. As they went further back, the air got colder, and Anna shivered. When they reached the back wall Daniel bent down and poured some wax from his burning candle onto the top of a wooden box and secured the candle onto it. He took a third candle from his pocket and lit it, placing it at the other end of the box. When the light settled Anna could see Daniel's face as he stared down at a similar box on the ground. They were not the familiar boxes in which the shoes were delivered, but large cases of dark-coloured wood, almost as long as coffins. Anna looked at Daniel as he slid the lid off the box at their feet. It came away easily, and Anna could see some dark shiny objects but could not make out what they were. Daniel reached up for her free hand and pulled her down towards the box. He took one of the shiny objects out and held it out to her. Anna jumped back, spilling hot candle wax on her skirt, and her hand shot up to her mouth. Daniel stayed where he was, with one knee on the ground, and held up the rifle for Anna to see.

"Oh my God, Daniel! How did they get here?" she shrieked.

Daniel placed the rifle back onto the pile in the box and stood up. "I don't know."

Anna looked around at the cases in a state of bewilderment. "How many are there?"

"Four crates," Daniel answered. "One hundred rifles in total."

Daniel slid the lid back onto the crate. He blew out the two candles and picked a dirty canvas off the floor and threw it over the four cases – the way he had found them.

Anna was now shivering uncontrollably against the coldness that had seeped through her skin.

Daniel took the candle from her and, taking her hand, negotiated their way to the door. There, he stuck his head outside and looked around before slipping through and allowing Anna to follow him. Outside, Anna rubbed her hands together and walked along the lane in the weak evening sunshine while Daniel closed and locked the door.

They walked back to the office in stunned silence.

Once inside, Anna sank onto the couch. Thoughts of Seán flooded through her mind as she began to piece together the dreadful possibility that her brother might have had something to do with this. Daniel took off his jacket, and placed it over her shoulders on top of her own coat. He walked over to her desk and leaned against it.

"How many people hold a key to that stockroom?" he asked.

Anna chewed the inside of her cheek and did not look at him. "There are only two sets of keys. Yours and mine."

Daniel leaned forward. "I want you to think hard, Anna. Could your keys have fallen into the wrong hands?"

Anna looked up fearfully.

"Did you give your keys to anyone else recently?" he asked.

"No," exclaimed Anna defensively.

"It could have been without your knowledge. Is it possible that someone may have taken your keys without your permission?" Daniel spoke evenly, with no trace of accusation.

Anna's eyes glazed over as she thought of Seán and the recent disappearance of her keys.

There had been a fleeting moment of suspicion that morning in the kitchen, but she had chosen to ignore it. Now she wondered how she could have been so stupid. Why had she not questioned him about it? Her head seemed to weigh a ton and her shoulders collapsed as the enormity of the situation hit her.

She put her hands up to her face and tried to breathe deeply. Daniel jumped from beside the desk and moved across the room to sit beside her. He prised her hands away from her face and his touch seemed to break something inside her. To her own surprise, Anna began to weep openly with loud sobs. Daniel's jacket fell away from her shoulders and he put his arms around her and tried his best to console her.

"I didn't mean to upset you, Anna! Please don't cry."

Anna sat up and tried to compose herself.

"I think I have a clean handkerchief," Daniel said, picking up his jacket and rummaging in the pockets.

He found it and handed it to her.

Anna dabbed her eyes and tried to wipe her nose as daintily as possible. Daniel sat quietly and waited for her to speak. After a few minutes, Anna turned to him and searched his eyes for any sign of anger, but she saw none.

"My family are involved with the anti-Treaty forces that are occupying the Four Courts," she said, looking away. "My father, my brother Seán and the man I was engaged to, Joe Maguire. They were all involved in the War of Independence until the treaty was signed. Now they've turned against the men they were fighting alongside." The word 'fighting' was said with a bitter shake of her head. "Joe is the hero. Everyone adores him. I honestly believe that he's prepared to die for 'the cause'." She wiped away another tear before she continued. "Seán, my brother, is just a young fool and I knew he'd end up in trouble. I kept begging Joe to keep Seán out of it, but he wouldn't listen." Anna turned to Daniel and her voice trembled as she continued. "Seán took my keys from my bag a few weeks ago. He pretended that he'd found them on the floor, but I know now he took them. I would never have thought he'd do something so terrible."

Daniel patted her back and listened intently as she spoke. Her face filled with dread as she looked up at him.

"Will he go to prison for this?" she asked in a thin voice.

Daniel smiled and wiped another tear from her cheek with his thumb. "I am not going to involve the police in this if your family are involved. I'm not some kind of monster that would send your brother to jail." He took her hand in his and moved closer. "I would like to meet your brother though. Perhaps the shock of being discovered will frighten him into seeing the error of his ways."

Anna nodded her head in agreement. "Thank you, Daniel. I'm so sorry for all of this. I have to take some share of the blame – he's my brother after all."

Daniel reached out his hand, gently turned her face towards his and looked into her eyes. "You cannot blame yourself for something you had no hand in." He leaned across and kissed her softly on the lips. Anna felt his moustache brush against her upper lip and it sent a warm shiver through her entire body. They looked at each other and knew that what had been building between them for the past few months was about to be realised.

"Anna," he whispered, "I've wanted to do this since the day I laid eyes on you."

They kissed again. This time his tongue glided along her lower lip and Anna could feel her heart pounding with pleasure. Their tongues touched slightly and, as they kissed, his hand moved upwards and caressed the skin at the nape of her neck. Anna put her arms around his waist and was surprised at how slender he seemed. The only man she had ever put her arms around was Joe Maguire with his huge frame, and Daniel felt so much narrower than the man she was used to. Anna didn't pull back or resist his touch. Daniel began to kiss her neck and Anna leaned her head back on the arm of the couch and closed her eyes, savouring every second of this feeling. When they stopped kissing, Daniel rested his head beneath Anna's neck and ran a finger along her protruding collar bone. She did not move, she hardly breathed for fear that the moment would end. They sat in the stillness of the deserted office until the twilight had turned to darkness.

Anna became aware of the time and gently moved Daniel's head away from her as she pushed herself into a sitting position.

"I think I should go home now."

Her hair had come loose and Daniel took the stray locks and tried to push them back into her comb. Anna smiled and pulled the comb out, letting her golden hair fall around her shoulders. She went to gather it together and pin it up again, but Daniel caught her hands and pulled them away.

"Let me see you with your hair down," he

whispered in the dim light.

Anna tried to hide her embarrassment – she felt naked as he stared at her unkempt hair tumbling over her shoulders.

Daniel ran his hands through the thick mass of curls and Anna fell back into his arms. "A last kiss goodnight," he whispered as he pulled her close to him.

*   *   *

Daniel walked into the living room and was greeted by the curious looks of his mother and grandmother as they sat by the fire. He loosened his collar as he was hit by the suffocating heat of the room. The brisk walk from the tram, mixed with his elation, had left him flushed with excitement.

"Why on earth are you sitting so close to the fire on such a warm evening?"

His grandmother smiled over at him. "Because, dear child, when you get to my age only fire is enough to warm such brittle bones."

"Where have you been? Surely not working till this hour," his mother asked. Then seeing his soiled shirt she exclaimed, "Goodness, Daniel, what on earth happened to you?"

Daniel looked down impatiently at the front of his shirt and saw the long line of black dirt just over the waistband of his trousers. It must have been from the dirty tarpaulin that he pulled back over the boxes, he thought as he tried to brush it away. His mother's constant questioning of his whereabouts was beginning to get on his nerves. Every time he came home a little later than usual, his mother was waiting for him, armed with the same set of enquiries. Daniel looked up and saw that the two women were waiting for an explanation. "Yes, I was working until this time, Mother. I'm trying to make better use of the space we have in the storeroom and that requires moving crates around. That's where I probably got this," and he pointed to the black mark on his shirt.

Irene sat up and stared at him in disbelief. "For goodness sake, Daniel, leave that to one of the delivery men, or ask one of the staff to do it. We don't expect you to go cleaning up the stockroom!" Then she looked across at Granny Jacob with a knowing smile. "Anyway, I think we may have some good news for you. Granny thinks she may have a man in Leeds who will take up your position in the company, and you'll be free to return to your studies!"

Granny Jacob nodded her head sternly. "Mind

you, I haven't discussed salary with him. No doubt he'll take advantage of our predicament and hold out for the highest *vage*." All her w's were pronounced as v's and the word *'vage'* rolled off her tongue with pointed disdain.

"Still," chirped Irene, "he has agreed to come over and start as soon as possible."

Daniel stood in the middle of the room feeling hot and angry with his mother for interfering in his life yet again.

"Darling, you look cross. Isn't that what you wanted all along? To go back to college?"

Daniel tried to pass the matter off nonchalantly, yet the thought of leaving his job in the shop made him panic inwardly. "I'm not cross, Mother," he said lightly. "It's just that there is no point in going back to college now. I'd be in no-man's-land. I've missed most of the year and I certainly don't want to spend the summer over there. The college dean has agreed that I can repeat the year starting next September, so until then I really have nothing better to do. I may as well stay here and make myself useful."

Irene gave her mother-in-law a worried glance and sat back in her chair.

"Well, if that's what you want, I can always arrange for Evans to hold on until September," Granny Jacob said, seemingly unaware of the change in atmosphere that had now entered the conversation.

"Fine," Daniel replied brightly. "I'm going to clean up and turn in for the night," he added, turning to leave.

"Goodnight, Daniel," Granny Jacob called behind him.

"Goodnight," muttered Irene as she twisted the pearls of her necklace.

When the door closed behind him, Irene looked up at Granny Jacob, her brow deeply furrowed with worry. "I told you. He's seeing her, that's why he won't go back."

The old woman swept a piece of dust from her skirt. "Perhaps he's in love with her, or hadn't that occurred to you?"

A glint of anger flashed across Irene's face. "What is that supposed to mean?" she asked, feeling a flush of heat about her cheeks. How did this woman always manage to get under her skin? She straightened her back in defence.

"I seem to remember a similar affair twenty-eight years ago, and I learnt a valuable lesson then. You can't stand in the way of true love." The old woman didn't show any humour as she spoke, but it was the first time she had ever admitted to interfering in the relationship between her son, and his then unsuitable fiancée, Irene Goddard.

Irene took no comfort from this placation. "Excuse me, I may not have been Jewish, but I certainly was of an equal social standing. This is a shop girl, working-class and uneducated. Forgetting the religious differences, what chance would they have of a life together?" She stopped herself from going any further, lest she said something she might regret. It wasn't often she got a chance to vent her hurt and indignation at the poor treatment she had received at the hands of her mother-in-law, but entering into an argument would be playing straight into the old woman's hands.

Granny Jacob looked at Irene and smiled acerbically. "I'm offering you some good advice. If he genuinely loves this girl then there is very little you can do about it – only hope and pray that it all comes to nothing. Learn by my mistakes. Let your feelings be known now – and you may have to live with the consequences for the rest of your life." With that said, Granny Jacob struggled to heave herself from the armchair and, without saying goodnight, she left Irene alone to consider her warning.

A faint smile played at the edges of Irene's mouth. Granny Jacob had actually admitted to being wrong about her son's choice of bride, and although it had taken twenty-eight years, it filled Irene with a certain sense of vindication.

★   ★   ★

Anna rocked backwards and forwards as the tram moved slowly out of Sackville Street. A strand of hair fell across her eyes. She had tried to secure her hair as best she could in the office, but she could feel the comb coming loose again. Her mind was crammed with conflicting emotions. Thoughts of Daniel and their blissful evening together were quickly overshadowed by the fury she felt towards her brother. There was no doubt in her mind but that he was the culprit. Her foot tapped rapidly on the tram floor as the gravity of the situation dawned on her. Thank goodness, she thought, it wasn't old Mr Jacob who had found the rifles – he probably would have called the police straightaway. And how kind of Daniel, to risk keeping those weapons there another night in order to protect her fool of a brother.

The hall was in darkness when Anna turned the key in the door. She took off her hat, placed it on the hall table and hurried downstairs to the kitchen where she could see a light through the glass pane in the door.

Seán turned around as she walked into the room. "Where have you been?" he moaned.

"Working late," Anna said, closing the door

behind her.

"I've no socks left. All these bloody socks have holes in them," he said, holding out a handful of odd socks. "You said you'd darn them for me weeks ago."

Anna stood with her back to the door and glared at the socks in his hand. "Where's Dada?" she asked, ignoring his request.

"He went to bed with a headache. Now will you do these tonight?"

Anna lifted her gaze from the socks and let her eyes rest on Seán.

"What?" he asked defensively.

"The cases of rifles in the storeroom, are they yours?"

Seán's mouth fell open in shock.

"Tell me now, Seán. Did you put them there?"

Seán swung towards the fire, his face hidden from Anna's view.

Anna walked over to him. "Answer me, Seán. Did you put them there?"

"Who found them?" he asked.

The tone of worry in his voice only served to confirm Anna's worst suspicions. "You did, didn't you?"

Seán stared into the glowing coals and muttered something.

Anna shoved the palm of her hand into his

shoulder making him fall backwards into the armchair by the fire.

"You stupid-lookin' eejit! What did you think you were at?"

Seán's eyes opened wide with fear. "What's going to happen to me?" he asked like a frightened child.

"You," hissed Anna. "That's all you care about! What about me? Did you stop to think for a minute how this would affect me?" Anna stood back and shook her head in disgust.

"How could you? My own brother."

"Who found them?" Seán asked again.

"Lucky for you it was Daniel Jacob. If it had been his father it wouldn't be me coming through the door tonight, it would have been the army to arrest you."

Seán shot her a worried glance. "What's he going to do?"

"I don't know," Anna snapped. "He wants to see you tomorrow. You're to call in to him after you finish work."

"What for?"

"I said, I don't know. But you can make arrangements for those guns to be taken away immediately."

Seán stood up and threw the handful of socks onto the chair.

"Do you hear me?" Anna shouted.

Seán turned around and glared at her. "Shut up, woman!" he shouted back.

"Don't you speak to me like that! You should be apologising for putting my job at risk. You're a disgrace to this family, Seán Barry. You should be ashamed of yourself!"

Seán sneered at her. "A disgrace! Look who's talking. Are you sure it wasn't you who discovered the guns and went running to your boss?"

Anna's mouth fell open. "Don't be so ridiculous," she said incredulously.

"Well, it wouldn't be beyond you. The way you've been carrying on lately it certainly wouldn't surprise me."

They stood facing each other in furious silence.

"Get out of my sight," hissed Anna.

Seán turned and went towards the door.

"You go straight to Daniel Jacob after work tomorrow," she ordered.

Seán walked out without answering and slammed the door behind him.

Chapter 15

Throughout the following day, the thought of Seán's visit to the office weighed heavily on Anna's mind. The same column of figures had been lying on her desk all afternoon and she made another attempt to tot them up, but as with her earlier efforts, her concentration waned. Her eyes wandered up to the clock: it read half past four. Another hour and Seán would be there, or would he? What then? thought Anna. Surely Daniel would have no alternative but to involve the law.

The whole day had seemed interminable. The intimacy of the night before had made it impossible to carry out a normal day's work alongside Daniel. Every time they had reason to brush by each other, a nervous cough or terse smile would emanate from one of them.

Anna stuck her head back down when she heard the familiar creak of Daniel's chair as he prepared to leave his office. He walked out and stood beside her, waiting until she looked up.

"If your brother is coming in to see me this evening, I think it would be best if you were not here."

Anna put her pen down slowly. "I feel so ashamed of him," she said, keeping her eyes on the desk.

Daniel moved closer and put his hand on her shoulder. "Anna, you have nothing to do with this. You cannot be responsible for his actions. That is why I want you to go home now. Whatever I have to say this evening only concerns your brother and no one else." He gave her shoulder a reassuring squeeze. "Now, off you go. I'll see you tomorrow."

* * *

Daniel sat in his office for another hour before he heard the heavy footsteps thumping up the stairway. Seán entered the room and looked around warily before he spotted Daniel in his office. Daniel stood and beckoned to Seán to enter. Seán pulled off his cap and walked boldly through the narrow doorway, his steel-tipped boots clicking defiantly against the wooden floor as he strutted into the room. Daniel nodded towards the chair on the other side of his desk. "Sit down," he said, without any greeting.

Seán pulled out the chair roughly and sat without taking his eyes off Daniel. His gaze was unbroken and impertinent and Daniel immediately forced himself to assume an air of authority.

"Before we start, I think it is important that you clear something up. The guns I found in the basement last night, were they put there by you?"

Seán chewed on his lower lip before answering. "Yes."

Daniel sat back, relieved that the admission had been forthcoming.

"Do you realise that I could have you arrested immediately?"

Seán nodded curtly. "I do."

"Apart from the obvious risks you were taking, did you ever stop to think about how this might affect your sister?"

Seán looked down at the floor and chose to ignore this question.

"She could have lost her job because of you."

Seán's face was expressionless. "I know," he mumbled.

"Anna tells me that you're involved with the anti-Treaty forces in the Four Courts."

Seán shifted in the chair. Daniel's question had obviously hit a nerve. "Anna shouldn't be talking about my business," he said gruffly.

Daniel sat back, his eyebrows arched in angry disbelief. "She didn't have much of a choice, you know. I don't think she enjoyed telling me about the illegal dealings you are mixed up in, in fact I'd say she was terribly ashamed of it. What did you expect her to do? Take responsibility for the guns herself?" Daniel tried to maintain his cool air of superiority but Seán's insolent almost challenging stare unnerved him.

The two men sat locked in silent combat and it became clear to Daniel that a different approach was necessary to enable him to penetrate the stubborn hard-headedness of this foolhardy lad.

Seán began to twist the cap in his hands. He sat forward on his chair, both feet planted firmly on the floor.

Daniel sighed loudly. "What do you think you're going to gain from this?"

Seán opened his mouth to speak but closed it again.

"Please, tell me," Daniel asked. "I am genuinely interested in hearing what you have to say."

Seán's mouth was closed so tightly that deep lines appeared around his lips. He stared at the floor like a bold child that would not finish his dinner.

Daniel rested his elbows on the desk and brought his hands up to his chin in a gesture of relaxed patience.

Eventually Seán shook his head. "You wouldn't understand," he said quietly.

"How can you say that? You don't know me," said Daniel

Seán twisted his cap until it had turned to a solid piece of rope between his hands.

"You're British," he said quickly.

The word '*British*' remained suspended between them for a few seconds before it dispersed into particles, making the air in the room seem charged with a dangerous atmosphere.

"I may be British, but I am not without a sense of justice."

Seán twisted his mouth into a cruel smile on hearing this.

"You are a young man with your whole life ahead of you – why are you getting involved in a lost cause? Because, believe me, that is what it is."

Daniel saw a shadow of doubt cross over Seán's face. He leaned forward and pressed on with his sermon.

"It's only a matter of time before every man down in the Four Courts will be arrested and jailed – possibly executed. Collins signed a treaty that wasn't perfect, but it was a beginning towards a peaceful solution, and people like you want to continue the fight."

"You wouldn't understand," Seán repeated flatly.

Daniel realised with disappointment that he was not going to get through to Seán the way he thought he might. In fact, he could see clearly that he was getting nowhere. "You're right," he said dismissively. "I don't understand."

Daniel reached for a set of keys that were on the corner of his desk and with the help of a silver letter-opener he levered the largest key off the metal ring.

"This is *my* key to the basement. I want you to get your guns off my property tonight. You can return the key to Anna when you have finished."

Seán stood up and stared down at Daniel. For a moment he looked as if he might be about to say something and Daniel held out the key slowly, anticipating an apology. But the moment passed and without uttering a word Seán pulled on his cap and snatched the key from Daniel's outstretched hand.

As Daniel listened to the heavy steps descend the stairs he was filled with disappointment. He had hoped to gain Seán's confidence, talk him into seeing how futile this war was, but he had failed miserably. Through his office window he could see Seán walking away from the building, shoulders hunched, hands thrust deep in his pockets, probably still clutching the key to the storeroom. His show of leniency had been met with shameless disdain, making him feel foolish, and he wondered as he watched Seán walk away, whether he had made the right decision by not informing the police.

★ ★ ★

The following morning Daniel was in work before any of the staff. During the night he had made the decision that if the guns were still there when he got in, he would have to involve the law. Seán's hostile attitude had dispelled any trace of compassion that Daniel had felt towards him before their meeting, but he was nonetheless pleased on discovering the empty space in the stockroom where the cases of guns had been. All that remained was the large dirty canvas sheet that was used to cover them. Daniel felt an immense relief, for he knew that the consequences of informing the police would have brought an immediate end to his relationship with Anna, both personal and professional. Now he felt worthy of a place in her affections, knowing he had acted with decency and honour towards her wayward brother.

When he got back up to the office, Anna was standing by her desk, her face pinched with worry. In her hand she held the key to the stockroom door that Seán had thrown across the breakfast table earlier that morning.

"Seán gave me this for you."

Daniel took the key. "Thank you," he said, taking it from her and slipping it into his trouser pocket.

Anna waited for an explanation but Daniel just smiled absently at her.

"What happened?" she asked impatiently.

"Nothing," Daniel answered. "We had a few words and he agreed to remove his belongings. That's all, nothing more." Daniel took a few steps towards his office and stopped. He turned to Anna who was standing in the same spot, nonplussed by his breezy behaviour. "Let's never mention this again," he said quietly before walking into his office and closing the door.

Anna sat at her desk and said a silent prayer to God for sparing her brother and keeping him from any harm.

*   *   *

Her heart pounded as they walked into the foyer of the Shelbourne Hotel on St Stephen's Green. His invitation had been unexpected and Anna was wearing a rather dull green dress, something that she would never have worn had she known that they were going out to tea that evening. All week, nothing had been said between them about Seán, or the night that they had kissed. In fact, by Friday, Anna had begun to worry whether it had all been just a bit of fun for Daniel – until he approached her as she was getting ready to leave the office and suggested that she join him for tea. The walk from the shop had been brisk as another heavy rain shower was imminent. Anna entered the foyer and discreetly scoured every corner for any familiar faces, but she could see none. She kept her head down as they were shown to a table. It was unlikely that anyone who knew her would be in the Shelbourne Hotel, but she couldn't help feeling nervous.

They sat down, and after a few minutes Anna relaxed, happy that there was no one in the dining room that she knew.

Daniel ordered sherry for each of them, and when the waitress left he turned to Anna, as if reading her thoughts. "This could always be a business meeting, you know."

Anna glanced around the room again.

"If anyone should see you, you can say we were discussing business matters."

She gave a terse smile. "I'm sorry if I seem nervous, it's just that being seen in public with someone other than Joe, well, I'd have a lot of explaining to do at home."

Daniel studied her face closely. "I understand," he said with a sincerity that made Anna want to reach across and touch his arm that rested just inches away on the table. A hint of mischief played at the corner of his eyes and he leaned across and lowered his voice. "A Jewish Brit. You'd have another war on your hands."

Anna put her hands up to her face and tried to suppress a laugh at his outrageous description, as if they were in school telling jokes behind the teacher's back. But a clawing feeling in the pit of her stomach reminded her that that is exactly what her father called the Jacobs.

The drinks arrived and Daniel handed Anna her glass of sherry and raised his own. "To you, Anna," he said, clinking his glass gently against hers. "You have been my saviour."

Anna looked at him in surprise.

"I mean it," he said seriously. "A few months ago I was the most miserable man alive, and since meeting you my whole world has changed. "You can't imagine how happy I was when I discovered your engagement was off."

His words seemed to come straight from the heart and Anna was touched by his honesty.

"Am I being too forward?" he asked.

"No," Anna blurted, not wanting him to stop.

"I really like you, Anna. I want to get to know you better, to spend more time with you." He looked into her eyes and held her gaze. "Is that what you want too?"

Anna's face broke into a smile. "Yes."

Daniel's high spirits drained away as he thought of the obstacles they faced. "What about your family? Is it going to be a problem?"

Anna looked down at the table and frowned. "Yes," she sighed.

Daniel pulled his chair in closer and leaned across. "I'll do anything to spend more time with you, even if it means meeting you secretly."

Anna looked into his eyes and at that very moment she knew that she was falling in love with Daniel. It amazed her that she could feel this way about a man who she had disliked intensely only months ago. His outer shell of arrogance and sulky abruptness had fallen away gradually since their early exchanges – revealing his true character, which was so different from the person she had first encountered.

"What would your father do if he found out about us?"

The mention of her father made Anna sit up in her chair. What could she possibly say that wouldn't hurt Daniel's feelings? She shrugged her shoulders. "He wouldn't be happy," was all she could think of to say.

Daniel gripped his empty sherry glass by the stem and pushed it around in little circles.

"Do you feel the same way as I do, Anna?" he asked, keeping his eyes on the glass.

"Yes," Anna whispered.

"Enough to risk the consequences should your father ever find out?"

The very thought made Anna's blood run cold and she hesitated for a split second. Daniel looked up anxiously and waited for her reply.

"Yes."

The muscles that were clenched around his jaw relaxed and he smiled at her.

"But, what about your parents? Won't they object?" Anna asked, as she suddenly thought of the two Mrs Jacobs and how they had looked at her with frosty stares the day she had met them at the hospital.

Daniel tossed his head defiantly. "They can object if they wish — it won't make a damn bit of difference to me."

*   *   *

Daniel threw his coat onto the hallstand and listened to the discordant sounds of Beethoven's 'Moonlight Sonata' coming from the living room. Irene was playing the piano, which was never a good sign. His mother had studied the piano as a young girl but had not been a gifted musician. Despite years of lessons her playing had always remained stilted and clumsy, without any natural flow. In recent years, she had only ever played to alleviate boredom or anxiety or in rare cases, anger. Daniel could tell by the way she chopped at each note that this was one of those rare occasions. He entered the room and saw Granny Jacob snoozing in her chair beside the fire. In the corner Irene sat at the piano, her head tilted to one side as she studied the upright music sheet. As soon as she heard the door open she stopped playing and let her hands drop to her lap. Granny Jacob opened one eye to see why the music had stopped, and quickly came to life when she saw Daniel standing by the door.

"Hello, dear, come in. Shut the door, there's a draft coming from the hall," she fussed.

"Good evening, Granny," he said, crossing the

room to kiss her.

"Mother," he looked across at Irene and saw the purplish marks of exhaustion under her eyes, "is everything alright? How is Father doing? I never made it in to see him today."

"Everything is fine," Irene said, lifting her face to kiss her son. "Father is no better but no worse. We spent all afternoon with him."

"I'll go to see him first thing tomorrow morning."

Irene closed the lid of the piano and stood up. "Have you eaten yet? I'm afraid we couldn't wait for you – we ate earlier."

"You should let your mother know when you are not joining us for dinner," Granny Jacob piped up.

Daniel looked at his grandmother but decided to hold his tongue – he knew from experience that the best way to deal with his grandmother's barbed comments was to ignore them.

"I ate already, thank you," he said to his mother.

"Where did you go?" Irene asked, moving back to the fire.

"The Shelbourne."

"Did you dine alone?" Irene asked as she settled into the armchair.

Daniel braced himself. "No, as a matter of fact, I didn't. Anna joined me."

Granny Jacob's eyes darted from Irene to Daniel

and back again, as if watching a game of tennis. Irene took a deep breath and looked across at her mother-in-law. It was a silent threatening look that said *'don't interfere'*. As if by some secret code, Granny Jacob received the warning and pulled her shawl tightly around her shoulders, casting her eyes down towards the floor.

"Well," Daniel said, breaking the wall of silence, "I think I'll turn in for the night."

"Goodnight," Irene said sharply.

"Goodnight, Daniel, sleep well, dear," Granny Jacob said, with unusual sweetness.

As Daniel put his hand on the door handle, he thought of something and turned to the two women. "You know, I should invite Anna home to dinner some evening. It would be nice if you could get to know her on a more personal level. Perhaps sometime next week?"

Irene's face was expressionless and for a split second Daniel thought she was not going to answer him. She turned her head slowly towards him and uttered, "Yes," faintly.

"Good," Daniel said cheerfully. "I'll let you know what day."

* * *

The women sat in silence after Daniel left the room. Irene stared into the fire, her face set in a tight-lipped frown.

"At least we'll get the opportunity to see what she is really like," Granny Jacob said tentatively.

Irene jumped up from her chair and gave her mother-in-law a murderous look. "If you had anything to do with this," she said, wagging her finger, "I will never forgive you."

Once again the black shawl was pulled defensively around the old woman's broad shoulders. "Excuse me," she barked, "how dare you suggest such a thing?"

"Never!" Irene repeated as she swept out of the room.

Chapter 16

Mary clattered the ladle against the side of the soup tureen and filled another bowl with the watery broth. Granny Jacob winced with displeasure at every ungainly move the girl made. Anna was unused to being waited on and she smiled over at Mary reassuringly. The two Mrs Jacobs sat at opposite ends of the large dining-room table, with Anna and Daniel facing each other in the middle. Anna felt a million miles away from Daniel even though he was only a few feet away – she may as well have been sitting on an iceberg, cast adrift in the Arctic Ocean.

Granny Jacob looked at the soup on her spoon as

if expecting to see something unpleasant floating on it. She sipped a small amount in through her rubbery lips and grimaced theatrically. "Oh dear," she said to Anna, "do be careful with the soup, it's scalding." She picked her napkin up and dabbed at the sides of her mouth.

Mary looked at Irene worriedly but Irene ignored the remark and arranged her face into a martyred smile.

"If you leave it a second, it will cool," she said. Then with a nod of approval towards Mary she said, "Mary always brings the food to the table nice and hot, the way we like it."

Granny Jacob gave Mary a jaundiced look and proceeded to stir her soup in large swirls.

"Please start, Anna," Irene said, picking up her own spoon.

Anna wanted to run from the room and not stop until she had reached her own front door. What had possessed her to accept Mrs Jacob's invitation to dinner? Daniel had mentioned it casually as they finished work the previous evening. "By the way," he had said, "Mother would like you to come to dinner tomorrow." At first Anna was terrified at the prospect of dining in Jacobs', but Daniel persuaded her to come along. "I want my mother to know you," he had exclaimed passionately. "Then she'll understand how I feel about you." Blinded by flattery, Anna had accepted the invitation, but as she sat in the tense atmosphere of the Jacobs' dining room she sorely regretted that decision. Her hand shook as she brought the soup towards her mouth.

"So, Anna, is everything going well in the shop?" Irene asked.

"Very well, Mrs Jacob," Anna answered obediently. "How is Mr Jacob?"

"He is very weak," Irene said sadly.

The four heads bowed towards their soup bowls in deference to the absence of Ben Jacob, the man they all loved.

"I hear you sold all the ladies' winter boots off for next to nothing," Granny Jacobs said admonishingly.

Anna could feel her face flush. "Well, they were not selling, and we needed the storage room."

"'Granny boots', that's what they call them," the old woman said to Irene, waving her spoon from Anna to Daniel.

Daniel looked over at Anna and grinned. "That is exactly what they are, Granny," he said.

"Granny boots indeed!" his grandmother responded. "They are made from good quality leather! The trouble with young people these days is that they don't appreciate good quality."

Daniel looked across at Anna and rolled his eyes

up to heaven.

Granny Jacob fixed her attention on Anna. "But they did sell, didn't they?"

"Yes," Anna replied meekly.

"Good," said the old woman. "Because I'm sending you another delivery, we can't shift them either."

"Why do you keep manufacturing them if nobody wants to buy them any more?" Daniel asked.

"Because that is what puts food on our table, young man." Granny Jacob rapped the table with a gnarled arthritic forefinger.

Anna took a sip of water and forced herself to speak. "May I suggest something?"

All eyes turned toward her and Anna was immediately sorry she had opened her mouth.

"Please do," said Irene with a bemused smile.

Anna turned to Irene, but her imperious gaze made her feel even more self-conscious, so she turned instead to Granny Jacob. "I think that ladies' boots are a thing of the past."

Granny Jacob narrowed her eyes.

"Two-inch heels with T-bar straps are what is being worn now. You see, as hemlines rise – "

"Hemlines rising, what next?" Granny Jacobs boomed, shaking her head.

Anna stopped and looked to Daniel for support.

He nodded his head reassuringly.

"Well, go on!" said Granny Jacob impatiently.

"As hemlines rise, women are beginning to put more thought into how the shoe looks. It must go with the skirt or dress they are wearing. It must be more fashionable. A black leather lace-up boot is no longer fashionable."

Daniel looked at his mother, searching for her reaction to Anna's assertion, but Irene seemed unmoved and maintained her usual upright composure.

Granny Jacob was still for a few moments while she absorbed Anna's words.

Eventually she shifted heavily in her chair. "Not fashionable," she mused. Then she looked at Daniel. "Your brother's been saying that for some time now, but I wouldn't take any heed. What would he know about ladies' shoes?" she snorted. "He doesn't even know any ladies!"

Daniel frowned at her. "Peter knows a lot more than you give him credit for – you should learn to respect his opinion."

Anna could see that Daniel was challenging his grandmother and tried to diffuse the situation. "If you could make less boots and concentrate on the design of a more modern shoe, I think we could sell a lot more," she said quickly.

Mary tripped into the room and set the empty silver tray on the sideboard with a noisy clatter. Anna moved to hand her plate up, but noticed that everyone else kept their hands on their laps and waited for their plates to be cleared away. She clasped her hands together and thanked Mary when her plate was taken from the table.

Granny Jacob didn't say much more over dinner. Anna wondered if it had seemed impertinent for her to make such a suggestion about the shoe designs to someone that had been in the business for a lot longer than her. The old woman tutted every now and again as she hacked at the meat on her plate.

"That beef was very tough," exclaimed Granny Jacob.

Mary had begun to gather the dirty dinner plates in her hands and looked like she might drop them at any moment.

"Sorry, Granny," muttered Irene. "Mine was perfectly fine. How was yours, Anna?"

"Very nice, Mrs Jacob."

"And yours, Daniel?"

"Fine."

Irene glowered over at her mother-in-law. "I'm sorry you didn't enjoy it."

Granny Jacob shrugged her shoulders, outnumbered. "I've had worse," she muttered under her breath.

After what Granny Jacob pointed out was a soggy apple pudding with cream, they moved into the front room.

Anna had been hoping that Daniel might suggest bringing her home, but to her utter dismay he seemed perfectly content to sit amongst the three women for the evening.

"Sit by me, Anna," ordered Granny Jacob. "I want to talk about an idea I have."

"Poor Anna," said Irene. "All this talk about work must be tiring you out."

"No, I enjoy it," said Anna with a smile.

Granny Jacob ignored Irene's comment and with an offhand wave towards the piano she said, "Why don't you play us a tune, Irene."

Daniel could see the two scarlet circles that had appeared on his mother's cheeks, a rosy glow that hinted at the vexation Irene felt at being dismissed from the conversation. She walked over to the piano and began to thumb through some sheets of music. When she had chosen a piece she sat down, secured the notes on the stand in front of her and proceeded to play Chopin's *Nocturne*. The anger of her playing did not match the lightness of the piece and Daniel smiled to himself at her choice of music – a funeral dirge would have been more appropriate for the mood she was in.

Over by the fire Granny Jacob was deep in conversation with Anna about her new idea to manufacture leather handbags that would match the new range of shoes for the coming season.

"Daniel, get me a pen and some paper – I need to write this down," she ordered and immediately went back to what she was talking about.

Daniel eased himself out of the chair and did as he was told. He found a pen and some paper in the drawer of the bookcase and brought them over to his grandmother.

Irene's playing had reached a crescendo and Granny Jacob looked up and gave her a disparaging look. "Not so loud, dear," she shouted over the piano. "We're trying to talk."

The playing stopped abruptly.

"That's better," Granny Jacob said with a smile that suggested she was oblivious to her insulting behaviour.

Daniel saw Anna's face contort with fright and he gave her a reassuring smile.

Irene stood up and looked as if she might hurl the piano at her mother-in-law, but again Granny Jacob remained raptly unaware of any upset she might have caused. Her head was bent forward as she scribbled some figures down on the sheet of paper that was resting on her lap.

"I think I will go and help Mary in the kitchen — she has had a long day," Irene said pointedly, and with one fluid movement from the piano to the door, she was gone.

Daniel smoked a cigarette and listened half-heartedly to the talk about shoes and handbags and profit margins, but he soon became bored. Anna looked very different now in contrast to how she had been when she had arrived earlier that evening — in fact, looking at her now it was hard to believe that she was the same person. Whereas an hour beforehand she was hardly capable of making conversation about the weather during dinner, now she was discussing the brass tacks of business without so much as flinching under the scrutiny of his grandmother. Daniel studied Anna's profile from his armchair. Her head tilted to one side as she listened to Granny Jacob, while Daniel followed the curve of her slender neck, letting his eyes rest on her face. Her blue eyes blinked slowly as she listened intently to what the old woman had to say. Her mouth was slightly open and Daniel stared at her lips, remembering how he had kissed them. He felt a stirring deep inside, as he thought of how much he would like to kiss her again. How he wished that his grandmother would leave them alone together, so that he might take her in his arms for just a few moments – but that was certainly not going to happen. Daniel slapped the palms of his hands on to his thighs and stood up.

"Now, Granny, will you please release Anna from your clutches. I have to get her home tonight."

Granny Jacob dismissed Anna with a wave of her hand and folded the piece of paper carefully.

"You have a good business head, young lady. So rare in a young girl these days," she added with a heavy sigh.

Anna stood up. "Goodbye, Mrs Jacob."

The old woman bent down and threw another log on the fire. "Call me Granny, everyone else does," she said, not bothering to look up.

Daniel took Anna's arm and led her from the room. They walked down the chilly hallway to the coat-stand beside the front door.

"I suppose I'd better tell Mother we're leaving. You stay there, I'll go into the kitchen and get her." Daniel disappeared towards the back of the hall and Anna reached for her coat and stood in the half-light. A slight noise made her look up, and she saw Irene coming down the stairs.

"Are you leaving already?"

"Yes, Daniel has just gone to look for you."

Irene walked over to Anna and helped her on with

her coat. "I am so sorry about Granny Jacob, she sometimes gets carried away with the business."

Anna smiled tightly. There was something about Irene's cool detachment that unnerved her and she wished that Daniel would hurry back.

"You seem to be running the place so well, Anna – we really do appreciate it. I am sure that you are long overdue some time off and we will arrange for you to take it, just as soon as Mr Evans takes up his position with us."

Anna looked at Irene blankly.

"Didn't Granny mention him?" Irene asked.

"No."

"Oh, I assumed that she told you. Mr Evans will take over when Daniel returns to college," Irene explained.

Anna felt a lump in her throat as she struggled to think of something to say.

"After all," Irene continued sweetly, "Daniel is only here temporarily."

Anna could feel an uncomfortable strain across her chest as if her heart was going to explode. She looked over Irene's shoulder to see if Daniel was coming, but the hall was empty.

It seemed that Irene was not finished what she had to say. She stepped closer to Anna and lowered her voice. "Daniel is an impetuous boy. He always has been, and he may have given you the wrong impression of his intentions for the future. But make no mistake about it, he will return to Edinburgh to continue his studies. Do you understand?"

"There you are. I've been looking for you," said Daniel, walking up the hall.

Irene swung around and replaced her steely expression with a serene smile. "Yes, I was just saying goodnight to Anna."

Daniel put his arm around his mother and kissed her cheek.

"That was lovely, Mother. I'll take Anna home now, don't wait up for me."

Irene glared across at Anna. "Goodnight, Anna, it was so good of you to come."

"Goodnight, Mrs Jacob," Anna said politely as she stepped out of the house.

It was almost nine o'clock and, though the light of the evening had faded, it was not yet completely dark. Daniel walked as close to Anna as he could without actually touching her. Anna turned Irene's icy words over in her head and tried to grasp their meaning. She felt hurt and confused that Daniel should be talking about seeing her in secret while still planning to return to Edinburgh. On the other hand she knew that there was a good chance that Irene might have been bluffing. As they strolled down the

South Circular Road, Daniel slipped his arm around Anna's waist and pulled her towards him.

"Daniel," Anna said looking around, but there was no one on the quiet street.

"Just one kiss," he pleaded. "All evening I've wanted to reach out and touch you, it's been agony."

Anna smiled at his dramatic plea and let him kiss her. His lips felt cold on the outside but the warmth inside his mouth sent a wave of pleasure through her. Anna moulded herself into his arms, until his mother's words came rushing back to upset her. What if it was true? She pulled herself free from Daniel's grasp.

"What is it?" asked Daniel.

Anna smoothed down the front of her coat. "Nothing. Come on, it's getting late."

"What's wrong?"

"Nothing," Anna replied quickly. "I should be getting home."

Daniel sensed her sudden sharpness.

"I'm sorry I stuck you with Granny for so long."

"Don't be sorry. I like your grandmother." Anna was now walking in long strides and Daniel had to hurry to keep up with her.

"Well, you seem upset, is something bothering you?"

Anna stopped and thought for a minute. "No,"

she said softly and resumed a slower pace. She would have to make sure that what Irene said was true before confronting Daniel about it.

Chapter 17

Mr Barry pulled down the window blind and began to clean up after a busy day. He went into the back room, took the sweeping brush and pan, and proceeded to sweep away the stray pieces of hair that had gathered on the floor. Behind him the bell gave a tinkle as the shop door was pushed open.

Seán stepped into the shop and pressed his back against the door as it closed behind him.

Mr Barry stopped sweeping and leaned his chin on the handle of the brush.

"Did you finish up early today?"

Seán shook his head. "No. I'm only here for a minute."

Mr Barry sensed his son's anxiety. "For what?"

"I need a favour."

"Go on," Mr Barry said cautiously.

Seán glanced about the shop before he continued. "We're shifting some guns tonight," he said, his chest expanding with importance. "They're going down to Wexford tomorrow, but we have to get them out of where they are by tonight. Can we leave them here?"

Mr Barry swept the pile of hair into a bundle and propped the sweeping brush against the wall with slow deliberate movements. "Don't bring any trouble on me, son."

Seán moved towards him. "I hate asking you, Da, but they have to be moved now or the law will be on to us."

"Have you nowhere else to keep them?"

"No. Nowhere safe. It was Joe that thought of you."

Mr Barry softened at the mention of Joe. "How many are you talking about? Sure there's hardly room to swing a cat in that back room."

"There's four crates. They'll fit in there no problem," Seán said, pointing towards the small room at the back of the shop. "We'll put them in tonight and be back for them tomorrow evening."

Mr Barry looked towards the room and frowned. "I

want to help, you know that Seán, but if I'm found out
…"

Seán jumped in immediately. "You won't be
found out, Da. We'll wait until after midnight to
move them, and the same again tomorrow night.
You have my word, there'll be no trouble."

Seán's reassurances did little to assuage Mr
Barry's concern. Possession of a firearm would result
in immediate arrest and imprisonment and, while he
wanted to help in the struggle, unlike his son Mr
Barry was not prepared to risk his personal freedom.

Seán looked at his father and waited for his
answer. Mr Barry stood with his legs set slightly
apart, arms folded tightly across his chest.

"Just the one night," he said finally.

Seán exhaled deeply. "Thanks, Da. You're really
helping us out. Joe is up the walls about it."

"Where are you moving them from?" Mr Barry
asked.

"Ah, it's a warehouse across town, it's not safe any
more. I better get back to work." Seán moved
towards the door. "Thanks, Da. I'll see you at home."

Mr Barry nodded his head and reached for the
sweeping brush again.

"I'll see you later," he said, and began to sweep
the pile of hair into the dustpan.

★　★　★

Anna sat at the kitchen table and thought about the events of the night before. Weeks before, when she had met Granny Jacob at the hospital, she had been terrified of the scowling old woman. But she hadn't turned out to be quite as fearsome as she pretended to be. Anna could see that once you got past her initial abrasive manner, Granny Jacob had quite an endearing quality. All evening she had been on her guard, waiting for the grandmother to pass comment on her relationship with Daniel, but to her relief nothing had been said. Instead, it had been Irene who had shocked Anna with her icy parting comments. Anna stirred her tea and thought of what Irene had said about Mr Evans taking over from Daniel. Her words had been delivered with such arrogance and contempt that Anna was now in no doubt how Irene felt about a relationship that might blossom between her, a lowly subordinate, and her precious son.

"Where did you go last night?" Mr Barry asked as he spread a dollop of jam across his slice of bread.

"I went to tea in Maureen's house." Already prepared for her father's questioning, she had decided to lie about being invited to Jacobs' for dinner. Anna hated telling lies, but she didn't want to risk arousing her father's suspicions about Daniel. She had already been in the Jacobs' house for tea in recent months, and saying that she was there again would only irritate him.

"Who?"

"Maureen Dolan, from the shop. It was her birthday yesterday and her mam invited some of us to tea." It had been Maureen's birthday, but Anna was fibbing about the invitation to tea.

Mr Barry nodded and stuffed the slice of bread into his mouth. He chewed it noisily and stared across at Anna and she knew instinctively what was coming next. He swallowed the bread with a gulp and reached for his tea.

"Have you seen Joe recently?"

Anna hung her head. "No."

Mr Barry took a slug of tea and set his mug down on the table. "Anna, you have to talk to him. Don't leave it like that – the poor lad is tormented."

"What do you want me to do?" Anna asked.

"I want you to have a chat with him, sort things out."

Anna lifted her head and met her father's stare. "Dada," she said slowly, "you have to accept that myself and Joe are no longer a couple. I know it's hard on you, you were so fond of him – but I can't continue to go out with him just because you want it. You have to understand that it's over between me and Joe."

Anna reached across the table and rested her hand on top of her father's, but he did not respond to her touch – instead he looked as if he might cry.

"I'm so disappointed," he said in a whisper.

Anna withdrew her hand and placed it on her lap. "I'm sorry, Dada," she said firmly.

Mr Barry looked across at her sadly. "Anna, you're making a big mistake. You'll never find the likes of Joe Maguire again. For God's sake, will you change your mind and settle down with him before it's too late? Because while you're larking about, he'll meet another girl and then you'll have missed your chance."

Anna could see that her father was struggling to control his emotions, but she couldn't let him think that there was any chance of her getting back with Joe again.

"Dada," she said, holding up a hand to stop him saying anything else, "it's over, and no amount of talking is going to change my mind."

Mr Barry stood up and leaned heavily on the back of his chair. "If that's the way you feel then I suppose there's little point in me trying to change your mind. I'm just afraid that you'll regret it." He paused and blinked a few times. "I always thought you and Joe were meant to be together."

"So did I, Dada." Anna was on the verge of tears, unable to bear the hurt that she was causing her father. "I thought that if we got engaged everything would be different … but I was wrong. I'm sorry . . . you were so happy about it."

Mr Barry pushed the chair back into the table and looked down at her with a weary smile. "I was happy because I thought it was what you wanted. I only want what's best for you, love." He leaned over and kissed her on the side of her face before walking slowly out of the kitchen.

★ ★ ★

The horse and cart rattled down Caple Street in the shadows of the dim orange glow of gaslight. Seán sat at the back and guarded the cargo. They had piled the crates on top of each other, and hidden them under the dirty tarpaulin that was used to secure any stray pieces of coal that the cart normally carried. Joe sat up at the front, dressed in the smelly black jacket of the coal merchant that had lent them his cart for the night. To anyone passing, they looked like two coalmen on their way home from a hard day's work. Joe pulled the reins outside the barbershop and the weary horse obediently came to a halt. Seán jumped down and moved quickly to the front door and unlocked it. The street was deserted. Joe stood up and stepped into the cart, throwing back the filthy canvas cover. He pushed the top crate towards Seán who stood waiting to receive it. Seán's knees buckled under the weight.

"Jesus Christ," he groaned.

It had taken them longer than expected to shift the guns from Jacob's storeroom to the shop on Caple Street, and their backs were breaking under the strain of lifting the heavy crates.

Joe jumped down from the cart and grabbed a hold of the rough wood and together they hoisted it onto their shoulders like two coffin bearers. Seán had been worried that the crates would not fit into the back room and might have been visible to customers the following day, but to his relief they fitted, leaving enough room to pull the partition door closed.

They had left black marks on the wall and door from where their jackets had rubbed up against them.

"Here," Joe said, pointing towards a tap, "get a cloth and clean off those marks."

Seán got two towels from a shelf and ran them under the water. He handed one to Joe and they began to scrub the evidence away.

"We've to do this all again tomorrow night," Seán moaned.

Joe stopped scrubbing and looked at him. "It's better than going to prison. You should be thanking God that that fella spared you."

Seán snorted loudly and ran his towel under the tap again.

"Why did he not report you?" Joe asked.

"He said it was because I was Anna's brother and he didn't want to see me going to prison on account of her," Seán answered derisively.

"Well, you've Anna to thank so."

Seán turned around, unable to hide his anger any longer. "My sister is nothing better than an informer. Why did she say they were mine in the first place? She should have kept her mouth shut."

"Who else would have put them there? It wouldn't have taken them long to find out. You should be glad that she came forward and said something. Sure isn't she the only one with a set of keys to the place?"

Seán shrugged his shoulders sullenly.

"By the way, did you get another set copied?" said Joe.

"I did," muttered Seán.

"Good. You never know when they might come in handy."

Seán scrubbed the coal marks off the wall in silence.

"She was protecting you, Seán, and you should be thankful to have a sister that cares about you," Joe said, stepping into his military role of superior officer.

Seán threw his towel into the sink. "I don't know why you're sticking up for her after what she's done to you," he muttered.

Joe flinched at the reminder of the humiliation of his recent heartbreak. He rounded his shoulders and looked at Seán gravely. "Whatever has happened between Anna and me should not make you look on her any differently. She's a good girl, Seán, and I know she'd do anything for you."

Seán looked down at the ground, still sulking.

"Come on, will you?" Joe said, springing into action again. "We have to get the cart back tonight."

* * *

As the curtain of the Abbey Theatre came down Anna applauded, then looked around as the house lights came up. Not that she knew many people who went to see Lady Gregory's plays at the Abbey, but still she wanted to be sure that there was nobody there that might know her. Being seen having dinner or a drink with Daniel could be explained, rather unconvincingly, as a business outing – but going to the theatre with him would not be as easily expounded. They walked out of the foyer onto Abbey Street and Daniel put his arm through Anna's as they strolled away from the crowd outside the theatre. Anna felt herself getting hot with panic and after a few paces she pulled away from him.

"Anyone could see us here," she said, looking across the street furtively.

Daniel frowned and walked alongside her. "I suppose you're right. No point getting caught if we can avoid it."

Anna gave him a terse smile as she quickened her pace.

"What exactly would happen if they found out?" he asked.

Anna thought of what her father's reaction would be. He was annoyed enough as it was, but if he discovered the main reason why she had broken it off with Joe, her life wouldn't be worth living. "I don't know," she answered quietly. "He wouldn't be pleased, I know that much."

They walked with a safe distance between them.

"Did you enjoy the play?" Daniel asked.

"Yes, thank you," Anna answered untruthfully.

The play had been boring and she'd had to stifle a few yawns towards the end. The part she did enjoy was during the second act, when Daniel had taken her hand and laced his fingers through hers, never once taking his eyes from the stage. Anna felt a rush of excitement race through her body as she felt the slight movements in each of his fingers. She sat rigidly in her seat, afraid to move a muscle in her hand for fear he would let go.

On the tram journey from Sackville Street, Anna sat opposite Daniel, never looking across at him once. When they reached Leeson Street Anna insisted on walking the last part of her journey alone.

Daniel shook his head and gave a weak smile. "I'm prepared to be discreet for your sake, Anna, but you have to think a little further ahead. We can't sneak around forever."

Anna had decided not to ask Daniel about his return to Edinburgh. If his mother was right then he would have to tell her soon, and she wanted to give him a chance to explain his intentions without her forcing him to do so.

"I know that," Anna said looking up at him. "It's just the way things have to be for the moment."

Daniel looked at her and leaned his face in slightly towards hers. "Let me kiss you," he whispered.

Anna looked around. An old woman was walking

away from them slowly, and on the other side of the road two girls about her own age were deep in conversation as they made their way up the street. Anna knew it was risky but she leaned in to Daniel and kissed him. When she went to pull away, he quickly slipped his arm around her waist and she leaned back into him and lost herself in his embrace. His tongue stroked the inside of her mouth making her weaken with desire.

She pulled herself away and whispered, "Goodnight," before rushing off, leaving Daniel standing in the same position, his head tilted forward and arms still bent around an invisible woman.

* * *

Joe Maguire stumbled up the quiet road with one hand clutching the spikes of the garden railings, to keep himself from falling down. At his front door, he searched his pockets for his key but could not find it. He dug deep into his trouser pockets but they were empty. He tugged at the pockets of his jacket until some coins tumbled out and tinkled against the porch tiles. A light came on in the hall, and through the thick glass panels of the front door he could see the distorted shape of his mother coming towards him.

"Joe, what are you doing at this hour of the night?" she whispered crossly as she tied the belt of her dressing-gown. "Come in."

Joe gave up his clumsy attempt to retrieve the coins and stepped into the hall, putting one hand against the wall to find his balance.

Mrs Maguire put her finger to her lips and pointed upstairs to where her husband was sleeping. "Come into the kitchen. I'll make you a cup of tea – you look like you need one," she said with an eyebrow raised disapprovingly.

It was only when he got into the silent, almost church-like atmosphere of his mother's sterile kitchen, that Joe realised just how drunk he was. Everything seemed to stand perfectly upright in its exact place – except him. He pulled out a chair and fell into it like an ape. His mother looked at him, her thin face lined with worry.

"Joe," she still whispered, as Mr Maguire's bed was directly over the kitchen, "what's got into you? You were never one to drink like this. What's going on?"

Joe gave her a baleful look and swayed slightly on the chair.

His mother abandoned her tea-making and sat down beside him. "Tell me," she implored.

It started deep within his chest and pushed itself

upwards into his throat, like a volcano erupting. His shoulders began to shake and Mrs Maguire looked on in shock as her son began to cry. His big arms fell onto the table and he let his head collapse down on top of them, surrendering to the pent-up grief that had lodged deep inside him for weeks.

"Joe, what is it?" his mother said soothingly.

"She's broken it off," he sobbed

Mrs Maguire nodded knowingly. It was just as she had suspected. "Ah, Joe, I'm sorry."

She patted his back gently. "I'm so sorry, son."

Joe sat up and wiped the tears from his face. "Sorry for crying like this, Ma," he apologised. The shameful expression that clouded his face reminded his mother of how he used to look as a young boy, whenever he was caught doing something wrong. She remembered a time long ago, when Joe and his brother Francis had been marched to the front door by the ferocious Mr Walsh. He had caught the two of them stealing apples from the trees in his back garden. Francis couldn't have been more than seven years old, making Joe only four. She remembered it as if it were yesterday: Mr Walsh standing there, his face as red as the apples the boys were still holding, Francis with his chin jutting out in defiance, holding the apples like trophies. She should have been mad with them, sent them to bed without any supper. But her heart had melted at the sight of the shamefaced four-year-old Joe, who stood quivering in the front porch, holding out the end of his jumper which was filled with the stolen apples, silently pleading with her to save him. When she had made her apologies to Mr Walsh she ushered the boys into the kitchen and gave them a long lecture about the evils of stealing. Then, to their delight, she set to work making a tart with the apples that Mr Walsh had forgotten to confiscate.

A pang of desperate loss shot through her chest like lightning as she thought of her darling dead son Francis. There were still some nights she woke and crept into his room – and imagined that she could make out the shape of his sleeping body under the covers of the empty bed.

Joe hung his head and sniffed loudly.

"Don't be sorry, Joe. It hurts, I know. But give it time and you will heal. Only God knows why it happened, but maybe Anna just wasn't the right girl for you."

Joe shook his head vigorously. "She's the only girl for me. That's why it hurts so much . . ." His voice trailed off.

Knowing there was nothing else she could do, Mrs Maguire stood up and hugged her son tightly. "I love you, Joe," she said gently and left him alone with his grief.

When she had gone, Joe reached into his breast pocket and pulled out his wallet. He flipped it open and stared at the photograph of Anna that she had given to him when they first started going out together. He ran his finger slowly down the line of her face and began to cry again.

Chapter 18

Anna locked the shop door and strolled down the street, oblivious to anything around her. Her thoughts were miles away, with a Mr Evans, and a university in Edinburgh that she had begun to despise, even though she had no idea where Edinburgh was exactly.

She had waited a whole week in the hope that Daniel might say something about his plans, but it seemed he could only tell her how madly in love he was with her. They had taken a day trip to Howth on the previous Saturday and walked along the seafront. Anna had purposely kept quiet to give him a chance to tell her, but Daniel had poured out his heart, about how he had never felt this way about any girl before. Of course Anna had been flattered and slightly embarrassed at his candid declaration of love, but her happiness had been thwarted by Irene's parting words to her: ". . . *he will return to Edinburgh . . .*"

"Tell me that you feel the same way, Anna," he had said as they sat against the pier wall and watched the fishermen haul the nets up from their boats.

"I do love you, Daniel," Anna answered demurely, and as the words left her mouth she was for the first time, truly aware of the depth of her feelings. And she knew that if Daniel did leave her, her whole world would fall apart.

That is why she had turned down his invitation to dinner earlier that evening. He had stood at her desk looking miserably dejected at her casual refusal.

"Why not?" he demanded.

"Because . . ." Anna hesitated and almost changed her mind. "Because we have been seeing far too much of each other. We've been careless, parading around the city as if it didn't matter who saw us."

"Oh, for heaven's sake, Anna! Your family have to find out about us sometime, and as for me, well, I've already told you, I don't care about what my mother thinks," Daniel said petulantly.

"Well, it's different for you. You're a man and men

can get away with doing what they want. I can't do that, Daniel. I have to think of the consequences."

"What consequences?"

Anna shook her head and knew she was entering dangerous territory. She had, so far, avoided telling Daniel too much about her father – he already knew about Seán and that was enough as far as she was concerned. The discussion had taken an unforeseen turn – Anna wanted to focus on Daniel's plans for the future, not her family.

"It's just too soon to tell my father about you. He's still annoyed with me about Joe, and … "

Daniel rolled his eyes. "You don't have to continue, I know the rest."

Anna took her handbag off the desk and got ready to leave.

"Anna, if you don't want to go out with me, just say so. Don't make excuses."

Anna froze. She wanted to shout at him: *If you love me so much then why are you going back to Edinburgh?* But she stopped herself.

"I'm not making excuses, Daniel," she said firmly.

He stood rooted to the spot and watched her gather her things together.

"I'll see you in the morning," Anna said as she moved to the side of her desk where he was standing. He turned his face downwards and sulked.

Anna hesitated and tried to think of something she could say that would lead around to his future plans – but nothing would come to her, and she left the office mumbling a brief goodbye.

Outside on the busy street, Anna walked towards the tram feeling hollow inside. Seeing Daniel look so disappointed had upset her; she wanted to spend every living moment with him and she was annoyed with herself for being so cold with him. She tried to imagine what her life would be like if he did go back to Edinburgh, and as she did she felt a lump in her throat. Her life without Daniel would be meaningless. Someone shouted her name and Anna pulled herself away from the morbid thoughts that filled her head, and turned to see Daniel cutting through the crowd of people behind her. A surge of happiness shot through her and she waited excitedly until he caught up. When he reached her he stood with his hands held by his side and looked around self-consciously as if he'd forgotten what he wanted to say.

"What is it?" Anna asked.

"If I promise that no one will see us, will you come to dinner with me on Saturday evening?"

"How can you promise that?" Anna asked.

"Never mind," Daniel said, letting a hint of secrecy creep into his voice. "Let me worry about that, but I give you my word that no one will see us."

Anna desperately wanted to stand her ground and not accept another invitation until she was sure that Daniel was serious about her – and not just filling a gap before he returned to his other life.

But she lapsed into a momentary weakness as he stepped closer, and whispered, "Please, Anna, say yes."

She looked at him for a few moments and knew that with all the will in the world, she could never say no. Her face broke into a grin. "Yes," she answered.

Daniel clapped his hands together. "Thank you!" He unclasped his hands and went to reach out to her, but quickly remembered where they were and put them down by his sides again.

Anna turned to go, but Daniel remembered he had something else to tell her.

"By the way, tomorrow is Friday."

Anna looked at him and laughed. "Yes, Daniel, I know."

"What I mean is," he said absently, "we're bringing Father home for a few days."

"That's great news!"

Daniel shrugged his shoulders despondently. "I don't think it's such a good idea, but Granny is insisting that we give it a try. Anyhow, I won't be in tomorrow and I possibly may not be in on Saturday."

Anna nodded her head and waited for him to continue.

"So, if it suits you we could meet at eight o'clock on Saturday evening?"

"Where?"

Daniel looked up and down the street. "Why don't I just see you outside the shop?"

Anna looked at him questioningly. "The shop?"

But Daniel just grinned and gave no clue as to what he might be planning. "Trust me," he assured her, "nobody will see us."

"I'll see you on Saturday," she said, looking slightly confused, "and give my regards to your father."

★   ★   ★

Anna buttoned up her good blouse with the silk collar, which she wore over a black wool skirt. She was sorry now that she had not insisted on finding out where Daniel was taking her. What she was wearing was smart without being overdressed, but if they were going somewhere glamorous, then she risked the possibility of looking quite dowdy. She looked over at the green silk party dress that was flung across her bed and realised that even if she wanted to wear it, she couldn't possibly walk out of the house so dressed up without her father becoming suspicious. Earlier that evening she had tried to sound as casual as possible, as she lied about her plans. Mr Barry had made a fuss about Anna not eating any dinner.

"I'm not hungry, Dada," Anna said as she handed him his plate of sausages and eggs.

"Will you sit down and eat something?" he insisted.

"I'll have something later in Maureen's house. Her mam has invited me to supper."

Mr Barry stopped eating. "Are you going out tonight?"

"Yes," Anna answered, trying not to blush. "We're going to the theatre."

Mr Barry nodded his head and began to chew his food slowly. A few moments passed and just as Anna thought the interrogation was over, he raised his head again. "Who are you going with?"

"Just myself and Maureen, from the shop."

Anna's heart raced as she heard the lies roll off her tongue with such ease.

Mr Barry sat forward and stared at Anna. "Are there boys bringing you?"

Her high-pitched giggle sounded nervous. "No, Dada, it's just the two of us."

He seemed satisfied with her answer and wiped

the remains of his egg off the plate with a hunk of bread. "Don't be too late. I don't want you walking the streets on your own at night. It's different when Joe is with you."

When Joe was with me, Anna thought as she nodded complacently and kissed her father goodnight.

★   ★   ★

A gust of wind swept up Sackville Street, almost blowing Anna's hat off. With one hand placed on top of her flat wide-brimmed velour hat, she stepped back into the porch of Jacob's shoe shop. It was already five minutes past eight and there was still no sign of Daniel. The click of the front door opening behind her made her jump, and she turned around to see Daniel standing in the shadows of the hallway.

"Come in," he beckoned.

Anna looked out into the street before she joined Daniel in the hall. He closed the door behind her and they stood in the darkness.

"Is this where you're taking me?" Anna asked jokingly.

Daniel took hold of her hand and began to lead her up the stairs, ignoring her mild protestations. When they got to the office, Daniel opened the door slowly, revealing the surprise he had prepared. All the office furniture had been pushed back against the wall to create a space in the middle where Daniel had laid a rug. The room was illuminated with the warm glow of the fire he had lit. The brass candle-sticks which had always stood empty on the mantelpiece, now held flickering white candles. He pulled Anna into the room and swept his hand about in a theatrical gesture. "What do you think?"

Anna looked around, completely taken aback. Daniel pulled her over to the picnic basket that sat beside the fire, and began to pull out some of the food he had brought. Cold meats, cheese and a bottle of wine.

"It's our very own restaurant," he said proudly, handing her a wine glass.

He opened the wine and poured some for both of them. Anna looked at the crystal glass in her hand and Daniel gave a mischievous smile. "Let's hope Mother doesn't notice her glasses are missing," he said as he clinked his glass of wine against Anna's. "But how rude of me, madam," he exclaimed, putting his glass down on the mantelpiece. "Please, let me take your coat and hat." He took Anna's glass, while she unbuttoned her coat and took it off. Daniel hung it on the coat-stand as Anna fumbled with her hat-pin.

"Please sit down, madam," he said, fussing over

her. "It's the best table in the house."

Anna laughed at his antics and sat down on the rug, tucking her legs in behind her and smoothing her skirt over her ankles. Daniel stuck his head into the picnic basket and pulled out plates and knives. "Mary made us some meat pies – I hope you like them."

"Mary?"

"Our housekeeper. You met her when you came to dinner."

Anna remembered poor Mary and how terrified she had been of the growling Granny Jacob. "Did you tell her what the food was for?"

Daniel took a bite of his pie and smiled slyly. "Not exactly, but she promised not to say a word so long as I return the crockery in one piece."

Anna tried to be as dainty as she could while eating the meat pie but it was impossible – pieces of pastry dropped onto her skirt and she tried to backhand them away discreetly.

It was a strange feeling sitting there in the semi-darkness of the office she worked in, looking across at her desk where she could see the work she had set aside for Monday morning.

Daniel could see what she was thinking and he smiled across at her. "It's the best I could do," he said with a touch of weariness. "I did promise that no one would see us."

"It's perfect." Anna hung her head to one side and gazed at Daniel with a smile that let him know he had made the right decision.

All afternoon he had been sick with nerves over whether to go through with his idea about the office picnic. One moment it seemed romantic and secretive, the next just plain foolish, but looking at Anna now he allowed himself to stop worrying and enjoy the few hours they had together.

When they had eaten their fill, Anna began to gather up the plates and cutlery but Daniel reached over and stopped her.

"That's my job," he insisted. "Please sit down and relax."

Daniel left the plates where they were on the rug and moved over to Anna. He sat beside her and put his arm around her shoulders and she let her body lean into his. They sat gazing into the fire, staying perfectly still, both of them acutely aware of how close they were to each other.

"I wish we could capture moments in our lives and keep them safely stored up. If that were the case, I would definitely treasure this moment and hide it away so no one could ever touch it."

Anna smiled drowsily. The glass of wine had made her sleepy, and the fire was making her cheeks burn but she didn't want to move an inch away from Daniel. She put her head on his shoulder and he kissed her forehead.

"I'm so happy, Anna," he whispered. "Meeting you has made me see how empty my life was."

"Surely it wasn't that bad?" Anna jibed, poking him playfully in the ribs. "Didn't you have girlfriends back in England?"

"Yes," Daniel said, "but that's what I'm talking about – it was all so meaningless. I spent my life escorting nice Jewish girls to dances, girls I hadn't got the slightest bit of interest in – just because my parents expected it of me."

The mention of his parents gave Anna the opportunity she had been waiting for.

"And how do they feel now?" she asked, still staring into the fire.

Daniel sighed deeply and pulled her closer to him. "If father were in the whole of his health he would probably be delighted that I have finally met someone as wonderful as you." His face darkened. "And as for my mother and Granny, I have already told you, Anna, I don't care what they think any more."

She could wait no longer. She let a few moments of silence pass before she spoke. "When are you going back to Edinburgh?"

His body stiffened. He put his finger on her chin and tilted her head upwards to face him. "What do you mean?"

Anna pulled herself away and sat up straight. "Your mother told me, the night I had dinner with you, that you were going back to university and a Mr Evans was taking over your position."

Daniel opened his mouth and stared at her incredulously. "My mother said that to you?" he asked in a strained voice.

Anna was immediately sorry she had said anything. The glazed look of contentment had vanished from his eyes – he leapt to his feet and began pacing the room like a tiger.

"Please don't be cross, I shouldn't have told you," Anna said, wringing her hands together.

Daniel walked to the other side of the room and smashed his fist into the palm of his hand. "Damn that interfering woman!" he hissed under his breath.

Anna hung her head and turned back to face the fire – which didn't seem as warm as it had been earlier.

Daniel clenched his fists and attempted to control his anger; he moved across to Anna and sank down beside her. "I'm sorry, but I can't help losing my temper when I hear of her doing things like that. It's so typical of her," he said, exploding again.

Anna bit down on her lip. "I shouldn't have told you," she said in a frightened voice.

Daniel shook his head and took her hands in his. "You were right to tell me. I'm sorry, I shouldn't have reacted so childishly." He looked away and glared at a spot on the floor before springing into action again. "It's just that my mother has always been so controlling. She has meddled with every decision I have ever made in my life, and it has got to stop."

"She's not happy about us, is she?" Anna asked, already knowing the answer.

Daniel threw his hands in the air. "Of course she's not happy about us, because she didn't arrange it. Did I tell you that my brother Peter broke off his engagement to a perfectly nice girl last year because *they* didn't like her?"

Anna could see his anger rising again.

"I mean," he continued in a high-pitched voice, "what exactly has my granny got to do with who he marries? Or my mother, for that matter? Honestly, sometimes I think they're in competition with each other to see who can meddle in our lives the most." He looked at Anna and saw the worry etched across her face. "Sorry, I'll shut up now," he mumbled as he bowed his head and rested it on her shoulder.

"Daniel, I don't want you to go. Ever since the night your mother told me, I've been so upset at the thought of you leaving. It's the reason why I wouldn't go out with you the other night. There's no point in getting any closer to you if you are going away."

Daniel pulled her face around to his and kissed her. It was a slow passionate kiss that seemed to last forever and Anna felt as if she would drown in his warm embrace. He kissed her face, and then her eyelids, whispering, "I love you, Anna," over and over. He pulled back and looked into her eyes. "I am not ever going to leave you. I know this might seem absurd and I don't want to frighten you off with my enthusiasm, but I am sure that I want to spend the rest of my life with you. I've never been more certain of anything." His eyes glistened feverishly as he spoke and all the doubt and uncertainty that had plagued Anna since that night in his mother's house vanished with his ardent declaration of love.

"I love you too, Daniel," she whispered through her kisses. "I was so afraid of losing you."

★   ★   ★

When she awoke she looked around and saw Daniel sleeping soundly beside her. The fire had turned to glowing ashes and Anna's bare shoulders felt cold. They had pulled the picnic rug around them afterwards, and fallen asleep in each other's arms.

Anna lay still and felt a rush of guilty pleasure as she thought of how easily she had given herself to him – sliding out of her clothes as if she had done it a thousand times before. She thought of Joe, and how patiently he had waited for that moment, a moment that had never arrived. Anna pushed the rug away from her and eased herself up from the floor. She was still wearing her slip – somehow it had felt more respectable to keep it on while they made love. The only light in the room now came from the candles on the mantelpiece and Anna dressed silently in the flickering shadows. Lifting one of the candles, she went across to the wall clock at the door and squinted to read the time – it was almost one o'clock in the morning. Her father would have a search party out for her if he knew she was still out. Anna closed her eyes and prayed that he hadn't waited up for her.

Daniel propped himself up and leaned on his elbow.

"What time is it?" he asked sleepily.

"Late," Anna answered. "We should go."

Daniel stood up and Anna turned away, embarrassed by his lack of modesty.

He walked over to her and put his arms around her waist.

"Daniel," she said, but made no effort to unlock herself.

He buried his face into the back of her neck and murmured an endearment that Anna couldn't hear. She wanted to stay there forever, but the thought of her father out searching the streets quickly dampened her passion.

"Daniel," she pleaded, "if my father catches me out at this hour, he'll have my life. Please get dressed."

"Of course, sweetheart," Daniel replied and began to rummage around in the dim half-light for his clothes.

When she was fully dressed, Anna put the plates and glasses back into the basket and folded the rug, smiling to herself. Nobody had ever called her "sweetheart" before. It sounded so grown-up and glamorous. Clutching the rug tightly to her chest, she looked over at Daniel as he pulled his shirt over his head, and for a moment she felt as if she might cry. In just one night her life had changed completely: she had become a woman, and somebody's sweetheart.

Chapter 19

The following Monday morning, Anna got into the office a little earlier than usual. They had left in a hurry on Saturday night and she was anxious to see that everything was in its right place. Thankfully, her father had remained sound asleep that night and Anna had managed to sneak into the house unnoticed. She hung up her coat and looked around slowly, surveying every corner of the room. They had moved the desk back into its usual position, and the furniture all seemed to occupy the same spaces. Her eyes stopped at the mantelpiece. The two candlesticks held the burnt-down remains of

Saturday night's candles. Anna went over and twisted the stubs of tallow out. Not that any of the staff really called into the office, but she wanted to make sure there was no evidence of their evening together. She left the ashes in the grate for the charlady, as it was not unusual for a fire to be lit on cold days.

The room was cold and empty and appeared bereft of the momentous occasion that had taken place within its four walls. Anna somehow expected that it would look different, but looking around she saw that it was only her and nothing else that had altered.

It was mid-morning by the time Daniel reached the office. When he walked in he looked around the room searching for Anna – she was not at her desk. He shook off his coat and threw it over the coatstand. Out of the corner of his eye, he caught sight of her standing at the cabinet in his office. His face softened as he looked in at her. He closed over the main office door and walked quickly in to meet her. Anna looked up shyly and smiled. All day Sunday she had thought about how to react when she came face to face with Daniel on Monday morning, and had decided that behaving as if nothing had happened between them was the best approach to take. After all, if they were to work together every day they would have to put some distance between their work and their romance. But his presence made her heart thump loudly.

Daniel hovered at the door uncertainly. "Good morning," he said.

Anna closed the cabinet drawer and looked up at him. "Good morning."

With a few quick steps, he was standing beside her kissing her with such force that she could feel the cabinet handle pressed against her back, the old walnut creaking with their weight.

He ran his hand along the top of her thigh and let it rest on her hip-bone, pulling her towards him. Anna knew that if anyone walked into the main office they would be seen almost immediately, but she could not find the strength to end this ecstasy. He moved his mouth down to her neck and breathed her warmth deep inside him.

"I've missed you," he whispered.

Anna closed her eyes and pushed him away gently until they stood facing each other.

"Daniel, we can't do this," she said, looking towards the door. "Not here, it's too dangerous. If anyone walked in … "

Daniel looked at her and, without taking his eyes off her face, reached down and found her hands and pulled her towards him again. He put an arm around her waist and kissed her gently. "You have to forgive me, I can't help it," he said, "I'm hopelessly in love and it is entirely your fault." A smile played at the corners of his mouth.

Anna raised an eyebrow and took a few steps back. "Daniel," she said weakly, "I mean it. We have to be careful."

Daniel stood at his desk and gave her a sheepish look.

"I must get back to work," she said, and walked briskly out of his office. She closed the door behind her and returned to her desk, trying to suppress the jitters of excitement in her stomach.

They managed to get through the day without exchanging another word. Anna stuck to her plan and behaved as if it was just a normal working day, and Daniel seemed to understand.

As the day drew to a close Daniel stepped out of his office and went to the coatstand. Anna watched him from her desk as he put his hat on, but she quickly looked away as he turned around to face her.

"They've taken Father back to the hospital."

"I'm sorry," Anna said with genuine sympathy.

"No, it's not too bad actually," he said. "In fact the weekend at home seemed to do him a lot of good. He was brighter, didn't sleep half as much. Granny even bullied him into trying to talk – she maintains that he can speak but is too embarrassed to try."

Anna smiled to herself at the thought of the fearsome old woman sitting by Mr Jacob's bed forcing him to speak.

"Anyway," Daniel continued, "she has come to an agreement with the hospital that we can take him home at weekends as long as he is strong enough."

"Well, if it does him some good, she may be right," said Anna.

"Mind you," Daniel said with a smile, "I don't know how it's going to suit Mother. The poor thing collapsed into bed after the ambulance took him away this morning." He pulled his watch chain out of his waistcoat and checked the time. "Almost half past five. I'm going to look in on him before I go home." He turned to leave but stopped and walked back to Anna's desk. "Would you come too? It would do him good to see a different face, especially yours."

Anna stared up at him and tried to decide what to do.

"Please," Daniel said softly.

"Yes," Anna said, rising from her desk. "I'd love to see him."

★　★　★

They climbed the stairs of the Adelaide Hospital. Mr Jacob was on a different floor this time – Granny

Jacob had seen to it that he was put in a private room. As they entered the small room Anna's heart sank as she saw the black silhouette of the grandmother, sitting motionless beside Mr Jacob's bed. The old lady turned her head stiffly and caught sight of her grandson.

"There you are," she boomed in her finest English accent. "I've been sitting here all afternoon alone. I thought you were coming in earlier."

Anna stood cowering behind Daniel, hoping to go unnoticed, but the old woman swung around on her chair to get a better look at her. "Anna, you have come as well?" she said sharply and turned back to the bed, not hearing Anna's timid "Yes".

Daniel caught Anna by the arm and steered her around to the opposite side of his father's bed. Mr Jacob lay sleeping soundly before them.

"He was in bright spirits earlier," Granny Jacob said to Daniel. "Pity you didn't come in then – he's worn out now."

Anna gazed at Mr Jacob and wished that the ground would open at her feet and swallow her up. It had never occurred to her that the old woman would be at the hospital. Even though they had got along quite well together on her last visit to Jacob's, Anna still couldn't help feeling intimidated by the old woman's towering presence.

"I was busy all day, Granny, I couldn't get away," Daniel said as he stroked the papery grey skin of his father's hand and ignored his grandmother's cold glare.

"Hhhmph!" she snorted. "You're father is more important than work! Can't Anna here look after things without you?" She nodded in Anna's direction.

Daniel made no attempt to meet his grandmother's beady eyes. He spoke directly to his father as if the sick man was taking part in the conversation. "Of course Anna is more than capable of running things without me," he answered slowly. "But the reason I am here is so Anna doesn't *have* to run the business alone."

Granny Jacob looked over at Daniel, her mouth held tight in disapproval. His tone carried a gentle warning, and she knew from years of disagreements with her grandson that another word could lead to an argument. Changing the subject, she turned to Anna. "I've been on to the factory at home and they will send you some samples of the handbags next week."

Anna nodded eagerly and wracked her brain for something intelligent to say. "I look forward to seeing them," she said.

Granny Jacob looked at the two of them and sighed heavily. "D'you know? I've been sitting here all afternoon without being offered so much as a cup of tea?"

"Poor Granny," murmured Daniel.

She stood up and clutched her handbag to her chest. "Daniel, you shall take me to a nearby hotel for some tea before I die of thirst," she announced.

Daniel shot a glance towards Anna. "We'd be delighted to, Granny," he answered breezily.

"You're coming too, Anna?" It was more of an statement than an invitation and Anna felt her heart sink.

"Of course," she answered faintly.

"Very well then," said Granny Jacob, bending over to kiss her sleeping son. "Goodnight, dear," she whispered tenderly, "I'll be back in the morning."

Anna stayed behind the old woman as they started to descend the wide staircase. From behind she looked like an enormous witch dressed all in black from her throat down to the toes of her boots that peeped out from her rustling skirts. She clutched the handrail tightly and carefully negotiated each step.

Daniel walked beside her. "Let me help you," he said, taking her free arm.

Granny Jacob prised her arm away from him, flapping it in his face. "Leave me be, will you," she said tetchily. Then, seeing that she had offended him, she pointed a short fat finger at the stairs beneath her. "There," she ordered, "walk in front of me. That way if I fall I shall land on top of you."

Daniel exhaled loudly and tramped down the stairs in front of his grandmother. Granny Jacob looked back at Anna and for a second Anna thought she could see a glint of mischief in the old woman's cunning eyes.

They walked around onto St Stephen's Green and Daniel stopped to think for a moment.

"I think the Shelbourne would be the best place to go."

Granny Jacob shivered. "So long as it's nearby I don't care. Lead the way!" she barked.

In the Shelbourne Hotel Anna and Daniel took off their coats and handed them to the waiter. Granny Jacob stood regally as the waiter turned to her.

"I'll keep mine on," she said loudly. "It's chilly in here."

The waiter shrugged his shoulders and walked away.

Anna spotted two couches by the fire and pointed towards them. "Let's sit by the fire," she suggested.

The two couches faced each other and between them was a low table set for tea.

Granny Jacob settled into one of the couches and patted the space beside her. "Come sit by me, Anna."

Anna looked over at Daniel, hoping that he would come to her rescue and swap places, but Daniel didn't seem to notice. In fact the old woman's tyranny didn't seem to affect him in any way.

The waiter came to take their order and Granny Jacob sat forward, ready to give orders.

"We'll have sandwiches and a pot of Earl Grey, thank you," she said in one breath.

Daniel raised his eyebrows as the waiter retreated. "Is that alright with you, Anna? Perhaps you would prefer coffee."

Anna smiled and shook her head agreeably.

"Of course she likes tea," boomed Granny Jacob. Then she leaned towards Anna and lowered her voice, "It's what the queen drinks," she said with a slight note of reverence.

"Really," said Anna, trying not to look at Daniel who was stifling a laugh. After a few minutes, Granny Jacob took off her gloves and undid the top button of her coat.

"Shall I take your coat now?" Daniel asked.

She immediately clasped the collar of her coat and pulled it tighter around her neck at this suggestion. "No. I am still cold," she answered petulantly.

The waiter brought the tray of tea and sandwiches and began to unload them ceremoniously onto the table under the watchful eye of Granny Jacob.

After a few minutes, Daniel sat forward on the couch and began to pour the tea. Glad to have something to busy herself with, Anna reached for the milk jug and poured some into her tea. Stirring in the sugar, she noticed that Granny Jacob had not moved from her position. She looked up and saw the old woman staring at her hand as she stirred the milky tea. Anna looked down at her tea and over at Daniel to see if she was doing something wrong, but Daniel just smiled back at her.

Granny Jacob continued to stare at Anna's teacup disapprovingly. "You've put milk in your Earl Grey," she stated.

Anna could feel her face redden under the scrutiny.

Granny Jacob clicked her tongue a few times and looked around the table, searching for something. "Did that chap not bring the lemon?" she demanded.

Daniel surveyed the table and put up his hand to attract the waiter's attention.

"No, Granny, it appears they forgot the lemon," he said wearily.

"For heaven's sake," she muttered crossly, "must I spell everything out to these people?"

The waiter appeared and Daniel ordered the lemon slices.

Granny Jacob looked into Anna's cup again and twisted her rubbery mouth into a half-smile. "It's nicer with lemon," she said to Anna.

Daniel looked over at his grandmother and gave her a warning glance.

Anna sat bolt upright and gulped her tea self-consciously.

"Perhaps," Daniel said snidely, "Anna finds lemons a little too bitter."

Granny Jacob sniffed loudly at this remark and dropped her newly arrived lemon slices into her teacup.

Each sandwich was opened and its contents inspected before the old woman would let it pass her lips. As she chomped on the last of her cheese sandwich she raised a finger to silence Daniel as he attempted to have a conversation with Anna.

"I want you to go outside now and get a cab to take us home, and on the way I want to stop at a kosher butcher's. I have the address here." She pulled her handbag onto her knee. Her hand disappeared into the huge bag as she rummaged through its contents to find a piece of paper. "Here it is," she squinted at the print as she read, "Rubinstein's of Camden Street." Then she turned to Anna and said, "Do you know that his mother doesn't keep a kosher kitchen?" Her finger wagged in Daniel's direction.

Anna stared back blankly as Granny Jacob waited for her reaction.

Granny Jacob looked over at Daniel and threw her hands in the air. "How would you be expected to know? Seeing that his home isn't a proper Jewish home. If it was, then you would know what kosher food means."

"Oh Granny, stop it. Anna isn't interested in things like that."

"I never heard of it," admitted Anna.

Granny Jacobs threw back her head and her bonnet wobbled precariously. "The best cooking in the world."

Anna smiled at her pronunciation: "the vorld".

"Unfortunately, Irene has shirked her responsibilities as a good Jewish wife and her family have lost their tradition."

Daniel rolled his eyes up to heaven and stood up. "I'm going to settle the bill and go outside to call a cab," he said, and walked away from the table, leaving Anna alone with his grandmother.

The two women watched him walk out of the room and Anna waited for the old woman to lead the conversation. To her utter surprise Granny Jacob leaned in towards her.

"I know he likes you," she said in an almost girlish way.

Anna was startled at her intimacy and searched for the right reply.

Granny Jacob reached across and patted Anna's hand, as if to reassure her that she would not bite.

"I know," she said, nodding her head sagely. "Young love is powerful and headstrong and sometimes we don't think of the path ahead."

Anna forced a smile and felt her heart pounding wildly.

"You like him?" the old woman asked matter-of-factly, as if Daniel was a handbag or a pair of shoes.

Anna took a deep breath. "Yes," she said bravely.

Granny Jacob lifted her shoulders and let them deflate as she sighed. "It's not a good match," she said gravely. "Too many differences."

Anna looked down at the carpet and bit her lower lip. "I know," she whispered.

"Life is hard, Anna – you'll learn that as you grow older." Granny Jacob's voice softened. "You must pick the right partner to spend your life with, because if you don't you will never have true happiness."

Anna kept her eyes averted and listened to what the old woman had to say.

"Social difference, religious difference, they don't make for a happy marriage. Each must find the perfect match, if true harmony is to be found. Do you understand what I am saying?"

"Yes," said Anna, looking up to meet the old woman's level stare. "I understand."

"Granny," came the sound of Daniel's voice from behind them, "the cab is waiting outside."

Granny Jacob stood up, still dressed in her coat and hat. "The fire has made me too hot. I'll wait for you in the foyer while you get your coats," she said, and walked towards the door.

Anna and Daniel waited for their coats to be brought

"I'm sorry," said Daniel, "was that awful?"

Anna looked around impatiently for the waiter and waved at him as he wandered about the room aimlessly.

"She's not as bad as she appears to be – I really think she likes you," he said apologetically, as he took the coats from the waiter.

Anna ignored him and slipped one arm through the sleeve of her coat. Her mind was elsewhere, still trying to grasp the meaning of Granny Jacob's portentous words.

Outside the hotel, Granny Jacob sat in the back of the horse-drawn cab and berated Daniel, who was standing on the side of the footpath holding the cab door open.

"Couldn't you get us a motor car?" she moaned, rubbing her hands together for warmth.

"Not unless you were prepared to wait and somehow I don't think that you were," Daniel answered impatiently. He turned to Anna, and put out his hand to help her into the cab but Anna stood where she was.

"Come on," urged Daniel, "get in."

Anna shook her head. "I'm going to walk, I need some air."

"Get in and close the door," barked Granny Jacob. "I'll catch my death."

Anna looked over at Daniel. "You go on. I'll be fine, I just need to stretch my legs."

Daniel clutched the door handle, looking completely confused.

"I'll walk you home and let Granny go on ahead," he said.

But Anna wouldn't hear of it. "No, Daniel, please go home with your grandmother, I'll see you tomorrow."

Daniel opened his mouth to say something but was stopped by Granny Jacob as she rapped her diamond ring impatiently against the window. Daniel abandoned any further attempt at persuading Anna to join them on the journey home and climbed into the cab with his grandmother. Granny Jacob smiled at Anna and lifted her hand slowly in a regal salute. Anna stared in at the old lady but could not muster up the enthusiasm to return her smile.

As the cab pulled off onto St Stephen's Green, Anna remembered how late she was and began to walk purposefully towards home. It was almost seven o'clock, and her father would be waiting for his dinner.

Inside the hall, she slipped out of her coat and left her hat on the hall table. Her hands patted some loose strands of hair into place as she made her way down to the kitchen. Both men stopped what they were doing and turned to look at her as she walked in. Mr Barry was down on his knees by the fire grate trying to blow on some smouldering kindling, but the only result was some thick grey smoke that blew out into the kitchen.

Seán had his shirt sleeves rolled up to his elbows and was peeling potatoes at the sink. As soon as he saw his sister he dropped the knife and potato onto the draining board.

"Where have you been? " he moaned as he pulled down his sleeves of his shirt.

"I've been at work," Anna answered curtly as she moved across to assist her father with the fire. She took a newspaper from the dresser and opened it out, then she stood before the fire and blocked the entire opening with the unfolded newspaper. Within seconds the kindling began to snap and spark as the fire began to ignite.

"I hope that's not today's paper," Mr Barry said as he brushed pieces of coal dust from the knees of his trousers. Anna's efficiency in getting the fire lit had only succeeded in irking him.

"No, it's not," she muttered, looking at the date on the paper as she twisted the pages into knots and threw them onto the flames.

"When will the dinner be ready?" Seán whined.

Anna ran her hands under the tap and wiped them with a dishcloth. She took up the knife and began to peel the potatoes that Seán had abandoned. "I'll be as quick as I can. There's some corned beef in the pantry – have it with a slice of bread if you're that hungry."

Seán went over to the loaf of bread that stood on a wooden board in the middle of the kitchen table and began to hack off a thick slice.

Mr Barry settled into his armchair, rolled a cigarette and watched his daughter as she prepared their supper with a determined vigour.

"Working till now?" he asked as he picked a stray piece of tobacco from inside his lower lip.

"Yes," answered Anna. "The grandmother is over from England – she wants to make some changes to the shop."

Mr Barry blew out his smoke loudly.

Anna put the potatoes into a pot of water and lit the gas flame beneath it.

"They're making handbags to match the shoes in the factory in Leeds, and she wants us to start selling them."

Mr Barry nodded his head with vague interest. "What's she like?"

Anna banged the lid down on to the pot. "A twisted old bitch!" she blurted.

Mr Barry's mouth opened with the shock of hearing his daughter swear.

Anna saw her father's reaction and turned back to the cooker. "Well, that's what she is," she said without any remorse.

Mr Barry began to chuckle to himself and Anna looked back disdainfully – she knew exactly what had tickled him. The fact that she had said anything derogatory about the Jacobs was enough to make him forget how long he had been waiting for his dinner, and bring a smile to his face.

That night as she lay in bed and thought about Granny Jacob's veiled warning about what a relationship with Daniel might lead to – Anna knew that she had reached a point where, once crossed, there would be no turning back. Granny Jacob obviously knew how deeply in love they were, which meant his mother did too, and Anna was well aware of Irene's disapproval of her son's poor choice. If they continued to see each other, it was only a matter of time before she would have to tell her father and he would surely disown her. Anna felt a knot of fear begin to grow in her stomach as she thought of how her father would react when she told him. Her eyes filled with tears as she thought of how she might have to make a choice between Daniel and her family. She couldn't imagine a life without her father or Seán, yet if she was really honest with herself, it was harder to imagine never seeing Daniel again.

Chapter 20

Joe Maguire lay back on a sandbag and closed his eyes. The waiting was interminable and some of the lads had begun to get irritable. The occupation of the Four Courts was into its eighth week, and there was no sign of any agreement being reached between the anti-Treaty forces and the Provisional Government. Morale was low and Joe had secretly begun to despair of the situation. Word had filtered through to the lads in the Four Courts that the British were putting pressure on the Irish Provisional Government to end the siege. Joe knew that if that happened it would surely mean civil war. He was prepared to die for the cause, but the thought of his parents losing another son brought him close to surrendering his position of volunteer in the Republican Army. He was disturbed from his morose thoughts by the chink of light that fell across the darkened room when the door that led to Chancery Lane opened for a split second and closed again. A man darted across the room and threw himself down next to Joe.

"How's it going?" he asked breathlessly.

Joe sat up and saw it was Seán, clutching some packets of cigarettes to his chest.

Seán ripped one open, took out a handful of cigarettes and pushed them down into Joe's breast pocket. "Here, you might as well take a few of these before the others get their hands on them."

Joe patted them down deeper into his pocket. "Thanks, Seán."

"No problem, Joe," he said, closing the box. "How are you keeping?"

Joe shrugged his shoulders and lit a cigarette. "Not bad. I've a pain in me arse sitting around here. I wish they'd hurry up and come to some decision."

Seán could hear the despondency in Joe's voice and he nudged closer to him on the sandbag. "It'll be over soon. They'll come to their senses and realise that we're right – there's plenty of support for us out there. The people are behind us."

Joe blew out his smoke and looked sideways at Seán. "Yeh," he answered doubtfully.

Seán stood up and grabbed the cigarette cartons. "Is there anything else you need? I'll be bringing in some food later on tonight."

Joe stood up and stretched his arms up over his head. "No, thanks, Seán. I think I'll go out myself later on. I've been here for three days without a break, I need to get out for a few hours."

"Fair enough," said Seán as he shuffled off to distribute the cigarettes amongst a group of volunteers on the other side of the room.

★ ★ ★

Daniel turned his key in the front door and, as he stepped inside, he could smell the furniture polish throughout the hall. It was Saturday and he had called into the office for a few hours, on the pretence of having work to do. He knew that Anna worked on Saturday mornings and he had only called in to gaze at her from his desk, and arrange a date for that evening. She had, reluctantly, agreed to meet him outside the office at eight o'clock. Now it was up to Daniel to think of somewhere they could go, without being seen. Perhaps, he thought as he unbuttoned his coat, he could swipe a few things from Mary's larder and surprise Anna with another evening in the office. His eyes misted over as he thought of the last evening they had shared there, lying by the fire in the dreamy aftermath of lovemaking.

"Oh thank heavens you're back!" Irene exclaimed as she came rushing towards him, her face pink with agitation. "Put your jacket back on, dear – I need you to go to the bakery and get some challah."

Daniel looked at her and screwed up his face. "What on earth do you want that for? Can't it wait till later?"

"No!" shrieked Irene. "It can't. Your grandmother took it upon herself to invite Rabbi Goldstein and his family around for Sabbath this evening."

Daniel opened his eyes wide and tried to disguise the look of amusement that spread across his face. "She did what?

Irene nodded her head gravely. "Can you believe it? She met him yesterday evening and invited him without my permission."

Daniel pulled his jacket back on and smiled sympathetically at his seething mother. "Since when did Granny ever need permission to do anything? Don't worry, I'll get the bread. Do you need anything else?"

"No, thank you, dear, Mary can manage

everything else." Irene fiddled furiously with the string of pearls around her neck. "I swear she does these things just to annoy me," she muttered to herself.

Daniel put his hand out to open the front door, but turned back when he thought of his own plans for that evening. "Mother, I won't be expected to join you, will I?"

Irene's face took on an even more pained expression. "Of course you will, Daniel!"

"Oh Mother, I'm afraid I've already made plans for this evening. I won't be here."

Irene clutched Daniels elbow. "I insist you cancel your plans. It's only one evening and I need you here."

Daniel stiffened at her orders.

"Well, what could be so important?" Irene asked indignantly. "Can't you put off whatever it is you're doing till another evening?"

"No, Mother," Daniel said, pulling his elbow from her grip.

"Where are you going?" Irene demanded.

"I'm taking Anna out for dinner."

His words seemed to shake Irene from the fit of anxiety she had been overcome by only seconds earlier. Her fretting over having the Rabbi to dinner was overshadowed by something even more worrying. Irene stared at Daniel coldly.

"Surely *that* can wait until another time." Her words were clipped and deliberate.

Daniel took a deep breath and glared at his mother. "I have plans for this evening," he said slowly. "And I am not going to cancel them." He opened the front door and turned to face his mother. "Unless of course … "

Irene's face lit up with anticipation.

"You would like to invite Anna to join us," continued Daniel.

His mother's smile faded and she pursed her lips together tightly. After a few seconds consideration, she replied, "No, Daniel, I don't think that would be a very good idea."

"I didn't think you would," mumbled Daniel as he walked out of the house.

★   ★   ★

Daniel stayed in his room for the rest of the afternoon, afraid that another confrontation with his mother might turn into a more serious argument. Along with the challah, he had bought some bread rolls and meats, which he had managed to smuggle into his bedroom unnoticed. Listening to the clanging of pots and raised voices coming from the kitchen he had decided that asking poor Mary to prepare any food for him was out of the question. He changed his clothes and freshened up. His plan was to get in to the office and light a fire before Anna arrived to meet him. As he combed back his hair, he was alerted to the sound of his grandmother's heavy footfall on the floor outside his room.

"Are you presentable, young man?" Granny Jacob asked from outside the door.

Daniel crossed the room and opened the door back a few inches, but his grandmother leaned her hand against the door and pushed it back fully. She walked into his bedroom and signalled for him to close the door behind her.

"Your mother tells me that you refuse to join us for supper this evening," she said as she sank down onto Daniel's bed.

Daniel walked back over to the mirror and continued to comb his hair. "I'm not refusing, Granny. I already explained to Mother that I have other plans."

"So she tells me," Granny Jacob said with a slight flare of her nostrils.

Daniel put the comb down on the dressing table and turned to his grandmother. "If you have been sent up here to bully me into joining you, then I'm afraid you're wasting your time."

Granny Jacob bristled at his suggestion. "I haven't been sent up here. I am here of my own accord and don't you be so impudent."

Daniel hung his head and accepted her admonishment.

"We just want you to join us for supper – is that such a terrible thing? To expect my grandson to eat with us?" Granny Jacob raised her hands upwards as if expecting the answer to come from above.

"Granny," Daniel reasoned, "I would gladly have joined you if I had been given some prior notice, but unfortunately I have other plans that I cannot break. Sorry."

The old woman let her hands fall limply onto her lap. "You are seeing Anna tonight?"

"Yes, I am," Daniel answered decisively. Then with an exasperated sigh he continued, "This could have been avoided. I suggested that mother invite Anna along this evening but she refused. It seems that she doesn't consider Anna's company good enough to dine with our Rabbi."

They both sat in the tense silence and listened to the muffled voices of Irene and Mary below in the kitchen.

Granny Jacob shook her head. "Daniel, what are you doing?" she asked wearily. "You can't be serious about such a girl."

Daniel clenched his fists and dug his nails into the palms of his hands. "Granny, I think it's about time that you realised exactly how serious I am about her," he said in a half whisper.

His grandmother looked up at him sadly. "It can't work. Don't you see? You come from different *vorlds*."

"How can you say that?" asked Daniel impatiently.

"Because I can see clearly what kind of girl she is," exclaimed Granny Jacob. "I like her, Daniel – she is a nice girl, but she is different from you. She is from a poor family, she has very little education and she works in your father's shoe store. Apart from all of that, she is not Jewish!" She raised her voice to stop Daniel interrupting her: "And you may not think that that is important now, but believe me it is. Our tradition is being watered down every time a mixed marriage takes place. Marry outside your faith and you will live to regret it. Have your fun with this girl, but don't get serious about her."

"For goodness sake, Granny!" Daniel shouted. "Not this again!"

Granny Jacob put her forefinger to her lip and with the other hand pointed downstairs.

"Lower your voice, I don't want your mother coming up here."

Daniel lifted a hand to his forehead and massaged his brow. "Granny, I don't think I want to continue this conversation," he said quietly.

He looked down at his grandmother and waited for her to leave, but the old woman remained seated and stared down at the carpet.

"Do you love her?"

"Yes." Daniel's voice cracked with emotion.

Granny Jacob stood up slowly and let her head hang down towards her chest as she moved towards the door. "In that case," she whispered, "there is nothing more I can say."

★   ★   ★

Daniel lit the fire in the office and waited until eight o'clock before he went downstairs to open the door. He stepped out onto the street and in the distance he could see Anna walking briskly towards him. Her head was bent downwards, at an angle that only enabled him to see the crown of her cloche hat. She had taken to walking bent in this manner whenever she was meeting Daniel. As she approached the office, she looked up and smiled broadly, seeing him waiting for her. Daniel reached out and took her wrist but dropped it again when he saw her eyes look over his shoulder to check the street, and who might be passing by.

They hurried in and climbed the stairway to the office. Inside, the fire was beginning to light. Bright orange flames grew higher as they licked across the dusty coals. The candlesticks were empty and no furniture had been moved back like the last time they had met there.

Daniel looked around despairingly at his hasty attempt at creating a romantic atmosphere and smiled wearily.

"I'm afraid things didn't go according to plan," he said, pushing the couch towards the fire.

"Don't worry," she said.

"I was going to get Mary to make me up some food but Granny went and invited people to supper without consulting Mother and ... " Daniel broke off and shook his head in exasperation. "I won't bore you with the details." He moved across the room and produced a bottle of sherry and some spiced beef from a paper bag. "This is all I could manage to take from the kitchen without being noticed." He looked over at Anna and saw the beginning of a smile. "Oh dear, what a mess I've made of the evening. Let's just forget about staying here and take our chances across the road in the Gresham."

"I am perfectly happy to stay here, Daniel. I had

to eat something earlier with Dada – he seemed a bit suspicious that I was going out again this evening so I had my tea with him."

Daniel opened the bottle of sherry and took two small glasses from the pockets of his overcoat.

"Do you think he suspects anything about me?" he asked, filling both glasses and handing one to Anna.

"No," Anna answered, her eyes widening dramatically. "Jesus, Daniel, I wouldn't be here if he had any suspicions about us."

Daniel nodded silently. Both of them sipped their sherries in the gloomy silence that had wrapped around them with the mention of yet another obstacle to their happiness.

"I'm sorry," Anna said. "But you might as well know now, Daniel, that my father would kill me if he knew I was here with you. Breaking up with Joe was hard enough for him to bear, but if he finds out about us . . . ." Anna stopped and swallowed hard. She had purposely not given much consideration as to what would happen if her father discovered where she had been going on her evenings into town. Her happiness had overshadowed the serious consequences, but now, thinking of what her father would do made her blood run cold.

Daniel sat down on the couch and gently pulled Anna down beside him. He reached out and took her hand in his and looked into her eyes intently. "I might as well tell you that my mother and grandmother are completely against me having any kind of relationship with you outside of work."

Anna gave a bitter smile. "Yes, I guessed that."

"I don't want to be the cause of any bother between you and your father."

"You won't," Anna said uncertainly.

Daniel put his glass down on the floor and a troubled look crossed over his face like a cloud. "Yes, Anna, I will." His voice was flat and serious. "We can't sneak around for much longer. It's only a matter of time before your father finds out, and you have to be prepared for that. You have to decide whether I am worth all the heartache."

Anna looked around the room as a wave of panic rose up inside her.

Daniel put his arm around her shoulders and pulled her close. "Anna, we have to make some decisions. This feeling I have for you is like nothing I have ever felt before. I have never been so sure of anything in my life. I know that nothing can ever come between us and I need to know that you feel the same way."

Anna looked up at him and her heart threatened to burst with joy. "Oh Daniel," she whispered in a shaky voice, "no one could stop me from being with you. I love you with all my heart."

Daniel jumped to his feet, beaming with happiness. He knelt down on the floor at her feet and took the empty sherry glass from her. He took both her hands in his and she could feel him trembling. "Will you come to Edinburgh with me?"

Anna's hand shot up to her chest as if he had struck her with the question.

"Well?" he said, his eyes boring into her as if his very life depended on her answer.

Anna could feel herself getting dizzy with excitement. "I ... I don't know what to say."

"Please, Anna, say yes. Say you'll marry me and come to Edinburgh."

Anna let out a high-pitched gasp and looked into Daniel's burning stare. "Marry you?"

Daniel leaned forward with one knee bended. "Yes, Anna," he said, "will you marry me?"

There was no doubt in her mind, no hesitations or second thoughts like there had been with Joe. "Yes," Anna heard herself answer.

Daniel pulled her hands to his mouth and began to kiss each of her knuckles. "I love you. I never want to be without you." He looked up at her and moved closer so his lips were brushing against her cheek. "I'll go back to college, and if you like Edinburgh we can settle there."

Anna felt as if she were in a dream, as if the moment weren't real at all. "I'll go anywhere with you," she whispered softly into his ear.

★   ★   ★

Anna fixed her stockings and pulled her skirt back on, while Daniel dressed quickly by the fire. Once again she had given herself to him so easily, yet felt no shame at all.

"It's late. I should get home soon."

Daniel turned to her and smiled. "I keep thinking that I'm going to wake now, and it will all have been a dream."

Anna went over to him and put her arms around his waist. "I know, I feel exactly the same way. I'm so happy and so frightened at the same time."

Daniel kissed her softly. "Don't be afraid. We'll pick our time carefully and tell them just before we leave – that way no one can do anything to stop us."

Anna felt a flutter of anxiety in her stomach.

"We'll do it soon," said Daniel decisively. "I'm sick of this sneaking around. But for now we will have to remain secretly engaged."

Again Anna's stomach turned over with nerves. "Secretly engaged," she murmured. How wonderful it sounded.

* * *

Joe Maguire squinted through the dusty window out onto the deserted street. He had dozed for most of the evening, waiting until he knew it would be safe to leave the building without being apprehended by any of the Free State Army who patrolled the streets directly outside the Four Courts by day. By night they relaxed their vigil, giving the men inside an opportunity to make their sorties. Joe pulled on a light overcoat – the night was mild but he needed something to hide his uniform. At the door he kicked the sleeping volunteer who was on night watch, and flashed his pass to leave in front of his face. The man opened one eye, then stood and unlocked the door. Once outside, Joe pulled his cap down low over his eyes and looked down at the street as he walked away from the Four Court buildings. The stagnant soupy smell from the River Liffey mingled with the distant bitter scent of hops that wafted down the quays from the Guinness brewery. As he turned onto Sackville Street, he slowed down and stretched his arms up over his head. It felt good to be outside again, walking freely like a normal citizen. His chest tightened as he passed Jacob's shoe store, and thought of all the times he had met Anna outside after work. Sometimes before a night out, or sometimes just to walk her home. He had tried to put her out of his mind and it had become a little easier in recent weeks with the occupation of the Four Courts. But standing outside her workplace made him realise just how much he missed her.

The bells rang out from a nearby church: it was midnight. Joe was to collect a sack of bread from a bakery on Parnell Square at four a.m. on his way back, but first he was going home to see his parents and have a wash. He continued up the street, but a sudden noise made him turn around. Two people stepped out from a doorway and the click of a door being shut startled him. Joe hid in the shadow of a shop front and watched a couple emerge from the doorway of Jacob's. He had taken a step forward when he recognised Anna. She stood alone on the street and waited for the other person to lock the door. Joe squinted to see who she might be working with at this time of the night. The person at the door extended a hand and Anna took it and was pulled back into the shadow of the porch. Joe left the doorway and edged closer until he could get a better view. He was hit by a sharp blow of dismay as the shadows took on a definite form, a tall fair-haired man was embracing Anna with a passion that made

Joe want to tear him apart with his bare hands. Edging back to the cover of darkness, Joe stood in numbed silence and looked on in disbelief.

★ ★ ★

Daniel nuzzled his nose into the warmth of the side of Anna's neck.

"Sweetheart!" he groaned. "Soon we won't have to say goodnight like this, and I will be the happiest man alive."

They embraced for the last time in the darkness of the shop porch and held each other tightly. Anna didn't feel the eyes that burned into her back as she strolled up the street, arm in arm with Daniel. Nor did she look back, for if she did, she would have seen the figure of Joe Maguire slumped against the wall in the shadows as he watched her walk away from him.

Chapter 21

Anna walked along the banks of the canal with her father as they made their way home from Sunday Mass. It was early June and the sun was pitched high in a cloudless sky. Mr Barry took off his jacket and, balancing the collar on his forefinger, with a circular motion swung it over his shoulder.

"Where were you last night?" he asked Anna.

Anna went to answer but stumbled over her words. "Just out, why?"

"Out where?" he persisted.

"With some of the girls from the shop."

"What did you do?"

Anna could feel the back of her neck begin to perspire. "We went to the pictures."

"Till after midnight?"

"No," Anna said quickly, giving herself time to think. "We went for a cup of tea afterwards."

"Where?"

"In the Gresham Hotel," Anna lied.

"That's too late for a crowd of girls to be out on the streets. It was different when you were with Joe, I knew you were being looked after. Girls roaming the streets at that hour are easy prey. Besides, there's going to be trouble in town any day now. I want you home by ten from now on."

Anna stopped and stared at her father, but Mr Barry looked straight ahead and continued to saunter towards the house.

"Dada," she exclaimed, quickening her pace to catch up with him, "I am a grown woman. You can't tell me what time to come in at."

Mr Barry swung his head from left to right as if admiring something up in the sky.

"You'll come in when I say so. As long as you're living under my roof, you'll do as you're told, young lady." With this said, he held out his jacket and fished around in the pocket for the front door key. He walked up the small garden path and opened the front door, standing back to let Anna in first. Anna glared at her father as she brushed by him and went directly to her room.

So this was her punishment, thought Anna, as she brushed her hair with hard furious strokes at her dressing table. She had wondered how long it would take her father to think of some way to make her suffer for her disobedience in not getting back together with Joe. He had been far too quiet about it lately – she had been expecting something like this. If he knew she had been with her fiancée last night! Anna smiled bitterly as she thought of what her father would have to say about that. She closed her eyes tightly and calmed herself with the thought that she would not have to endure this for much longer. "Soon I'll be married," she whispered to her reflection in the mirror. "Soon I'll be Mrs Anna Jacob."

Downstairs she heard the front door slam and the sound of Seán's heavy steps as he plodded down to the kitchen. Anna put her brush back on the dressing table and stood up. It was easier to be with her father when Seán was around. Anna walked into the kitchen and noticed the dark circles around Seán's eyes – he looked as if he hadn't slept in weeks. She had looked into his bedroom earlier and seen that his bed had not been slept in.

Seán nodded in her direction and poured himself

a mug of tea from the pot.

Mr Barry looked up from the page of his newspaper. No matter who walked into the room they were never important enough to make him look up from whatever he was reading until he had finished. "Howya, son," he said and shook his paper closed.

"Howya, Da," answered Seán flatly.

"Where have you been?" asked Anna.

Seán looked up at her scornfully. "Working."

Anna gave him an innocent look. "I didn't know you worked on Saturday nights."

"I'm a volunteer with the Irish Republican Army, and I'll work on Saturday nights or any other time they need me."

On the table was a square of paper. Anna took it up and turned it over in her hands. It was a pass, giving Barrack Staff no. 167 permission to enter and leave the Four Courts. Anna threw it down on the table and gave an exasperated sigh. She saw a complicit look pass between her father and Seán, making her feel like an outsider in their company, which is what she had become lately.

"It makes me laugh," she said to her father. "You want me in by ten o'clock, in case I get up to anything when I'm out with my friends. Yet your son is running wild around the streets, doing God knows what for that crowd of Irregulars in the Four Courts, and you don't raise an eyebrow."

Seán stood up. "Don't you call us that, you brazen bitch!"

Anna stood her ground. "That's what they're all calling you. The Irregulars."

Seán swung around to his father who was staring at a spot on the oven door. "Da," he wailed, "listen to what she's saying!"

Mr Barry rubbed his chin roughly. "Get out, Anna."

Anna put her hands on her hips and looked over at him. "What?"

"Get out!" roared Mr Barry without moving a muscle.

Anna jumped with fright. "Dada, it's – "

"Out!" he shouted again, pointing to the door. He stood up from his chair like a bull and Anna began to inch towards the door.

"Get up to your room!"

Anna looked at Seán, but he turned his eyes away from her. She opened her mouth to say something, but when she saw the glint of anger that flashed across her father's eyes she fled from the room.

Mr Barry followed her to the foot of the stairs. "Don't come down until you're ready to show some respect."

Anna stamped up the stairs and back into her bedroom, slamming the door behind her. Angry tears began to gather at the back of her eyes but she blinked them back. She kicked her shoes off, sending them flying across the room, and collapsed onto her bed. Her outward defiance dissolved in the privacy of her room. She laced her shaking hands together tightly and rested them against her forehead. Her heart was pounding and her father's rough voice reverberated violently through her head. She turned onto her side and a wave of emptiness washed over her as she looked at her mother's face, gazing out at her from behind the dusty glass of the picture frame. Her head was tilted slightly to one side, as if she knew exactly what was happening. Anna reached over and took the photo frame into her hands. If only her mother was here, if only she could talk to her for five minutes, she'd know what to do. "Mam," she whispered, "please give me the strength to leave, and help them to understand why."

When Seán knocked at her door later in the morning, Anna was going through her wardrobe, deciding which clothes were good enough to take with her when she left for Edinburgh. She knew it was Seán, she recognised the conciliatory three taps.

"Come in," she said.

Seán opened the door but only took a step in,

keeping one hand on the door handle.

"I'm off now."

Anna stared at him coldly.

Seán looked around the room, searching for the right words to say. "Look, I didn't mean to get you into trouble like that. I didn't think he'd get so annoyed with you."

Anna nodded but remained silent. She was touched by her brother's attempt to make peace between them but slow to show it.

Seán let go of the door handle and took another step into the room. "Anna, I'm doing what I have to do and Da's right, you should have some respect for me. You don't have to agree with it, but stop fighting with me all the time. You don't understand what it means to me." He stood before her, scratching his head childishly.

Anna looked at her foolish headstrong brother and sighed. "You're right, I don't understand."

"I don't expect you to understand," Seán said, clutching at the thread of clemency he had been thrown. "It's something in here," he said beating his fist against his heart.

"Oh Seán," Anna said heavily.

But before she could embark on a lecture, he broke in. "Just don't get involved in my life, Anna, and I won't get involved in yours."

Anna thought about this for a moment and smiled sadly as she thought of how Seán could never honour this pact if faced with the knowledge of what she was about to do. If he knew what her plans were, he would undoubtedly be the first person to try to stop her.

"I think that's a good idea," she said matter-of-factly.

Seán stood before her, his eyebrows knitted together in confusion.

"You mind your own business and I'll mind my own." Anna took up a dress and began to arrange it on a hanger.

"Fine," said Seán. He stood there for a few seconds looking at Anna while she hung up the dress and closed the wardrobe door, then seeing that the conversation had ended he turned to leave.

"Just be careful, Seán," Anna said in a sisterly way. It was a tone that Seán had not heard in some time.

He turned to her and an impish smiled flashed across his face. "I will," he assured her and stepped out onto the landing.

★ ★ ★

Irene lifted the slices of cold roast chicken onto her plate.

"Daniel, some chicken?"

Daniel pushed his plate over to her.

Granny Jacob began to chew her food with a scowl. "Why is it cold?" she asked.

Irene kept her eyes on the plate and tried to smile. "Because Sunday is Mary's day off and she prepares a cold meal for us on Saturdays."

"Hmph," grunted Granny Jacob.

"How was Rabbi Goldstein?" Daniel asked.

"He was well," Granny Jacob said in her most pronounced Yiddish accent – *vell*. Then shaking her fork in his direction she said, "It was rude of you not to be here to meet him." Then looking across at Irene she added, "Lord knows, he doesn't get invited too often."

Irene cut her chicken with such vigour that it made her knife scrape along the plate, causing everyone to wince at the unexpected screech. After that, she had no appetite and pushed her food from one side of the plate to the other, being careful not to lean too heavily on the cutlery. When she saw Daniel take his last mouthful she stood up and dropped her napkin onto the table.

"I'm going to check on your father," she said, and left the room.

"Cold chicken," Granny Jacob said as soon as Irene was safely out of earshot. "I wouldn't feed it to a pig." She threw her knife and fork down onto her plate with a noisy clatter.

"Really, Granny," Daniel said with measured indifference, "why make such a fuss about it?"

"I'm not making a fuss. I'm simply saying that just because the girl is off on Sundays –"

"Mary is her name," Daniel interjected.

"Whatever," Granny Jacob said waving her hand at him dismissively. Remembering servant's names was not something she had ever wasted her time on. "Just because there is no staff on Sundays is no excuse to serve cold meat. I always found the time to prepare food for my children, *and* ran a factory," she exclaimed proudly.

"I'm sure you did," said Daniel lighting a cigarette. "But father is very sick and Mother needs all her time to look after him now," he said, surprising himself by jumping to Irene's defence.

Granny Jacob reached for the decanter and poured herself another glass of sherry. Daniel could feel her menacing stare as he drew on his cigarette, as if she was trying to read his thoughts.

"Where were you last night?"

"I told you already, I was out with Anna."

There was a brief silence as she raised the sherry glass to her puckered lips. "Where do you go?"

Daniel looked at her with surprise. "Why do you

want to know?"

Granny Jacob shrugged her shoulders. "I'm interested to know where you go together."

"Here and there," Daniel said quickly.

"And her family, what do they think of you, Daniel?" Her eyes narrowed as she watched him shift uneasily in his chair.

"I don't know," Daniel snapped.

"Well, do they like you? Do they *approve* of you?" The old woman was like a dog with a bone, not letting go until she was satisfied.

Daniel stubbed out his cigarette and waited a few seconds before speaking. "I haven't met her family."

Granny Jacob sat back in her chair and gave an annoying nod of satisfaction. "So, it can't be too serious then, if she hasn't brought you home."

Daniel gripped the edge of the table until his knuckles turned white. "That's what you would like me to say, Granny, but I'm sorry to disappoint you, it is very serious."

"She can't bring you home, can she?" the old woman shot back.

Daniel hung his head. "No," he answered.

"They wouldn't want their daughter going with an Englishman."

Hearing her speak the words so plainly made Daniel feel strange, as if he should be ashamed of himself.

Granny Jacob leaned into the table. "Daniel, forget about her. A girl like that will bring you nothing but trouble."

"I've asked her to marry me," Daniel said quietly.

Granny Jacob recoiled in horror, and muttered something that sounded like a Jewish prayer as she shook her head from side to side.

"Please don't say anything yet," said Daniel, already regretting his burst of confidence. "I wanted to tell you and mother together."

"Oh Daniel," whispered Granny Jacob, "I beg you, don't do anything foolish. Take your time and think this through very carefully."

"I have," Daniel answered.

"You haven't even met her family," Granny Jacob said, trying not to raise her voice.

"I know that," Daniel said, throwing his arms out in a gesture of helplessness, "and I probably never will. Her mother is dead. Her father and brother sound like the type that would have me shot if they caught me anywhere near Anna."

There was a hint of desperation in his voice and Granny Jacob sat back and listened for a change.

"They're both involved in the anti-Treaty forces."

Granny Jacob struggled to keep quiet but the mention of anti-Treaty made her sniff loudly.

"Anna was engaged to her brother's friend, Joe.

He is some kind of Republican hero and her father and brother are furious with her for breaking off the engagement." Daniel paused for a few seconds and waited for his grandmother to say something, but she sat motionless in her chair. "If we are to marry, it will be against everyone's wishes, I know that," he looked down and lowered his voice, "but we are both so very sure of how we feel."

He looked over at his grandmother and steeled himself for her reaction, but, just at that moment it seemed that the old woman had lost her will to denounce him any further.

Perhaps it was the look of sheer misery in his eyes, or a distant memory of what it felt like to really love someone. Whatever the reason, for a brief moment she allowed her softer side to emerge. The flood of compassion for her grandchild took her by surprise, and she reached across and put her ample, jewel-encrusted hand on top of Daniel's.

"You really love her," she said in a hushed voice. It was more of an acknowledgment than a question.

Daniel nodded his head in assent and swallowed hard.

The old woman's bosom heaved as she let out a long sigh. "Oh Daniel, you are making a hard road for yourself." She paused for a few seconds and drained the last of the sherry from her glass. "I am going to lie down for a while." She stood up slowly from the table and Daniel rose from his seat. Granny Jacob looked at him sadly and waved her hand, to indicate that there was no need for his show of politeness. Daniel slumped back down into his seat as his grandmother shuffled out of the room weighed down with the news he had given her.

Chapter 22

Joe sat alone and watched the light fade from his corner of the room. He had remained in a state of deep depression all day, not uttering a word to anyone. His back ached from sitting in the same position for so long, but he didn't have the energy to get up and move around. He replayed the events of the night before for the umpteenth time, and wondered how it had never crossed his mind that Anna might have met someone else.

It all made sense now, he thought grimly. The hasty end to their engagement, how she hadn't wanted him next or near her from the day she had broken it off. He thought of Mr Barry and Seán – did they know? Was that why they were treating him with such sympathy? The overwhelming grief and disappointment that had paralysed him all day turned to anger as he thought of who else might know about Anna's new man. His stomach turned over as he remembered the arch of her back as she was pulled willingly into her lover's arms, just steps away from where he was standing. Anna, his girl, being kissed by another man – it was like living through a nightmare. The door at the end of the room banged and Joe could see three volunteers entering the room. One of them was Seán. They were all in high spirits as they sat down in a group against the opposite wall. One man produced a bottle of whiskey from under his coat, which sent a wave of muffled laughs throughout the small group.

Seán broke away from them and weaved his way through the sandbags to where Joe was sitting.

"Joe," he said cheerily. "Come on over to the lads! Mooney's wife had a baby boy this morning and we're wetting the head with a drop of whiskey."

Joe looked up at Seán and shook his head, mumbling something inaudible.

"What?" asked Seán.

"You go on and drink to the baby. I'll stay here."

Seán stepped closer to Joe and sensed that

something more than the usual was disturbing him. "Come on over," he said, "don't be sitting here on your own."

Joe stared out the window and ignored Seán's enticement.

"Come on," said Seán, grasping Joe's arm. "You're coming over for one." He pulled Joe to his feet and Joe, too exhausted to argue, numbly gave in to him.

Over in the darkened corner the lads passed the whiskey bottle from one mouth to the other, giggling like schoolgirls about the consequences of getting caught with alcohol whilst on active duty. Joe loosened up a little and tried to participate in the jovial banter – the few swigs of whiskey had succeeded in lightening his heavy mood. He smiled over at the grinning Mooney who was still in a state of euphoria having just visited his newborn son in the Rotunda Hospital. The men drained the bottle of whiskey and chatted about the fight that was now imminent. The general election had resulted in a victory for the Treaty supporters and the Provisional Government was now in a strong position, a government that only months before had stood shoulder to shoulder with the same men that now occupied the Four Courts. The resistance to the Treaty had turned brother against brother and each man knew that if they were to take up arms against the opposition, it would result in a bitter end. A door opened on the other side of the room and the men stopped their lively debate and began to disperse. Lurking in the shadows was Commandant Quinn, a man of little mirth who took a dim view of alcohol at the best of times. Seán quickly swept the empty whiskey bottle under his coat and crept to the other side of the room after Joe.

"Can you keep it down in there?" Quinn said in his thick Kerry accent.

His order was met with a sea of mumbles as the lads quietened down and returned to their game of cards. Over by the window, Joe lit a cigarette and stared out into the darkness. Seán sat down beside him and they smoked in silence for a few minutes.

"What's up with you?" Seán asked innocently.

Joe blew out his smoke and threw him a scornful look.

"You seem a bit down, Joe."

Joe gave a short caustic laugh at this remark. "Do I?" he said sarcastically.

Seán looked over in confusion, detecting the contempt in Joe's voice. "Have I done something to annoy you?"

Joe brooded over this for a few minutes before saying anything. He cleared his throat and met Seán's eye. "You might have told me," was all he said.

"Told you what?"

Joe crushed his cigarette butt with the heel of his boot and gave Seán a hard stare. "About Anna," he said quietly.

"What about Anna?" Seán retorted impatiently.

"For fuck's sake, Seán, she's seeing that fella from the shop. You could have told me about it. I had to wait until I nearly ran into them down on the street before I found out." He spat the words out angrily.

Seán jumped up as if Joe had pointed a gun at him. "I don't know what you're talking about."

Joe shook his head disappointedly. "I thought you knew me better than that, Seán. I thought you had more regard for me."

Seán paced up and down the narrow stretch of the bay window. "Joe, I swear to God. I know nothing about this."

Joe thought about it for a moment and sucked in a deep breath. "Well," he said, uncertain whether to believe Seán's plea of innocence. "I saw them with my own eyes."

"Who?" asked Seán, trying to control his agitation.

"I told you! Anna and that fella from the shop. They were coming out of the shop last night, and from what I saw, they weren't working late." He said this with a knowing nod that made Seán's jaw drop.

"Jacob?" he asked in a thin voice.

Joe, annoyed at his own petulance, shrugged his shoulders roughly. "I can only suppose that's who it was. I didn't introduce myself. All I'm saying Seán is that you should have told me."

Seán stood before Joe with his mouth open. Defending himself was something that always came naturally to him but now, faced with the most unjust accusation, Seán could find no words to rescue himself.

Joe stood up and Seán made a grab at the sleeve of his jacket. "Joe, honestly … "

Joe shook Seán's hand away. "I'm going to get some kip," he mumbled and walked away into the darkness, leaving Seán reeling with shock.

★ ★ ★

Anna clattered the dirty dishes into the sink and rinsed them quickly in an attempt to hurry her father and Seán as they dallied over their dinner plates. She reached over to take Seán's plate but he pulled it back towards him and began to pick at the bone of his pork chop. Anna gave him a murderous glare and returned to the sink to wait until they had finished.

"In a hurry this evening?" asked Seán slyly.

"No," said Anna trying to disguise her impatience.

"You're flying around the place like a bluebottle," Mr Barry remarked as he put his knife and fork down and indicated to Anna that he was now finished eating his meal.

"I'm just a quick worker, that's all," said Anna breezily as she swooped her father's plate from under him.

"Are you going out tonight?" Seán asked.

"Yes," Anna answered with a hint of trepidation.

"Where?"

Anna looked over at Seán and wanted to box his ears for asking questions like that in front of her father. "Nowhere special. Just out."

"Make sure you're in — " said Mr Barry, but Anna finished his sentence for him.

"Yes, I know, ten o'clock," she said, drying her hands on a cloth.

She glanced at the clock on the mantelpiece, it was already half past seven. She had yet to change her clothes and be in town by eight o'clock. Upstairs, Anna put on a fresh blouse, and smoothed out the creases of her skirt with the palm of her hand. She looked at herself in the mirror and sighed — it would have to do. Any more time spent getting ready and she would be late for Daniel. He had booked a table in a small restaurant on Nassau Street, and Anna had agreed to the arrangement at first, but now her nerves were beginning to play up as she worried about the risk they were taking. At the front door, she stopped to put on her hat and shouted goodbye to her father before rushing out of the house.

As she stormed down Harcourt Street, her eyes fixed straight ahead, Anna was unaware of her brother who had left the house just after her. At a distance safe enough not to be seen, Seán trailed behind her ready to dive for cover should she look behind. Anna was too intent on getting to the restaurant on time and kept up a quick pace. When she reached the end of Grafton Street, she turned the corner and slowed down her frantic pace. Seán stayed at the corner and watched his sister as she examined the doors of the buildings, as if she was looking for something. At the doorway to a restaurant, she stopped and checked her reflection in a pane of glass before stepping inside.

★   ★   ★

Anna was led to a small table at the back of the restaurant. Daniel looked up from his menu and grinned at her.

"Is this private enough for you?"

Anna sat down and surveyed the quiet restaurant. There was only one other table in their corner, and it was unoccupied.

"Yes," she said in a whisper, as if someone might hear them.

They ordered their meal and Daniel reached across and took Anna's hands in his. "Won't it be nice to do things like this without looking over our shoulders all the time?"

Anna thought about this and smiled. "Yes, I can't stand all the lying every time I leave the house."

Daniel pulled his chair closer to the table. "We have to plan this carefully. I've already told my grandmother about us getting married, so there's only my mother to worry about now."

Anna's face dropped. "You told your grandmother?"

"Yes," said Daniel.

"What did she say?"

Daniel shrugged his shoulders. "She was surprised, of course, but I think she understands how I feel. Sometimes she's not as fierce as she pretends to be."

Anna felt a tide of panic surge through her veins. Hearing this made it all seem so real and she worried that she might not have the nerve to go through with it. Daniel looked over and saw the doubt in her eyes.

"Anna. You are going to marry me, aren't you?"

She reached for her glass and took a gulp of

water. "Yes," she said.

"This is such a huge decision for both of us. Please tell me if you are having any doubts. I'll understand if you need more time. Don't rush into this unless you are sure of what you are doing."

It was a huge decision and it was making Anna increasingly anxious. Marrying Daniel would mean turning her back on her family forever. She knew that whatever happened, her father and brother would never find it in their hearts to forgive her.

"I want to marry you, Daniel, more than anything else in the world. But it will mean losing my family. I will never see them again." Anna could feel her voice beginning to break.

Daniel looked down at his hands. "Am I asking too much of you?"

"No," whispered Anna.

"Will you be able to live with your decision?"

Anna smiled sadly. "I'll have to," she said resolutely.

"Are you going to say anything to them at all?"

Anna shuddered at the thought. "No. I will have to leave and never come back. If I told my father, you would probably never see me again. I don't want it to be like this, but it's the only way we can be together. I'll leave him a note."

"I love you Anna," Daniel whispered. "I hate that

you have to do this, but I swear I'll make it up to you. You won't ever be sorry."

Anna felt a rush of joy as she thought of their future together.

"Let's pick a time now," said Daniel. "We should go soon. I've written to a friend of mine in Edinburgh asking him to find a suitable house we can rent. I have some money put by that will keep us going for a while. He can also arrange for a church wedding – I presume you want to get married in a Catholic church."

"But Daniel, how can we marry in a Catholic church?"

Daniel waved this question away with his hand. "I'll convert," he said nonchalantly.

Anna looked at him in shock. "You would change your religion?"

"I would change anything in my life to be with you," Daniel said quietly. "I would sleep out on the streets every night if it meant being with you."

Anna gazed over at him and smiled broadly. "Daniel, can you believe it? We are actually getting married."

Daniel leaned over and kissed her forehead – but quickly sat back down again as the waiter approached with their meals.

"How about two weeks' time?" Daniel asked as he

cut into his steak.

Anna pursed her lips together and fell silent.

"Is that too soon?"

"No," Anna said, thinking of what she would write in the farewell note to her father. "I suppose the sooner we leave the less chance we have of getting caught."

"Right, I'll press on with the arrangements then." He put his knife and fork down and looked across at her solemnly. "It feels right Anna, doesn't it?"

Anna knew exactly what he meant, even though she was going against everything she was brought up to believe in. Deep down she knew she was doing the right thing. "Yes, it feels right," she answered.

*   *   *

On the corner of Nassau Street, Seán stamped his feet impatiently. It had been almost two hours since Anna had entered the restaurant and Seán's determination had begun to waver with the boredom of standing around for so long. He went to light up another cigarette, when out of the corner of his eye he spotted her. He dropped the match and put the unlit cigarette behind his ear. Stepping backwards, he pressed himself against the wall and prepared to run if Anna looked towards him. She seemed to hesitate outside the restaurant, then turned and walked away from Seán in the direction of Kildare Street. Seán waited a moment, and just as he moved out to follow her, he jumped back again as he saw Daniel Jacob coming out of the restaurant. Seán noticed that he moved with the same air of lofty arrogance that had made him hate the man from the moment he had met him. At first, he couldn't physically move. Even though he had been waiting all night to catch them, seeing them together was shocking. Seán felt strangled with rage as he watched them walk up the street together. He put his fist up to his mouth and bit down hard leaving a white tooth mark across his knuckle. It was all he could do to suppress his anger at the sight of his sister and the man she had thrown Joe Maguire over for.

★   ★   ★

Seán leaned against the warm wall of a tobacconist on Sackville Street. The day's heat had baked into the stone and Seán basked in the heat that came from it. It was Saturday evening, and Anna had said that she would not be home from work as she was going out with some girls from the shop. Seán had waited outside and watched the shop girls as they left without his sister. It was seven o'clock, the shop had been closed an hour and still there was no sign of Anna. Seán sat on the saddle of his bike, which was propped against the wall, and waited impatiently. He should have been down at the Four Courts by now. The lads would be clamouring for the cigarettes he had stuffed deep inside his coat. He knew there was a dispatch waiting to be brought to *Poblacht na h-Éireann* for publication – he would have his job as runner taken away from him if he failed to show up. He stared up at the building where his sister worked and felt the hairs on the back of his neck bristle, as he thought of what she might be doing with that pompous Brit. Another twenty minutes passed and Seán pulled his bicycle from against the wall at the same time as the door to Jacob's opened. There were still enough people on the street for him to be unseen. He sat on the saddle of the bicycle and stared across as his sister and Daniel Jacob emerged from the building together. He blinked quickly in disbelief as he watched the blatant show of affection between the two of them. They were linked together, arm in arm like any normal courting couple. In the porch, Daniel locked the door, then turned to Anna and kissed her before they stepped out onto the street. The knuckles on Seán's hands turned white as he gripped the handles of his bicycle and peddled off in a blind fury towards the Four Courts. His anger grew as he thought of the disgrace his whore of a sister would bring on the family when people discovered what she was up to. He thought of Joe, and a lump rose in his throat. Did he honestly believe that Seán would stand by and cover up for Anna while she made dirt of herself with that no-good Brit. And what about their father? He reached the Four Courts building and threw his bicycle against the back wall in a rage. Had Anna lost her mind altogether? Had she not thought of what her father would do to her?

Chapter 23

Anna arrived home from work and quickly went upstairs to her bedroom. Her hands were full of the bags of clothes she carried. It was foolish, she knew, bringing them into the house at all, but it was only for one night – she would take them into the office and hide them there – and her father rarely went into her bedroom. The bags rustled as she emptied the contents out onto her bed. The wedding dress was simple, made in cream silk with a dropped waist and some beading around the hem. Anna folded it back into the bag and hid it at the back of her wardrobe. The shoes were also made in cream silk, with a pearl button to one side – these were also pushed to the back of the wardrobe. Seán's heavy footfall pounded on the stairs and Anna stepped outside her room onto the landing, in case he spied anything inside her bedroom.

Seán stood at the top of the stairs, his arms folded tightly across his chest and prevented Anna from passing.

"Where's Dada?" Anna asked.

"Gone out," he answered gruffly.

Anna went to pass Seán but he stepped to one side, blocking her again.

"Seán, let me by."

"I know what you've been up to," he said menacingly.

"What?" Anna asked, feeling her mouth go dry.

"Don't act the innocent with me. I know," he said, raising his voice.

"Seán, for God's sake!" Anna was frightened now – she could tell that Seán was furious.

He took hold of Anna's arm and pushed her backwards.

"What are you talking about?" she cried.

Seán pinned her against the wall and Anna gasped loudly.

"You and that fuckin' Jew boy. I saw you together, more than once. Is that who you've been with since you threw Joe out?" His mouth was inches away from her as he spat the angry words into her face.

She looked away, but Seán gripped her jaw roughly and pulled it towards his. "Answer me, Anna, is that why you finished up with Joe?"

"It's none of your business!" Anna shouted defiantly.

Seán tightened his grip on her face. "You answer me, you little whore, or I'll smash that pretty little face to bits. Is he the reason you finished up with Joe?"

Unable to move from his grip, she kept her eyes averted as he waited for her to speak. "Yes," Anna whispered hoarsely.

Seán looked at her in disgust. He turned away and leaned on the handrail of the banisters, then with another wave of violence he kicked the wooden spindle, sending splinters of wood flying into the air. He turned and pointed a shaking finger at Anna.

"How could you?" he shouted.

Anna wrung her hands and looked down towards the front door. "Please, Seán, Dada might come in," she pleaded.

"I hope he does!" Seán continued to shout. "I hope he comes in right now and I can tell him what a lying little whore of a daughter he has!"

A terrified sob escaped from Anna and her body

shook with fear. "Please, Seán, don't tell him!" she cried.

Seán looked on as Anna fell to pieces before him. His body slumped against the creaking banister as he mulled over what to do next. Never before had Seán had the upper hand in an argument with his sister and although he was truly disgusted with her behaviour, there was a certain pleasure in hearing her beg for mercy.

"What the hell are you at, Anna? Bringing disgrace on our family like that. How could you do it to Joe?"

Anna wiped her tears away. "Seán, you don't understand."

Seán's furious glare stopped her from saying anything else. "Shut up," he barked, moving towards her. "I don't want to understand." He took a deep breath and grabbed her shoulders roughly. "This is what you are going to do. You give that Jew boy his marching orders and find yourself another job." Anna's eyes widened, but Seán paid no attention to her. "You get back with Joe Maguire. If he'll have you."

Anna took a step backwards and shook Seán's hands away. "What are you saying?" she said, her fear now replaced with outrage.

Seán stared at her coldly. "You do that, and I

won't tell Da about it."

"Are you serious?" Anna shrieked.

"Deadly," Seán answered. He turned and walked down the stairs slowly. When he reached the last step he looked back over his shoulder. "Do it quick, or I swear to God, I'll tell Da everything."

★   ★   ★

The yellow sunshine spilled across the office, illuminating the tiny particles of dust that floated in the morning light. Anna had been alone for over an hour, anxiously awaiting Daniel's arrival so she could tell him what had happened with Seán.

At half past ten, he bounced up the stairs and stopped in his tracks when he saw Anna's stricken face. "What's wrong?" he asked, closing the door behind him.

"Oh Daniel! Seán knows about us. He's been spying on us."

Daniel leaned back against the door and closed his eyes tightly.

Anna resumed her frantic pacing. "He's threatening to tell Dada if I don't stop seeing you. He wants me to leave Jacob's and … " She looked over at Daniel and put a hand over her mouth as if trying to stop the words escaping.

"And what?" Daniel asked.

"He wants me to get back with Joe." All of the colour had drained from her face and she looked as if she might faint.

Daniel pushed himself from the door and went to her.

"That's utterly unreasonable," he said, taking Anna into his arms.

Anna let her head rest on his shoulder and breathed in the warm scent of cologne that had become so familiar to her. He ran his hands along the length of her spine and his reassuring touch made Anna feel immediately safe and protected.

"Don't worry," he whispered. "We'll just have to speed up our departure."

Anna pulled back and looked into his eyes.

"Are you ready?" he asked.

Anna nodded slowly.

"You play along with Seán's orders. Tell him you are working out your notice. I don't know what you're going to do about Joe."

"I'll try to think of something," Anna said.

"I'll look into booking our passage to England straight away. Anna, tell me again, tell me you're sure of what you are doing."

Anna took his face in her trembling hands. "Daniel, I am so sure that I love you and I will love you always."

Standing in the pool of sunshine, they held each other tightly and all their worries dissolved in the warmth of their tender embrace.

★   ★   ★

For the next few days Anna managed to avoid Seán. He had been spending his nights up at the Four Courts, which had given her some time to compose more lies. Daniel had booked tickets for the boat to England – she had five more days to spend with her family and every time she thought of leaving, the knot would tighten in the pit of her stomach. It was too risky for her to pack at home, so Daniel had taken his suitcase into the office, and little by little she had taken her belongings into work and packed them alongside his.

"We'll get engaged properly on the boat," Daniel said to her as he pushed the suitcase behind his desk.

Anna gazed into the mirror of her dressing table and was overcome with excitement as she thought of how Daniel would place the ring on her finger. Her dreaming was interrupted by the thud of the front door closing, and her excitement turned to dread, as she heard Seán kicking his boots off in the hall.

Down in the kitchen he kept his back to Anna

when she entered the room.

"Where's Da?" he muttered.

"Gone around to the pub for an hour. He should be back soon."

Seán proceeded to hack a lump of bread free from the loaf and spread it with butter. He swaggered over to the table and collapsed wearily into a chair.

There was silence while Anna made tea and placed the teapot and a mug before him.

"Have you finished up in Jacob's?" Seán asked without looking at Anna.

"I'm working out a week's notice," Anna said without faltering. Months of practice had made her a master in the art of lying.

Seán snorted at this. "Notice my arse," he said.

Anna stood behind him and threw some coal on the fire; it was easier to speak to him without making eye contact.

"Did you tell the Jew boy you wouldn't be seeing him again?" He tore another lump of bread off the loaf with his unwashed hands.

Normally Anna would have scolded him for being so uncouth, but this evening she held her tongue – she was hardly in a position to admonish.

"Yes," she answered shortly.

She looked at the back of Seán's head and

watched his ears rotate as he chewed his bread.

"What about Joe?"

"What about him?" Anna said.

Seán turned around and gave her an icy stare. "Have you tried to contact him?"

Anna could feel her face redden with anger. "No," she answered.

Seán turned back to the table and drummed his fingers against his mug of tea. "He's up in the Four Courts all the time. Write him a note, tell him that you want to see him, and I'll take it up."

Anna stormed over to the table and Seán jerked around in his chair.

"Are you not happy now? I've given up my job, I've done all that you asked of me." She was afraid to mention Daniel's name out loud. "Can you not just leave it at that without involving Joe?" She could no longer hold in the anger at her brother's outrageous demands.

Seán shook his finger in her face. "You do exactly as I asked you to do, or I'm telling Da. That's the deal."

"The deal!" exclaimed Anna, throwing her hands in the air. "Is that what it is? What do you think I am?"

Seán stood up, throwing the chair out from under him. "You shut your mouth!" he shouted, pointing his finger in Anna's face.

Anna slapped his finger away. "I've had enough of you!" she shouted back. "You're taking advantage of the situation, trying to get me back with Joe. It's making me sick! If you like him so much why don't you go out with him yourself?"

Seán stepped up to Anna and poked a finger into her chest. "Tell me something," he roared, "were you whoring for your Jew boy when you informed on me?"

"What?" cried Anna.

"Go on, answer me!" Seán yelled.

The door burst open and Mr Barry stood in the doorway glaring at them. They hadn't heard his key in the hall door over the shouting.

"What the hell is going on here?" he roared.

Mr Barry marched over and grabbed Seán by the collar of his shirt. "What did I hear you saying?"

Seán looked at Anna as if he were about to burst into tears. "Nothing, Da," he said, trying to free himself from his father's tight grip.

Mr Barry slapped Seán hard on the side of the head.

"Stop it, Dada!" Anna screamed.

Mr Barry stopped and looked over at Anna. "Tell me, what are you fighting about?"

Anna looked over at Seán beseechingly. Mr Barry

landed another blow to the other side of Seán's head. Seán put his hands over his ears and pulled himself free.

"She's running around with that Jew boy," he blurted, pointing to Anna.

Mr Barry took a step back and swayed slightly – the few pints of stout had suddenly made him feel dizzy.

He looked over at his daughter and ran the palm of his hand over his chin. Over and back, over and back, making a bristling noise.

"Is this true?" he asked, staring down at the table.

"She broke it off with Joe so she could carry on with him. I followed them, I've seen them together!" Seán couldn't stop now, it all came tumbling out of his mouth uncontrollably. "It's her who informed on me about the guns, that's why we had to move them to your place!" he cried.

Mr Barry stood with his mouth open and listened to Seán as he heaped the damning evidence on his sister's head. Anna wept openly as she watched her father turn pale with rage. The three of them stood in the frigid silence that followed Seán's outburst.

Mr Barry took a deep breath. "Get out, Seán," he said quietly, keeping his eyes firmly fixed on the table. Seán looked over to Anna and saw the shadow of fear that crossed her face, but it was too late to do anything. He knew the damage had been done and there was nothing he could do to save her now.

Seán walked slowly out of the kitchen, rubbing the side of his head, making sure to close the door as he left.

Mr Barry rolled forward on the balls of his feet, swaying to and fro.

"Is all of this true, Anna?" he asked solemnly.

Anna wrung her hands together and gulped back her tears. "It's true about Daniel but I never informed on Seán. Daniel found the guns and I knew it was Seán who put them there, Seán stole my keys and hid them –"

Anna didn't see it coming. Her father's fist connected with her jaw sending her crashing to the floor with a loud thump. She lay crumpled in a heap, her head resting against the warm oven door.

"Get up!" her father shouted.

Anna rubbed her jaw but it felt completely numb. Mr Barry leaned down and pulled her to her feet. Before she could say anything, he smashed his fist into the other side of her face sending her reeling backwards into the dresser. Anna slid down the side of the dresser like a rag doll, the taste of warm salty blood filling her mouth.

Mr Barry stood before her breathing deeply.

"Believe me, Anna. That hurt me more than it

hurt you," he said and turned to walk towards the door.

Anna pulled herself up from the floor with both hands and leaned heavily against the dresser, sending two plates smashing to the floor. "Is that what you told Mam every time you hit her?" Her voice sounded strange. Her lips were swollen and the words sounded thick and clumsy.

Mr Barry swung around and with another heavy fist he sent Anna flying back down onto the floor where she landed in a heap amongst the broken crockery.

★　★　★

There was an atmosphere of gloom amongst the men in the Four Courts. Earlier in the day, the volunteers had learned that the British government had ordered their surrender. Now, they had to sit it out and see if the Provisional Government would act on their orders and fire the first shots on the men they had once fought alongside. Joe sat beside a window and ran a rag over his rifle. All of the men had been ordered to keep their arms close by and ready to use. Fr Albert and Fr Dominic were doing the rounds of the men, hearing confessions and trying to keep the spirits of the volunteers up. Fr

Albert spotted Joe by the window and made his way over to him.

"Joseph."

Joe put his rifle down and stood up. "Hello, Father."

Fr Albert sat down beside Joe and gave him a warm smile. "How are you?"

"I'm grand, Father. Getting a bit anxious, but I'm fine."

"I was with your mother last night, Joseph – she's praying for you night and day."

Joe nodded grimly. Fr Albert had been with Joe's brother Francis when he was killed. The priest had whispered the last rites into the dying boy's ear as he lay bleeding to death outside the GPO on Easter Monday.

Of course his mother was praying, Joe thought, her knees were probably worn out from praying.

"It's a hard time for your parents, but it's a hard time for you as well," Fr Albert said in the way only a priest can in times of difficulty. "Is there anything you want to say to me, Joseph? Would you like me to hear your confession?"

Joe thought for a few minutes. "Yes, Father," he answered.

Fr Albert leaned towards Joe and made a sign of the cross in the air.

Joe blessed himself. *"In the name of the Father, and of the Son, and of the Holy Ghost, Amen. Bless me, Father, for I have sinned."*

Fr Albert nodded his head and looked down. "Tell me your sins."

"I've had murder on my mind, Father, not the kind I may have to carry out on active duty. I want to murder someone else, someone who took my girl away. My fiancée. I swear if I had the chance to kill him, I don't know if I'd be strong enough to walk away from it." Joe's voice shook with emotion.

Fr Albert nodded his head and waited, but Joe had nothing more to say.

"For your penance say a decade of the rosary," Fr Albert said and made the sign of the cross again: *"Et ego te absolvo a peccatis tuis in nomine Patris, et Filii, et Spiritus Sancti."*

"Amen."

Both men leaned against the window ledge and the priest let a few moments pass before he spoke.

"Your mother told me that you're not engaged any more," he said carefully.

"No, Father, she broke off the engagement," Joe said, trying to cover up the hurt in his voice.

Fr Albert shook his head slowly. "Sometimes it's hard to understand what the Good Man has planned for us all. Perhaps she wasn't the right woman for you."

Joe forced a grim smile. "Perhaps she wasn't," he agreed, "but it still hurts."

Fr Albert put a hand on Joe's shoulder and squeezed it gently. "I'm sure it does, son, but say your prayers and I know that God will be good to you. You're a great man, Joe, and I know that you would never murder anyone for taking your girl."

"You're probably right. Thanks, Father," he whispered.

Joe watched from the windowsill as Fr Albert went to talk to another volunteer. Across the room he saw Seán rushing across to talk to him. He was the last person Joe wanted to see at that moment. He was annoyed with himself for saying anything to Seán about Anna – after all she was free to see whoever she wanted to now that they were no longer engaged, and Joe knew he would have to get used to it.

Seán settled himself on to the window ledge beside Joe.

"How are you?"

Joe picked up his rifle and began to clean it again. "Grand," he answered.

Seán kicked his legs against the wall and struggled to find something to say. After a moment he looked over at Joe, uncertain how to begin.

"What?" Joe said.

"It's about Anna."

Joe looked back down at his rifle and remained expressionless.

"I just want you to know it's been sorted out."

Joe looked up and raised his eyebrows.

"She won't be seeing that fella again," Seán said, a touch of pride entering his voice.

"How's that?" Joe asked slowly. He put his rifle down and fished inside his breast pocket for a cigarette.

Seán immediately pulled out his and offered one to Joe.

"Thanks," said Joe, taking one.

Seán struck a match against the wall and lit Joe's cigarette. Joe took a long pull and breathed the smoke deep inside his lungs.

"Honestly, Joe," Seán continued. "I had no idea what she was at, and if I did, I certainly would never have hidden such a thing from you."

Joe looked at Seán wearily; his constant adoration had become hard to stomach lately.

"Would you have her back, Joe? Would you take her back again if she was to beg you?"

Joe sat up and stared at Seán. "What are you saying?"

"Da had a good talk with her and she's seen how foolish she was – she knows now that she made a big mistake breaking off her engagement with you."

Joe's eyes narrowed as he listened to Seán ranting.

"She's going to write to you. I told her I'd give you the letter when she's written it." Seán was speaking fast, reeling Joe in with every word.

Joe's heart thumped wildly as he pictured Anna trying to compose a letter to him explaining how she wanted him back again.

"Would you have her, Joe?" Seán asked.

Joe looked up at Seán crossly. "Never you mind. I'll go and talk to her myself."

Seán jumped up. "Not now, Joe. She said she wanted to write to you first, to explain what happened."

"I can't bloody well go now, can I?" Joe exclaimed impatiently. "We're about to fight a war any minute."

Seán backed away. "I might be out again tonight. If I am, I'll drop home and see if she has anything for you."

Joe slumped back down on to the windowsill and nodded at Seán dismissively.

Would he take her back? Of course he would, even though things would never be the same between the two of them again. Joe let his head rest against the cold windowpane and shut his eyes. Would he take her back? He would take her back in a heartbeat.

Chapter 24

Daniel packed some more clothes into his side of the trunk, taking great care not to crumple any of Anna's dresses. He pulled out his watch chain and looked at the time. It was almost midday and Anna had not been into the office yet. He knew that it wasn't a good sign and frowned to himself as he put the watch back into his pocket. There was no way of finding out what was wrong. Calling to her house was out of the question; he just hoped that her brother hadn't done anything foolish. A muffled knock came from outside on the main office door. Daniel came out of his room and crossed Anna's office to answer the door and froze when he saw who the caller was.

"Can I come in?" Seán asked.

Daniel stood back, let Seán into the room and closed the door behind him.

Seán stood in the middle of the room, feet set apart in a cocky stance.

Daniel pointed to a chair but Seán refused it.

"I won't take up too much of your time," he said.

"What is it?" Daniel asked worriedly.

"I'm here to tell you that you won't be seeing Anna again."

Daniel shot a cautious glance across at Seán. "What do you mean?"

"I mean," Seán said slowly, "that Anna will not be returning to work in this office. You will never see her again, do you understand?"

"What have you done?" Daniel asked with growing concern.

"Never you mind," said Seán, the corners of his mouth twisting up into a cruel smile. "Anna will have nothing to do with you any more."

Daniel held his hands stiffly by his sides and clenched his fists. "Did you tell your father?"

Seán took a step closer. "Don't you ever go near my sister again or I'll blow your head off."

They both stood in the thick silence and glared at each other.

It was a different Seán that had sat twisting his cap apologetically on his last visit. Daniel looked across at this vindictive monster and cursed himself for showing any clemency about the hidden guns.

"Do you understand me?" Seán asked, moving closer again.

Daniel met his stare coldly. "I understand that you are a poisonous bastard," he said, trying to disguise his fear. He knew that Seán could finish him off with one blow from his fist if he so wished. He was no match for him. "I am only sorry that I didn't have you arrested."

Seán looked down at Daniel and sneered. "You just remember what I've said. Don't ever go near her again."

Seán turned and left the office, leaving the door swinging open behind him. Daniel sank onto the couch and tried to take in Seán's words. What had he done to make Anna stay away? All morning he had known that something was wrong but he had pushed the dreaded feelings to the back of his mind. Now he feared that the worst had happened.

★ ★ ★

Anna rose from her bed and sat down stiffly at her dressing table. The sight was shocking to her – it looked even worse than it had the night before. Her left eye was twice its size and a gaudy purple in colour. Her lower lip was puffed out, and divided in the middle by a red gash, where it had split. There was swelling to the side of her face, and her jaw was still completely numb. She had lain in bed for most of the morning. What point was there in getting up? She was not leaving her room until she looked normal again. Anna jumped as she heard the thumping on the front door. Her father had risen early and left for work, and Seán was not in the house. Anna looked about wildly – she could not let anyone see her like this.

The thumping grew louder. Anna went to her window and pulled back the lace curtain a crack. She jumped back in shock and pressed her back against the wall as her whole body started to shake.

"Anna!" Daniel shouted from outside.

Anna buried her face in her hands and started to cry. How could she let him see her like this?

"Anna!" Daniel shouted louder. "I know you're in there! Open the door!"

Anna went to the window again and looked out the side of the curtain. Daniel had stepped back and was looking straight up at her.

"Open the door," he pleaded.

Anna made her way slowly downstairs, every bone

in her body aching with each step she took. At the front door she stopped and took a deep breath before opening it. She slowly pulled back the door and revealed herself.

Daniel put his hand to his mouth and looked at her in horror. Anna couldn't bear it and looked away, completely ashamed of her appearance.

"Don't look at me," she whispered.

"Oh God!" cried Daniel, turning her around to face him. "Oh my God, what have they done to you?" Anna watched the tears stream from his eyes, and put her hand to his face.

"You have to go, Daniel. If they catch you here they'll kill you."

Daniel stepped into the hall, closing the front door behind him. He put his arms around Anna and felt her tremble against him.

"You can't stay here any longer. We'll leave immediately – come with me now."

Anna sank into his embrace and wanted to stay like that forever. "Daniel, I don't think I would be up to a journey right now. It hurts to breathe."

Daniel took her face in his hands and winced when he saw the damage that had been done to her beautiful face. "When, Anna? We have to go soon."

"I can't go anywhere like this!" Anna began to cry and pressed her fingers over her stinging lip.

"You have to," Daniel urged. "Before they discover anything else, we have to go."

"Oh Daniel, I can't think any more. Everything is ruined … "

Daniel pulled her closer. "Nothing is ruined. We still love each other and that is all that matters. Now listen carefully – meet me tomorrow evening on Leeson Street Bridge."

Anna shook her head. "No, Daniel. I will not go anywhere looking like this."

Daniel looked down at her bruised and swollen face – and tried to hide the disgust that welled up inside of him. "We can't waste time. If not tomorrow, then the following day at the latest. Will that give you enough time?"

Anna nodded mechanically.

"Now listen carefully. Be on Leeson Street Bridge on Thursday at four o'clock. I'll be there to meet you. The boat sails at seven o'clock. Can you make your way there on your own?"

Anna looked down at the floor and nodded again.

"You will be there, Anna?" Daniel asked as he saw the blank expression on her face.

"Yes," she whispered. "Now please go, Daniel. I'm afraid you'll be seen."

"Four o'clock on Thursday," Daniel repeated. "Where?"

"Leeson Street Bridge," said Anna.

Daniel pulled her face close to his and kissed her gently on the forehead. Anna closed her eyes and felt the heat of his breath soothe her battered face.

"I love you sweetheart," he whispered in her ear.

"I love you too."

Daniel stepped outside the front door and hurried away from the house. As he walked along the canal a strange sensation rose up inside him and he was gripped by an overwhelming desire to vomit.

★　★　★

The Major General stood on top of a desk in the middle of the round hall of the Four Courts. In his hand he held a scroll of paper which he read from.

"At nine a.m. this morning we received a note signed by Tom Ennis demanding on behalf of the government our surrender at four a.m. when he would attack." He dropped the piece of paper and continued to speak to the assembled volunteers. "You boys are glorious, and will fight for the republic to the end. How long will our misguided former comrades outside attack those who stand for Ireland alone?" A cheer went up from the men on the floor.

Outside the troops from the Free State army lined the streets surrounding the Four Courts. Rifles, machines and field pieces had been brought out to attack the anti-Treaty forces. Joe looked out the window and watched the men in grey uniform as they thronged the streets holding back the curious public. Seán came up behind him.

"Would you look at them?" he said, nodding towards the street. "Mercenaries wearing the Irish uniform, have they no shame?"

Joe gazed down, not bothering to register Seán's comments.

"They won't dare to fire the first shot," Seán said, pointing down to them.

Seán waited for Joe to say something but he remained silent as he fixed his eyes on the big gun that was being wheeled to the other side of the river in preparation for the attack. Inside he felt hollow; he was weary before the battle had even begun.

Chapter 25

Daniel reached the end of the stairs and paused in the hall, bracing himself for the evening ahead. He entered the front room and saw his grandmother sitting in her armchair.

"Hello, Granny," Daniel said and bent to kiss her. "Where is Mother?"

"With your father at the hospital, she should be home soon."

Daniel sat down facing his grandmother and breathed out heavily.

"You look unhappy," she said instinctively.

Daniel lifted a hand to his forehead and closed

his eyes.

"What has happened?" Granny Jacob asked.

Daniel looked over at her, deciding whether to tell her or not.

"Something is wrong," she said, her brow creasing with concern.

"Yes," Daniel said nodding his head. "Something is wrong."

"Tell me," she demanded.

"Anna's brother found out about us and told her father. One of them, I presume the father, beat her black and blue … " His voice trailed off and Daniel stared up at the ceiling and waited until he could speak. "You should see her, Granny – her beautiful face is destroyed."

Granny Jacob raised her fist and beat her breast-bone several times. "Poor girl," she said, shaking her head with genuine sadness. "Daniel, I warned you. It can't work for the two of you. Leave her alone before anything worse happens."

Daniel sat forward. "Granny, listen to what I have to say. Anna and I are leaving here. We are getting the boat to England on Thursday and travelling on to Edinburgh. We will be married as soon as possible."

Granny Jacob's eyes filled with tears. "I am begging you not to do this," she said hysterically.

Daniel stood up quickly. "No, Granny, it's too late

for that. We are going to be married and I want your blessing."

Granny Jacob looked up at Daniel with wet eyes and scowled.

"You know Anna, I know you like her," he said. "Please say you'll give us your blessing."

"It's not a question of whether I like the girl or not!" exclaimed his grandmother, hitting the arm of the chair as she spoke. "She is not suitable for you!"

Daniel walked to the door and turned to his grandmother. "Please, Granny," he said hoarsely.

"No," she said firmly, staring straight ahead of her.

Daniel stood at the door and looked over at her.

"I'll be in my room. Please tell Mother to come upstairs when she gets back."

* * *

Irene peeled off her white lace gloves in the hall and went straight into the front room where her mother-in-law was waiting for her arrival.

"There you are," said Irene brightly. "Have you eaten yet?"

"No. I was waiting for you," Granny Jacob replied.

"I'm ravenous," Irene said. "Let's go inside now.

Is Daniel home?"

Granny Jacob looked at Irene gravely. "He is upstairs in his room. I think you had better go and speak to him."

Irene stopped and looked down at the old woman. She knew immediately that something had upset her mother-in-law. "Is something wrong?" She looked closely at Granny Jacob and saw that she had been crying. Her back stiffened with anxiety. "Please tell me what's wrong," she demanded.

Granny Jacob waved a finger towards the door. "Go up to him," she said.

Irene tapped gently on Daniel's door and entered the room. Daniel had been lying on his bed and stood up to greet his mother. He crossed the room and kissed her on the cheek.

"Daniel," exclaimed Irene, "Granny seems upset. What's going on?"

Daniel took her hands and led her towards the bed. "Sit down, Mother. I have something important to say to you."

Irene sank onto the bed and clasped her hands together on her lap.

"You know I have been seeing Anna," Daniel said. He walked to the chest of drawers and leaned against it for support.

Irene's face dropped at the mention of Anna's

name. "Yes," she said coldly.

"Her family didn't know about it. Her father would never have agreed to her seeing someone like me, and he was annoyed with Anna for breaking off her engagement. Anyway, her brother found out about us and told her father, and he beat her to within an inch of her life."

Irene's mouth gaped open and her stern expression faded as she listened to Daniel. "Oh dear! Poor Anna!"

"Mother, I didn't intend to shock you like this, but we are leaving the day after tomorrow for Edinburgh. We are getting married."

Irene looked up at Daniel in shock.

"I love her, Mother," Daniel added softly.

Irene stood up slowly and went over to him, treading lightly, as if she was afraid that the floor would be pulled from under her feet. "Married?"

"Yes. I wanted to give you some notice, but we have to leave straight away. I'm sorry about the shop – but if Granny can get that Evans fellow over a little sooner than planned . . ."

Irene's face had caved inwards with bitter disappointment, making her look suddenly older than she was. "Daniel," she said shakily, "please do not do this."

Daniel turned away, unable to meet her stare. "It's

too late, Mother. We have made our plans."

"Listen to me, Daniel," Irene said, moving around to where he could see her. "You are making a big mistake. You are infatuated with this girl. A marriage between the two of you will never work. How can you make a life with a shop girl who has come from such a different background? She will never fit into your world, Daniel."

"Oh shut up, Mother!" Daniel shouted.

Irene jumped back in horror at her son's sudden outburst.

"Do you ever take people for what they are, or is it all about money with you?"

"How dare you!" she hissed.

"You only care about what people have, how big their houses are, how much money they earn. Did it ever occur to you that I might be different? I love Anna for who she is. And if she doesn't speak as well as you or read the same books then it makes no difference. I love her, Mother. Please try to understand that.

"I will never try to understand it," Irene said through her clenched teeth. "I forbid you to go near that girl again, and that is final."

Daniel looked at his mother and laughed scornfully. "You forbid me?"

"*Yes!*" screamed Irene.

"You seem to forget that I am a grown man."

"A grown man who depends on this family for an income," shouted Irene. She walked across the room and stopped as she reached the door. She stood perfectly still for a few seconds and when she turned to face Daniel her icy tone had been restored. Her eyes glistened with the strength of her conviction. "If you run off with this woman, you will never get a shilling from us again. I speak on behalf of your father. I know that he would never agree to such a marriage."

Irene stood before Daniel and waited for his reaction, to see if the prospect of poverty would bring about a change of heart, but he remained unmoved by her threat.

"Is that all you have to say?" he said quietly.

"Yes," said Irene briskly. "I hope by tomorrow morning you will have found some sense."

Downstairs in the living room Granny Jacob turned as Irene opened the door. Irene went to enter the room, but quickly changed her mind as she looked across at her mother-in-law's expectant face.

"I won't be dining with you this evening," Irene announced. "I am going to lie down."

Before Granny Jacob could reply to this, Irene had retreated from the room.

★ ★ ★

The first shafts of dawn light fell across the murky green waters of the River Liffey. The city slept, under an eerie veil of stillness, holding its breath in anticipation of what was to come. On the other side of the river from the Four Courts, the army was having trouble operating the big machinery that had been sent from England for the occasion. An army car inched its way through the mute wall of soldiers and stopped across from where the gun had been wheeled. A small man jumped from the passenger seat and made his way confidently through the group. He stood behind the big gun and altered its settings, then he marched over to the embarrassed soldier who had been trying to operate the machine and had a few words with him.

"Ready?" he asked briskly.

The soldier nodded his head.

"Stand back," he ordered loudly. "Ready to fire."

A massive boom reverberated across the walls of the Liffey and a crash of metal on brick exploded through the stillness of daybreak.

Joe and Seán rolled over several times on the floor, narrowly escaping the spray of concrete that landed where they had been lying. A flurry of panic swept through the men in the Four Courts sending bodies running in every direction.

"They've fired!" shouted Seán. "They've fired the first shot. They've declared war."

Joe inched forward on his belly and grabbed the butt of his rifle.

"By God," exclaimed Seán. "They don't know who they're up against." He spoke with the childish bravado that Joe had come to despise.

A hail of bullets sprayed through the windows and Joe put his hands over his head and pressed his forehead into the wooden floor. Three volunteers jumped across Joe's body and took their positions beside the window and began to fire back at the men below. Another explosion rocked the foundations – this time it came from the other side of the building and blew a hole clean through the wall, leaving Joe completely deaf in one ear.

* * *

Anna sat down slowly at her dressing table and felt her heart sink as she saw the hideous face that stared back at her. Her trembling hand reached across for the tin of face powder, and she slowly patted the purple welt that had formed on her cheek with the powder puff. Even the slightest touch to her face made her wince in pain but she knew that she would have to try to conceal the ugly bruising if she was to travel the following day. She put on her oldest house dress, as all of her good clothes were now packed safely away in the suitcase that Daniel would take from the office. Down in the kitchen, she cleared the dirty dishes that had been left in her absence and waited for the kettle to boil. Looking around the room Anna was gripped by a sharp pang of loneliness when she realised that she would never see this room again. She thought about her father and Seán. Even though they had done such a terrible thing to her, turning her back on them seemed so final. Anna tried to think of some way she could make things right between them, but deep down she knew that the only way to do that was to walk away from Daniel. The thought had crossed her mind several times in recent days, but having had time to think about it Anna was certain now that she could never give him up. She thought of her mother, and felt a lump rise in her throat – she was the only person that would have understood exactly how Anna felt.

The sound of the front door being slammed jolted Anna from her thoughts. She wondered who could be coming in at this time of the morning: it was only after ten.

Mr Barry burst into the kitchen and looked about the place wildly.

"Where's Seán?" he shouted.

Anna looked up at her father and his eyes bulged out at the sight of his daughter. They had not seen each other since the night before last when he had given her the beating and it was as if he had forgotten about it. He took a step back and looked around for anything he could rest his gaze on, anything but his daughter.

"Why are you home?" Anna asked.

"I want to know where Seán is," he said with less urgency.

Anna shrugged her shoulders. "I don't know."

"They've attacked the Four Courts. They're up there, firing on their own men."

Anna remembered the boom she had heard earlier that morning and it suddenly became apparent to her why her father was looking for Seán. "Did he go to work this morning?" she asked.

Mr Barry shook his head. "No, I called in to check but he hasn't been in for days."

Anna jumped up and took the boiling kettle off the gas. "I told him," she blurted. "I told him that this would happen." She turned around to her father who was staring down at the floor, unable to look at the results of his vicious temper.

"We don't know for certain that he's there," Mr Barry said doubtfully.

"Of course he's up there," Anna exclaimed.

As she said this, Mr Barry's face collapsed with worry.

"Is it bad?" Anna asked.

Mr Barry took a deep breath. "It's very bad. They're using heavy artillery – the boys haven't got a hope."

Anna pulled out a chair and sank down into it. "Oh Jesus!"

Mr Barry moved over to the table and stood for a minute gazing down at his daughter. "Say a prayer for him, Anna," he said in a strangled voice. "And Joe too – he's sure to be up there as well."

Anna looked up and nodded. Mr Barry pointed to her face and looked away in shame. "I didn't mean to do that," he whispered.

Anna's face froze at the mention of what had happened. She had blocked it out of her mind and the brutal memory now came flooding back in all its violence. A hot tear rolled down her bruised and tender cheek. The only sound in the kitchen was the heavy breathing that came from Mr Barry as he struggled to contain his emotions. He reached across slowly and patted Anna's hand gently.

"Don't be crying, love." He patted her hand

several times and then straightened up and cleared his throat. "I'm going back out to see if I can find him."

$$\star \quad \star \quad \star$$

The shelling had continued intermittently for almost twenty-four hours, and the casualties had begun to pile up. Joe lay on the floor and tightened the tourniquet which he had fixed to his upper arm. An earlier blast had sent a piece of metal ripping through the flesh and with every hour that went by the pain grew worse. Seán lay beside him. Another explosion blew a hole in the wall beside them and both men were thrown backwards with the force of the blast. Joe crashed down to the floor, landing on his shoulder. The pain seared through him like a sharp knife. "Oh Christ Almighty," he groaned. His mouth had filled with dust and he spat on the floor to rid himself of the choking particles of grit.

The explosion had come from within the building. Orders had been given to mine the Records Office, as surrender was now imminent.

Beside Seán lay the dead body of Mooney who such a short time before had celebrated the birth of his son.

Seán got up and scrambled across the floor to

where Joe was lying. "There's talk of surrender," he said despondently.

Joe nodded and grimaced as he tried to move his arm.

"To hell with that!" said Seán. "I'm not surrendering to those bastards."

"There's not a lot you can do about it," said Joe, breathing heavily against the pain.

"I'm going to try to get out before they get to us," said Seán. "Are you coming? A few of the lads made a run for it earlier over the roof."

Joe looked at Seán and shook his head. "You go on, Seán, I'd only slow you down with this."

"Come on, Joe, if we wait till it gets dark we can try and get out then. Mooney gave me the address of a safe house in Mountjoy. You can make it that far, can't you?" Both of them looked across at Mooney's body lying against the opposite wall.

Joe pursed his lips together and frowned. He looked around at the other dead bodies that had been pulled into the far corner of the room and knew that there was a good chance that he would end up piled on top of them.

"Alright. I'll go with you."

Seán gave him a gentle punch on his good shoulder. "You keep the head down and as soon as it gets dark I'll come and get you. There's a window down the hall that leads out to the roof. We'll go that way."

The firing abated during the late afternoon and Joe could feel his eyelids getting heavier by the minute. His head drooped down and rested on his chest and, as his blood pressure dropped, he gave in to the overwhelming desire to sleep. What seemed like minutes later, someone was shaking him roughly and a fresh wave of pain from his arm jolted him into wakefulness.

"Are you right?" Seán whispered hoarsely.

Joe rubbed his eyes and sat up.

"Come on, will you? It's gone quiet out there. We'll try to make a run for it now." Seán helped Joe to his feet. "Are you sure you're able for this?"

Joe looked at him and nodded dumbly.

"Come on then, follow me." Seán proceeded to weave between the sandbags and bodies and Joe put his head down and followed him.

Outside the big room, they ran down a long hallway and through a door that led to a narrow staircase. Joe gripped the handrail and leaned heavily on it as he climbed the steps, trying to keep up with Seán. At the top of the stairs was another narrow passageway. At the end of it Joe could see a ladder propped up against a wall. As they approached the ladder, Joe spotted the tiny window it gave access to.

"Jesus, Seán, we'll never fit out there."

Seán was looking over his shoulder to make sure that no one had seen them deserting.

"Go on, you go first. It's not as small as it looks, you'll fit out."

Joe gripped the ladder with his good hand and climbed it slowly, leaving his injured arm dangling by his side.

"Hurry," Seán said in a raspy whisper from below.

The window was slightly wider than it had looked from the floor. Joe had to inch his way out slowly, trying not to roar with the pain as he tried to raise his injured arm to fit out. Outside on the roof, both men crawled along the flat valley that led to a rusty ladder which was fixed to the wall. It had been put there in the event of a fire but did not extend completely to the ground below. It stopped short of the ground, leaving a ten-foot jump to the alleyway beneath them. Joe tried to descend the ladder as quickly as possible, he knew that all it would take was for one soldier to see them and they would be shot down immediately. Seán was climbing down like a monkey just above him, urging him to hurry and stepping on his only functioning hand at every second rung.

"Come on, come on," he whispered loudly as Joe tried to quicken his step. The jump to the ground was excruciating and when Seán landed on top of him

Joe let out a high-pitched whine. Seán slammed his hand roughly over Joe's mouth and pressed down hard to shut him up. They both stood up and looked around the alleyway. There was no one patrolling it.

Seán got a hold of Joe's arm and tugged at it. "This way."

Seán had made this journey many times over the past three months and could do it in his sleep if required. It was a moonless night, and the two men moved unnoticed through the darkness of the back streets and laneways that led towards the safe house in Mountjoy Square.

Seán ran up the steps and banged on the door of number thirty-two, the address he had been given a few days ago by Mooney. A girl with a pinched-looking face opened the door a crack and peered out.

"What do yez want?" she said sharply.

"Tell your da it's Seán Barry, I've come from the Four Courts."

The girl closed the door and left them standing outside. Seán pulled his jacket collar up around his face and stared down at the ground. Joe leaned against the railings breathing heavily, the short journey had made his arm throb so much it felt as if it would burst. The door opened again and this time a red-faced man stood glaring out at them. He raised his candle and took a look at their faces.

Seán went to step into the hall but the man put out his hand and pushed him back out.

"You can't come in here," he said, looking over Seán's shoulder out on to the street.

Seán looked at him in dismay. "What do you mean? We were told we could use your place."

"I know that, but the army were around yesterday – they're on to me. I sent word up to the Four Courts earlier – this place isn't safe any more." The red-faced man was getting agitated and put his foot against the door to stop Seán pressing it in.

"Jesus man, can't you see we're desperate? Let us in for a few minutes till we get our breath. Joe here is injured."

The man looked at Joe who had slumped against the railings. "For Christ's sake, what are you bringing him here for?" He opened the door and extended his head outside, scouring the street for anyone that might be watching them. Then he stood back and beckoned for them to come in. "Come on, quickly – if you're seen coming in here I'll be done for."

Seán helped Joe down to the kitchen where the young girl was waiting with her mother. They both wore their nightgowns and sat in the candlelight staring at the men.

Seán nodded to the two of them and helped Joe into a chair.

"Take this off and let me see the damage," he said, opening Joe's jacket and undoing the already loose tourniquet.

Joe eased his arms from the jacket and clenched his teeth as the pain shot through him. The young girl gasped as Joe's arm emerged, soaked with dark blood. The woman stood up quickly and began to fill a basin of water.

"Thanks for letting us in," Joe said in a strained voice.

The man looked down at the bloody arm sympathetically. "It's no bother. I'm glad to help out, it's just that this place isn't safe. I don't want to put my wife and daughter in danger, it's not fair to them. I'm behind you lads all the way – sure isn't me own brother-in-law fighting with you up there. Willie Mooney, do yez know him? His wife had their first baby boy a few days ago – she's beyond in the other room sleeping."

Seán and Joe glanced at each other in silent dread and didn't answer.

The young girl held the candle over Joe as her mother began to dab at the blood that surrounded the gaping hole in his arm. Her brow creased with concern when she examined it closely and she turned to her daughter. "Molly, run down and see if Mrs Ward is at home and tell her to come quickly." When the girl had left the room, the woman turned to her husband and put the towel down on the table. "There's something stuck in there, it'll have to come out."

The man began to pace the kitchen floor anxiously. "He can stay here till the women fix him up, then he'll have to go. But you'll have to leave now," he said to Seán. "Sheila will make you a bit of supper to see you right, but after that you'll have to get out of here. Is there somewhere you can hide out for the night?"

Seán was about to argue, but he stopped and put his hand into his trouser pocket and felt around for the set of keys to Jacob's. They were still there. If he could get back up Sackville Street without being seen, he could spend the rest of the night in there, and possibly even the next day. All the shops in the area had been told to close up until the firing had stopped.

"I appreciate your help and I'll be off after I've had a bit to eat, if that isn't any bother," Seán said solemnly.

Molly arrived back with Mrs Ward, and the three women huddled in the corner discussing Joe's injury.

"Is she a nurse?" Seán asked, looking at the rusty tin of implements that Mrs Ward had laid on the table.

"Sort of," said the man dismissively.

The women helped Joe up from the chair and steered him towards a room down the hall. As he left the kitchen, Joe turned to Seán. "Don't go home, Seán. They might be waiting for you there."

Seán got up and squeezed Joe's good shoulder gently. "Don't worry, Joe. I still have those keys to Jacob's, remember?"

Joe nodded. "Be careful," he warned, as the two women walked him out of the room.

$$\star \quad \star \quad \star$$

Seán edged up Sackville Street with the deftness of an alley cat. He shot in and out of shop fronts, staying in the shadows of the buildings, for fear of being seen by anyone. The street was like a ghost town – completely deserted and in total darkness. When he reached the porch of Jacob's, he fumbled in his pocket for the set of keys. The locksmith he had given Anna's keys to had only had a few hours to copy them and Seán prayed that they would work. The first one slid into the lock easily and turned with a gentle click. Seán breathed a sigh of relief as he pushed the door open. Upstairs in the office he looked about in the dark. He could see the shape of the leather couch just inside the door. He threw himself onto it and was immediately hit by an overwhelming feeling of exhaustion. He had had little sleep during the past two nights and every muscle in his body ached from being thrown around by the explosions. He knew he was taking a risk by staying in the office, but he couldn't stand the thought of hiding out in the damp cold storeroom below. He needed to get some sleep and then, at first light, he would move down to the storeroom until it got dark again and think of what his next move would be. He took off his jacket and pulled out the revolver from the inside pocket, sliding it under the couch. With a loud yawn he rolled his jacket into a pillow and placed it under his head, settling down into the only bit of peace and comfort he had felt in days. Minutes later he was sound asleep.

★ ★ ★

Daniel walked downstairs for breakfast dragging a heavy heart. This was the last meal he would have with his mother for some time, and he knew that it was not going to be a pleasant experience.

He pushed open the door and entered the room. Irene sat alone at the table, her eyes fixed on the steaming amber flow of tea that Mary was pouring for her. In her right hand she clutched a crumpled handkerchief.

"Will you have an egg this morning, Daniel?" Mary asked, setting the teapot back down on the stand.

"No, thank you, Mary." His stomach heaved at the thought of food, his anxiety had dulled his appetite.

Mary left the two of them alone and Daniel pulled out a chair and sat down.

Irene looked across at him and, exercising her usual restraint, she asked, "Are you going somewhere this morning?"

Daniel met her steely gaze. "Yes. I have to go into the office."

Irene gave a short laugh, as if this amused her no end. "My dear, the city is being torn apart as we speak. You'll do no such thing. Besides," she said, pointing to the morning paper, "people have been asked to stay away from that part of town until the trouble is over."

Daniel grabbed the paper and ran his finger slowly down the column as he read about the shelling of the Four Courts. He poured himself a cup of tea and looked over at his mother.

"I have to get something in the office today, and I really should go in for a while in case of looting."

Irene looked at him sternly. "I care more about

your safety than any looting that may occur. Don't go near the place today."

Mary entered the room again, carrying a plate of toast, and Irene immediately turned to her. "Daniel wants to go into the office this morning. Tell him what it's like down there, Mary."

Mary placed the toast beside Irene and shook her head vigorously. "I nearly had the heart frightened out of me," she said, rolling her eyes dramatically. "There were guns and canons firing in every direction. I had to run down the quays for fear of getting shot myself."

Irene nodded her head carefully as she listened to Mary's tale of escape from near death. Mary picked up the teapot and tapped the side to feel if it needed replenishing. She clutched the warm teapot to her breast and continued. "To see those blackguards firing on their own countrymen, it's enough to make a body's blood run cold! There isn't a true Irishman among the lot of them!" With this said, Mary walked from the room, still clutching the teapot.

Irene gazed after her with a look of mild astonishment. "I don't remember asking for an opinion," she said to Daniel, with a thinly concealed smile.

Daniel almost threw his hands up and agreed not to go, but remembered the suitcase. It wasn't important to him – he had more clothes upstairs that he could take, but Anna's wedding dress was sitting at the top of the suitcase – and she had been through enough without having to leave that behind. Daniel drained the remains of his tea and stood up purposefully.

"I'm afraid I have to go in. I won't be long." He hesitated before continuing. "My boat sails from Dun Laoghaire at seven this evening. I'll be home later to say goodbye."

Irene looked up in dismay. "You mean, you are really going through with this?"

Daniel stared straight ahead. "Yes, Mother."

Irene put her elbow on the table and cradled her forehead with the palm of her hand. "Daniel, please don't do this to me."

"Nothing will change my mind, Mother."

A tear plopped onto the tablecloth and Irene dabbed her eyes with the crumpled handkerchief. Daniel knelt on the floor beside her chair and put his arm around his weeping mother. "I don't want to hurt you, Mother. I know I said some terrible things to you last night and I am truly sorry. I just want to be with Anna, and I wish you could accept it."

Irene was gripped by a fresh wave of tears as she realised that there was nothing she could do to stop her son from making such a terrible mistake. She listened to his words but made no attempt to argue any further. She had made her position more than clear. Daniel stood up and looked down at the crown of her head that was hanging in sorrow and felt a lump in his throat.

"I'll be home later," he said softly and left the room.

* * *

The trams had stopped running and as Daniel walked towards O'Connell Bridge, he began to wonder if he had made the right decision in coming so close to the gunfire. Every few minutes, a fresh burst of artillery exploded along the quays, and Daniel quickened his pace in the direction of the shop. All the shops on Sackville Street were in darkness and remained closed for business until further notice.

"Where are you going?" A soldier from the Free State Army approached Daniel, putting his hand out to stop him going any further.

"I'm Daniel Jacob, from Jacob's shoe store down there." Daniel pointed.

"You can't go down there," the soldier said, blocking Daniel's path.

Just then another explosion came from the Four

Courts, rocking the ground beneath them.

The soldier turned and looked up the quays, then turned back impatiently, anxious to get back to the action. "Look, no one is allowed up here today. Go on home."

Daniel stepped closer and ran his hand through his hair. "I have to get something in the office," he pleaded. "It's urgent. I'll only be five minutes."

The rat-a-tat of machine-gun fire rang out in the air. The soldier frowned at Daniel's persistence and looked around to see if anyone was watching them.

"Please!" Daniel implored.

"Go on then," the soldier said with a toss of his head. "Be quick and stay on the other side of the road."

Daniel broke into a run and began to cross to the other side of the street.

"Must be very important," the soldier shouted after him.

Daniel looked back and smiled. "It's my fiancée's wedding dress!"

The soldier gave a comical look of comprehension. "Ah, why didn't you say that in the first place!"

Daniel held on to his hat and ran as fast as he could until he reached the porch of Jacob's. He let himself in the front door and hurried up the stairs, taking them in twos and threes. Just as he reached the top step, the boom of another explosion sent him flying across the top landing. The whole building seemed to sway with the shock of the blast. He picked himself up and put a shaking hand on the wall to steady himself, but a second later he was thrown back down again as another explosion burst through the air. Daniel stayed down on the floor on all fours and waited for another blast to throw him, but nothing happened. Picking himself up slowly, he pushed open the office door and jerked backwards in fright as he saw Seán Barry scrambling to his feet.

The two men stared at each other in stunned silence. Seán eyes blinked furiously as he tried to get his bearings. He had fallen into a deep sleep during the night, surrounded by the sound of gunfire which mingled with his dreams. The shock of being thrown from the couch so suddenly and seeing Daniel standing at the door made Seán think that he might still be dreaming.

"What the hell are you doing here?" Daniel demanded as he stepped into the room.

Seán looked around like a trapped animal.

Daniel looked at him and sneered. "I thought you'd be up in the Four Courts defending your precious country, or did it all get a bit too much for you"?

Seán stood up slowly and Daniel saw the look of raw hatred in his eyes.

"Did the men with big guns frighten you?" Daniel continued contemptuously. "Perhaps you should just stick to beating up girls? It's a lot easier isn't it?"

Seán clenched his fists but remained silent. Daniel brushed by him and went into his office. He pulled the suitcase out from under his desk. He pressed down the catches and locked them before dragging it out to the main office. Seán was standing beside the couch, putting on his jacket.

"Going somewhere?" Seán looked over at the suitcase and spoke with a newly found confidence.

"As a matter of fact I am," answered Daniel as he went to open the door out to the hall. "You'll be glad to hear that I'm leaving tonight, and you may as well know that Anna is coming with me. We intend to be married as soon as possible."

Seán's mouth fell open.

"That's right. So the beating she was given was all in vain, because it didn't stop her. She's coming with me and nothing will get in our way."

As Daniel spoke, Seán's face contorted into a malicious grin.

"You're going nowhere with her, you uppity little Brit," he said under his breath.

Daniel shrugged his shoulders impassively and

turned to go down the stairs. As his foot landed on the first step he heard a click behind him and turned to see Seán pointing a revolver at his face.

"Put that thing away," he said, trying to disguise the quiver of fear in his voice.

"My sister is engaged to Joe Maguire, did she forget to mention that to you?" Seán's lips twisted into an ugly grimace as he spoke.

Daniel shook his head and tried to reason with Seán. "You know that's not true. You know she broke it off with him months ago. Why won't you accept it?"

Seán's face had turned to stone and his hands shook as he gripped the trigger.

Daniel clutched the suitcase tightly and turned to leave.

"You take one more step and I'll blow your head off," Seán shouted hysterically.

Daniel stopped and turned around slowly. He took a step towards Seán and raised his hand in a gesture of surrender. "Put down the gun," he said evenly, taking another step forward.

"Get back," Seán shouted, but Daniel continued to walk towards him. Seán closed his eyes and squeezed his finger around the trigger of the gun. A deafening shot rang out through the air, echoing off the walls in the narrow stairwell. Daniel's head snapped back for a second and his body swayed with the force of the bullet. He lost his grip on the suitcase and it began to fall slowly down the staircase with a series of dull thuds. Daniel's eyes flickered, he put his hand up to his head and felt the gaping hole in his temple. He stepped backwards, losing his footing on the first step. With both arms outstretched, his body took flight, sailing through the air until the hard crack of his skull sounded on the tiles below.

Chapter 26

Anna drank the remains of her tea and looked around the empty kitchen. On the ground beside her feet was a bag containing the few belongings that she had not put into the suitcase. The shelling of the Four Courts had continued all day, and the explosions had echoed through the city like thunder. The piece of writing paper lay in front of her, and Anna stared down at the blank whiteness wondering what last words she could find to leave to her father. Her trembling hands reached out for the paper and she pulled it towards her slowly. There were no words that would explain what she was about to do, but her father's show of brutality had made it a little easier for her. Anna bent her head and with grim determination began to write.

Dear Dada,
I am leaving today and will never return to this house.
My life is with Daniel, and there is nothing you can do that will ever stop me from being with him. My heart is broken, but you have forced me to make this decision.
I am praying for Seán's safety. Tell him I said goodbye.
Anna

She picked up the letter and folded it quickly, not wanting to dwell on it for too long, for fear that she would change her mind. The few lines seemed so little to say, but no amount of words would ever be enough to make her father understand, and she couldn't walk away without leaving him some form of farewell. She lifted the sugar bowl from the middle of the table and slid the note underneath it. After allowing herself one last look around the empty kitchen, she picked her bag up off the floor and walked out the door. At the hall table, she put her hat on, pulling the wide brim down to hide the bruising that had turned a purplish yellow colour around her left eye. The only way to disguise her swollen lower lip was to keep her head bent as she walked.

The streets around Portobello were unusually quiet. The huge explosions in the Four Courts had blown every document in the Records Office to the four corners of the city. Flurries of grey cinders and burnt-edged pieces of paper swirled through the air like confetti. People had stayed in their houses, away from the war that was being waged in the city. Anna approached Leeson Street Bridge at five minutes to four. She looked around for Daniel but he was not there. She walked over the bridge and back again, looking out all the time for the cab that he might arrive in – for how else would they be getting to Dun Laoghaire? After half an hour of waiting, Anna began to grow anxious – she knew something was wrong. On the bridge, she stopped and looked down the canal. A low mist clung to the water, giving it a ghostly grey stillness. Her hands rested on the cold granite of the bridge and a deathly chill shot through her. Something was wrong, she could feel it in every bone, something was wrong. For almost an hour, Anna stood motionless and stared into the canal, unable to move.

"Are you alright, Miss?"

Anna swung around, startled by the closeness of the voice. Behind her, was a man about the same age as her father, his head cocked to one side as he looked at Anna with concern.

"You've been here a long time – are you lost?" He tilted his head a little more and looked directly at Anna's face, his eyes widening as he registered her injuries. "My God, are you hurt?"

Anna put her hand to her mouth and cast her eyes downwards in shame. What did she look like to this gentleman, standing alone on the bridge with her face so battered and bruised.

"No, I'm not lost," she said.

"Where do you live?" the gentleman asked.

"Just over there," Anna said pointing up the canal.

"Well, you should go home now, Miss. The streets are not safe today, especially not for young ladies."

Anna looked back up Leeson Street but there was still no sign of Daniel and in her heart she knew that he was not coming.

"What time is it?" she asked, as she bent to pick her bag from the ground.

The gentleman pulled out his pocket watch and flicked it open. "It's ten minutes past five," he said. A large plop of rain fell directly onto the face of the watch and he closed it quickly and put it back inside his waistcoat. He put his hand out and looked up at the darkening clouds.

Anna felt the thud of a heavy raindrop as it hit the crown of her hat.

"You'll get along now, Miss, won't you?" he asked,

still surveying the gathering rain-clouds. "It's going to lash."

"Yes," Anna said. "I'm going home now."

The rain started to clatter down on them. Huge drops like silver knitting needles bounced off the gentleman's hat as he stood on the bridge and watched Anna walk away – her head bent low against the summer downpour.

She walked through the river of rain that had gathered on the path outside her front door. Her feet were wet through, and a steady trickle of water poured from the rim of her hat down the back of her neck. Her heart felt as cold as stone as she turned the key in the door, entering the house she had only hours before left forever. She walked down the hall and pushed the door open into the empty kitchen. In the middle of the table, still in the same position she had left it, was her letter lying under the sugar bowl. Anna picked it up and crumpled it in her hand then she turned around and walked slowly upstairs to her bedroom. Her sodden clothes were stuck to her skin and she peeled them off, leaving them in a bundle on the floor, and pulled on a flannel nightgown. The bag she had packed earlier that morning was also soaked through. Reaching inside she felt around and pulled her mother's photograph out and replaced it on her dressing table. Only then did she realise that her teeth were clattering together with the cold. An icy feeling spread throughout her insides, making her shiver uncontrollably.

Anna pulled back her bedclothes and climbed wearily into bed. Never in her life had she felt as desolate as she did at that moment.

★   ★   ★

Anna waited to hear her father leave the house before she went downstairs the following morning. This should have been the first day of her new life in Edinburgh with Daniel. Anna couldn't face going downstairs to eat breakfast with her father, as if nothing had happened. Her world was falling apart and she doubted whether she could maintain her silence for very much longer. Her sleep had been fitful and was broken several times, with nightmares in which she ran through streets that were empty, searching for Daniel. At her bedroom window, she watched her father as he walked down the road with short purposeful strides. He had been spending hours on end, pacing the streets around the Four Courts in the hope of hearing any news, or perhaps getting a glimpse of his son.

Anna dressed and went down to the kitchen to make herself some tea. She had not eaten since the same time yesterday and was weak from lack of food. The gas flame flickered under the kettle as she absently spooned the tea leaves into the pot. The familiar rattle of a key in the front door made her stop what she was doing. She stood still, resting her hand on the lid of the tea caddy. The heavy steps plodded towards the kitchen and Anna strained to hear if they were Seán's or her father's. The kitchen door opened and Mr Barry stepped in, carrying the morning newspaper under his arm. Anna saw him flinch slightly as he looked at the bruises on her face that had fused together into a mottled yellow pattern. She turned away quickly but felt a certain satisfaction at witnessing his shame.

"Are you not going to work?" she asked.

Mr Barry unfolded his newspaper and threw it on the kitchen table.

"How can I?" he said flatly. "The city is in turmoil. The Four Courts has been shelled to smithereens, the boys have all surrendered, and the ones that weren't killed have been taken to Kilmainham jail."

Anna turned her head to look at the picture of the burnt-out remains of the Four Courts.

"Jesus," she whispered under her breath. "Is there any news of Seán?"

Mr Barry sank down into his armchair and

exhaled loudly. "I don't know. They've printed the names of those arrested, but Seán's name isn't there. He's not one of the injured or dead either. No one knows where he is."

"What about Joe?"

"I heard he escaped with a few others – I just hope to God Seán was with him," Mr Barry said, keeping his eyes averted, unable to meet his daughter's gaze.

"Will you have a cup of tea?" she asked.

Mr Barry stared into the empty fire grate and nodded his head. "I will."

They sat without talking and sipped their tea, both of them distracted with their own worries. The hot liquid scalded Anna's lip every time she put the cup to her mouth. The heat of the tea mingled with the dried blood made her feel nauseous and she pushed the cup away. Neither of them could find a way to break through the silence that hung so heavily between them. Anna forced herself up from the table and walked over to the door.

"Anna!" her father said sharply.

Anna stopped but did not look around.

"I'm truly sorry," he whispered.

Anna stood for a few seconds facing the door and let his words bounce off her back. It was not the cuts and bruises that she could not forgive him for – like any scars, they would fade and be forgotten about in time. But no amount of contrition on his part would be enough to ever heal the emotional wounds that had cut her so much deeper. When she was sure that her father had nothing more to say, she reached for the door handle and left the room noiselessly.

Back in her bedroom, she paced the floor and tried to think of all the possibilities that could have prevented Daniel from meeting her the day before. The clawing feeling of despair that had gripped her yesterday afternoon had returned to torment her. For a while, when she had woken early that morning, she had convinced herself that there must have been a simple explanation as to why Daniel had let her down – but now that seemed quite unlikely. Anna stopped suddenly and clasped a hand to her forehead. Perhaps, she thought excitedly, it was Mr Jacob. Wasn't it possible that he could have taken a bad turn and Daniel had been delayed at the hospital? Anna felt a glimmer of optimism and convinced herself that this was the only possible reason for their broken arrangement. He would hardly take the chance of calling to her house again and Anna wracked her brain to think of where she could find him. He could be waiting in the office, or have left a message there, she thought, as she hurried downstairs to the hall. The hat she had worn the day before was still too wet to wear – she threw it aside and grabbed another one from the peg on the wall. Her hands shook as she secured it hastily with a pin. The front door closed quietly behind her and she rushed away from the house before her father could run out behind her asking questions. At O'Connell Street Bridge she could see the thick black smoke that rose from the shell of the Four Courts. The heavy smell of artillery fire hung in the air. A barricade had been put across the top of Sackville Street and no one was allowed through. Anna approached the barricade and waved to a soldier that stood smoking a cigarette a few paces away. He threw his butt on the ground and walked towards her.

"No one's allowed down here, Miss."

"But I need to get to work," Anna said, pulling the shop keys from her handbag as proof.

"Have you not heard?" he said with pointed sarcasm. "There's a war going on. No one's working in those buildings." He took a closer look at her face. "You look as though you were doing a bit of fighting yourself."

Anna ignored his remark and looked over his shoulder, down towards the shop. There was no one on the street and she suddenly felt very foolish, trying to get to work when the city was in such chaos. Her hopes faded as she realised that Daniel certainly wouldn't be waiting for her and she looked up at the soldier and forced a smile.

"I work in Jacob's," she said, putting the keys back into her bag. "I suppose there's no point in trying to get into work today."

The soldier's face dropped at the mention of Jacob's and he looked down at his boots. "No, you'd better go on home," he muttered, and walked back to where he had come from.

Anna turned back in the direction of home and tried to think of how she would make contact with Daniel. She could call to his house, but her heart sank as she thought of how Irene would react to Anna calling at their door with a beaten-up face. God knows, she was low enough in his mother's estimation without allowing herself to sink any further.

Anna turned the key in the door and was met by her father. He stood in the hall, his face set in a fierce expression, and waited for her to come inside. He turned an envelope over in his hands and looked at it closely, before handing it over to Anna.

"This came for you," he said.

Anna snatched it from him and stared down at it.

Mr Barry lifted his short thick forefinger and pointed at the telegram. "If that's from who I think it is, I'll burn it."

Anna ignored him and ripped the envelope open. Her eyes scanned the letter and, at first glance, she could see it had been sent by the Jacob family. The bold black print that imparted the message of Daniel's death didn't make sense to her, and she read it again carefully. Anna's hands began to shake as she tried to focus on the print that swam before her eyes.

Mr Barry stood behind Anna and tried to read the telegram from over her shoulder.

Anna put her hand on the hall table and felt the ground being pulled from under her feet. Mr Barry snatched the telegram from her and swung his head from side to side as his eyes read the message.

A deep moan came from Anna's throat and forced its way up through her windpipe. Mr Barry crushed the telegram in his hand and put his arm around her.

"It's alright, pet," he said, his voice thick with remorse as he watched his daughter reeling with shock.

The touch of his hand on her shoulder made Anna suddenly came to her senses, as if she had been struck with a bolt of lightning. With a sudden movement, she straightened up and shook her father's hand away.

"Don't touch me!" she screamed loudly, causing Mr Barry to jump back with fright.

He squeezed the crumpled telegram in his fist and let it drop to the floor. "Anna, calm down," he said soothingly.

"Don't come near me!" her voice was shrill with hysteria. "Don't touch me!"

Mr Barry stepped closer, keeping his tone even and calm. "You've had a shock, Anna, come down to the kitchen and I'll make you some tea." He put his hand out to her but she took a step back and refused it. He took another step closer and Anna drew out and slapped him hard across the face.

"Get away from me!" she screamed again, pushing herself back against the wall.

Mr Barry's hand shot up to his stinging cheek and he glared at his daughter in disbelief.

Anna edged away from him, her eyes searching the floor. "He can't be dead," she whispered fearfully as she dropped to her knees and grabbed the crumpled telegram. Opening it out, she read it again and Mr Barry looked on helplessly as she began to sob uncontrollably.

Chapter 27

A chink of white daylight fell across the floor of Anna's bedroom. Outside, she could hear the sounds of the children as they played in the street, their voices muffled and far away – they seemed to come from another world. It was after midday and Anna had slept on and off since the night before. It was all she wanted to do, sleep and never have to face another day again. It had been three days since Daniel's death and Anna had spent most of the time in bed. She had not spoken to her father or enquired of Seán's whereabouts. He had not come home, and Anna was too wrapped up in her own grief to think of where he might be. There had been a mention of Daniel's murder in the newspaper. It said he had been shot by an intruder on the premises of Jacob's shoe shop. Anna pulled herself out of the warm cocoon that her bed had become and, without washing or doing her hair, she pulled on a dress and went down to the kitchen. Her father's dirty breakfast dishes lay scattered on the table and Anna cleared them away into the sink. The tea she made tasted bitter and she pushed the slice of bread she had cut for herself away – she had barely eaten for the past few days and felt sick just looking at the food.

A knock on the front door made her heart skip a beat and she ran out to the hall, thinking for a second that it might be Daniel, that perhaps the past week had just been a bad dream. Through the front door glass she could make out the figure of a woman dressed in black.

Anna opened the door and found herself face to face with Granny Jacob. Behind her, a cab waited in the street, its engine still running. Anna had not seen anyone from the Jacob family since Daniel's death, she had not been informed of the funeral arrangements and had thought it better not to attend.

Granny Jacob was dressed from head to toe in black. The sorrow she had experienced in the days following Daniel's death had stripped her of her usual fierce and haughty demeanour. She stood in front of Anna, weighed down with her immense grief, and Anna was once again gripped by the cold reality of what had happened. Being alone most of the time in the house, she had avoided the pain of speaking about Daniel's death and at times even managed to persuade herself that it hadn't happened.

Anna stepped aside and silently gestured for Granny Jacob to come in.

Granny Jacob turned and instructed the cab driver to wait for her. Anna led the old woman into the parlour and pointed to a chair.

"I won't sit down. This will not take long."

Anna looked at Granny Jacob and could feel the tears pricking the back of her eyes.

Granny Jacob opened her handbag and took out a small velvet box. "Daniel was carrying this the day he was killed. He would have wanted you to have it." She held out the box for Anna to take.

Anna reached across and carefully lifted it from Granny Jacob's trembling hand. She walked over to the couch and sat down holding the box out in front of her. When she opened it and saw the diamond ring, she breathed in sharply and could feel her throat constricting.

"It was to be your engagement ring."

Anna stared down at the ring, unable to speak.

Granny Jacob's bottom lip trembled as she looked across at Anna.

"I am leaving Dublin in a few days." Her voice grew thinner. "I have lost a grandson and my own son will not live for much longer." She put a gloved hand inside her handbag and brought out a handkerchief to dab her eyes. "I know about your wedding plans. I know Daniel loved you very much, he told me so. You were both prepared to give up everything for each other." She looked across and pointed towards Anna's yellowing bruises. "He told me what your father did."

Anna put her hand up to her face. She had forgotten about the fading bruises and had gone beyond caring how she might look to anyone else.

Granny Jacob blew her nose loudly. "Now," she said, sniffing back her tears. "This is what I came to tell you. I think you have nothing left here, and I am certainly finished with this place. I return to England in a few days and if you want, you can come with me. I am getting old and the factory could do with a girl like you to run it."

Anna listened to her, all the time never taking her eyes off the ring. She lifted her head slowly and her eyes met Granny Jacob's intense stare.

"Why would you ask me now? After all that's

happened," Anna asked, breathing shallowly to stop herself losing control of the eerie calmness that had settled over her during the past few days. Granny Jacob had brought the true horror of Daniel's death back to Anna, and the well of anger and bitter injustice she had hidden in the depths of her being were now clawing at the back of her throat, fighting to get out.

Another tear glistened in Granny Jacob's eye. "I am honouring Daniel's memory. I give you my blessing now, when it is too late. But it is all I can think of to do." A large tear fell from her eye making a wet line in the powder on her cheek. "You don't have to answer me now. Think about it for a few days and let me know," she said in a quivering voice. "I sail for England on Monday morning."

Anna walked over to Granny Jacob and touched her arm gently. "Thank you," she gasped through her tears. For the next few minutes neither woman said anything. They stood together, and wept bitter tears for the loss of a man that bound them together.

At the front door Granny Jacob turned to Anna. "I have the suitcase you left in the office, it still has all of your things in it. If you don't come, I will have it returned to you."

Granny Jacob walked out to where the cab was waiting and turned to Anna as she opened the door.

"Please let me help you," she said, patting Anna's arm with her black gloved hand.

Then she turned and climbed slowly into the cab, looking straight ahead as the car moved away.

★ ★ ★

Later that night as Anna prepared for bed she opened the black box that Granny Jacob had given to her and took out the diamond ring. Its brilliant shine seemed to light up the room and she slipped it onto her finger and held it out to admire. Around her neck was the gold chain which held the miraculous medal that her mother had given to her as a child. Anna reached behind her neck and undid the chain, holding it open she slid the diamond ring onto the chain beside the medal and fixed it about her neck again. As she lay in bed and waited for sleep to come, her hand fumbled for the ring and brought it up to her mouth. The rough edges of the diamond felt cold as she pressed it against her lips. "Daniel," she whispered into the darkness, "Daniel my sweetheart, we're engaged at last."

★ ★ ★

The last rays of evening sunshine slowly retreated

from the parlour as evening began to fall. The ticking of the clock on the mantelpiece seemed to fill the room with a steady hypnotic rhythm. Anna sat in the armchair, her hands neatly folded on her lap and gazed ahead at nothing. Ever since Granny Jacob's visit, Anna had fallen into a deep torpor, unable to move from one room to another without summoning up every bit of strength she had left. Down in the kitchen, she could hear the sound of her father's chair being pushed out from under him. They had not spoken since the telegram arrived – both moved about the house avoiding the possibility of a conversation. There had been no news of Seán, and Anna knew that her father was out of his mind with worry, but she was too paralysed with her own thoughts to think about anyone else.

The parlour door opened softly and Mr Barry stepped into the room and looked over anxiously at Anna.

"Would you like me to get you something to eat?" he asked.

Anna shook her head.

Mr Barry stood by the door and thrust his hands deep into his trouser pockets. "Anna, you have to eat something. You'll make yourself sick if you go on any longer like this."

"I'm not hungry, Dada," Anna whispered. It had

been days since she had spoken and her voice sounded weak and distant.

Her father sighed and moved across to the window. "Still no news of Seán," he said, looking up the street as if he expected to see his son out there.

He turned to face Anna, anticipating her reaction – a sympathetic glance, a word to express her concern – but she stared back at him impassively.

"I'm going around to Lawlor's to see if anyone might have heard any news. I'll be back shortly." Then, with a certain amount of trepidation, he added, "Sure maybe we'll have something to eat together later on."

Anna shook her head. "I think I'll go back to bed now. I'll leave your tea ready for you."

Mr Barry's face dropped at her reply. "Fair enough," he said abruptly and closed the door behind him.

On hearing her father leave the house, Anna let her stiff shoulders relax and she sank back into the chair, lulled by the ticking of the clock.

Later on, in the kitchen, Anna placed the dinner she had made for her father in the warm oven. It was only seven o'clock, too early to sleep, but Anna did not want to risk being up when he returned from the pub. Besides, she was feeling tired again. She had done nothing but sleep for the past few days, and with each bout of sleep her exhaustion seemed to grow heavier. She gathered her things and prepared to turn in for the night.

Up in her room, Anna drew the curtains. The bedspread was still warm to the touch from the evening sun and she lay down on top of it and turned her face to the wall. Her finger ran along the outline of the sprig of flowers on the wallpaper which had become so familiar to her, and she blinked slowly as she tried to clear her mind.

A sharp banging woke her and Anna opened her eyes and gazed around the room. It was almost dark. She had fallen asleep fully clothed on top of the bedclothes. Again, the door-knocker sounded and Anna stood up and slipped on her shoes. Her father must have forgotten his key, she thought, as she walked down to the darkened hall.

"Is that you, Dada?" she asked as she approached the hall door.

"No," came a deep voice. "Anna, open the door."

Anna could feel her heart quicken as she recognised Joe's voice. She opened the door and Joe stood there wide-eyed and stepped into the hall before she could say anything. Once inside, he pushed the door closed behind him. They both stood in the dim light and looked at each other. Anna went to the hall table and lit the gas light above it. Down the hall, the kitchen was in darkness, which meant that her father had not returned. She walked back over to Joe and took a closer look at him. His arm was held in a grubby-looking sling, and he looked worn out. His hair stood on end, and around his eyes were dark circles that made him look as if he hadn't slept for weeks.

"I can't stay, there's a car waiting for me at the top of the road."

"Is Seán with you?"

"No," Joe answered solemnly.

"No one knows where he is – Dada's searched everywhere."

"The lads that escaped got out of town quickly – maybe he's one of them," Joe said hopefully.

Anna pointed to his arm. "Are you hurt?"

He looked down at the dirty sling. "I'll live," he said with a strained smile.

He looked at Anna in such a way that she became conscious of her dishevelled appearance. With both hands raised behind her neck she tried to gather her hair back into the loosened combs.

"Dada's up in Lawlor's."

Joe took a step towards Anna. "I came to see you. Last week when I saw Seán, he said that you wanted to see me. He was going to bring me a letter you had for me."

"What?" Anna patted her hair into place and tried to make sense of what Joe was saying.

Joe reached across and grabbed her hand in his. "I know everything, Anna. I know you were seeing the fella you work for, but Seán told me you'd finished up with him and I'm prepared to put it all behind us now."

Anna pulled her hand free from his grip and walked away from him, into the dim circle of light. Her hands rested on the lace cloth that covered the top of the hall table. "You don't know," she said faintly.

Joe moved towards her and went to put his arms around her waist but Anna swung around to face him. "Stop, Joe," she pleaded.

Joe's eyes narrowed. He reached over and caught her face between his hands and turned her towards the light. When Anna realised what he was doing, she cast her eyes downwards as he examined the fading bruises.

"Jesus," he groaned.

Anna struggled out of his hold and retreated back into the shadows.

"Was it your da?" he asked, struggling to contain his anger.

"It doesn't matter," Anna said, staring at the floor.

"Was it all lies, what Seán said, about you wanting

to see me?" Joe put his hand against the wall and prepared himself for her answer.

"Yes," Anna whispered.

He looked up at the ceiling and swallowed hard.

"You'd better go now," Anna said, but both of them stiffened as they heard the click of footsteps outside the door. Joe looked around frantically and bolted past Anna down the darkened hall. Anna held her breath, until she heard the familiar rattle of her father's key in the lock.

"It's alright. It only Dada," Anna whispered over her shoulder to him.

Mr Barry stepped into the hall, bringing with him the sour smell of stout on his breath. His eyes opened wide in disbelief as he saw Joe appear, like a ghost, from the end of the hall.

"Jesus, Joe," he said, reaching out to touch him, to make sure he was real. "What are you doing here? Is Seán with you?" he asked, looking around.

"No," Joe answered gruffly. "I don't know where he is."

Mr Barry lifted a hand to his forehead and shook his head. "No one knows where he is. It's like he vanished into thin air. When did you see him last?"

Joe looked at Mr Barry and said nothing.

"Please, Joe, tell me, I'm beside myself with worry," Mr Barry pleaded.

Joe shrugged his shoulders. "We left the Four Courts and got as far as a house in Mountjoy, but it wasn't safe. I was wounded too badly to go any further and the people in the house looked after me, but Seán went on. I've been hiding out in a back room for the past week, I haven't seen anyone. I'm being shifted down to Wexford tonight. A few of the lads are down there, maybe Seán is one of them."

"Where did he go when he left you?" Mr Barry asked, getting excited at the prospect of even the tiniest morsel of information.

Joe looked down at his feet and mumbled. Mr Barry shot Anna a look that told her to leave them alone. Anna silently obeyed and began to walk slowly towards the stairs.

Joe continued in a hushed voice and Anna strained to hear what he was saying.

"He needed somewhere to hide out for the night, and, I shouldn't be telling you this but he had a set of keys for Jacob's. That's where he said he was going."

Anna heard this as she started to climb the stairs and every muscle in her body froze as the words reached her ears.

"Sshh," Mr Barry said to Joe.

Anna turned and with a trembling voice asked, "What night was that?"

"Wednesday, that's the last time I saw him," Joe

answered, oblivious to Mr Barry's frantic attempt to stop him.

Slowly Anna descended the stairs and moved towards the two men. "But that's when Daniel was shot!" A slight note of hysteria had crept into her voice.

"He was shot?" Joe asked incredulously.

Mr Barry pinched the bridge of his nose and squeezed his eyes shut.

"He was shot dead by an intruder," Anna cried.

Mr Barry jumped in to defend his son. "Now, Anna, we don't know anything for sure. Don't go upsetting yourself."

"Did Seán have a gun?" Anna shouted at Joe, ignoring her father.

Joe looked at Anna with a pained expression. "I'm sorry, Anna," he said.

Anna took hold of his jacket lapels and shook him roughly. "Did he have a gun when he left you?" she shrieked.

Mr Barry put his hand across his mouth and walked down the hall, unable to hear what Joe was about to say.

Joe stared down at Anna and their eyes locked.

"Tell me, Joe," she gasped, as the tears rolled down her cheeks.

"Yes, he did." His words echoed through the

narrow hallway.

Anna let go her grip on him and breathed in sharply. She turned from Joe to face her father who stood like a statue with his back to her – without looking back, he gripped the banisters and walked slowly up to his room. Anna turned her face to the wall and rested her forehead against its soothing coolness. Hot angry tears ran down her cheeks as she closed her eyes and wept.

"Anna, I'm so sorry. I would never have come here tonight if I'd known."

Anna sniffed loudly and nodded her head. "I know."

For a few moments Joe stood and watched helplessly as the only woman he had ever loved grieved for the loss of another man. He reached out to touch her, but just as his fingers brushed her trembling shoulder he withdrew his hand – knowing anything he said would be hopelessly inadequate to bridge the distance between them.

"I'll go now," he said and turned to open the door.

"Goodbye, Joe," Anna whispered hoarsely.

The door closed quietly behind him and Anna was left alone. As she listened to his footsteps retreat on the pavement outside she was filled with a sense of panic, and knew that she would have to talk to him before he left. Outside on the street, she ran as fast as she could to catch up with him. Her combs fell on to the pavement and her hair fell down in tangles around her shoulders. Joe turned around in fright on hearing the running footsteps behind him.

"Anna," he said with a glimmer of hope in his eyes.

"Joe, will you do something for me?" she asked, wiping the tears from her face.

"Yes."

"I'm going to England tomorrow. Daniel's grandmother has offered me a job running the factory in Leeds, and I'm taking it."

A faint frown spread across his face. "What do you want me to do?"

"I want you to tell Dada after I'm gone. I'm not telling him, he'll only try to stop me."

"So you're just taking off like that, without saying anything?"

"Yes," she answered.

Joe stared into the canal and thought for a few minutes. "Alright," he said quietly. "I'll tell him."

"Thanks," Anna whispered.

Joe looked down at her and brushed a piece of hair from her face. "Anna," he said, stepping closer. "Please don't go."

Anna shook her head. "Don't, Joe," she pleaded.

"We could start again. Put all this behind us. I was

thinking that maybe we could go to America and start a new life together."

Anna looked into his eyes and saw the Joe she had once fallen in love with, and wished with all her heart that she could put her arms around him and say yes, and really mean it. But if Anna was certain of one thing, it was that her heart did not belong to Joe Maguire.

"No, Joe," she said softly.

Joe's face seemed to collapse inwards.

The horn of the car parked on Portobello Bridge sounded twice and the driver waved a fist out the window, indicating his impatience.

Anna kissed Joe on the cheek and stepped back. "You'd better get going," she said looking up towards the car. "I wish you well, Joe."

Joe blinked back his tears and accepted that this was her final word. He squared his shoulders and let his eyes rest on her one last time. "Good luck in England, Anna, I really mean that. I'll get word to your da in a few days." As soon as these words were said, he turned and ran towards the waiting car. When he reached it, he climbed into the back seat and looked out the window at Anna, who was still standing on the canal bank looking across at him. He raised his hand and waved to her as the driver revved the engine and sped away.

Chapter 28

Granny Jacob pulled her sable stole tightly around her shoulders and shivered against the chilly morning air that blew in from the sea. The cab driver swore under his breath as he pulled the heavy trunks from the back of the car. The old woman's ferocious demeanour drew stares from the other passengers as they hurried past her towards the ticket office. With slow deliberate movements, she pulled off a glove and felt about in her purse for the cab fare.

"Careful with that," she barked, as the cab driver struggled with the weight of the heaviest trunk. "Don't bang it about like that."

He threw her a murderous stare and began to mutter furiously again.

"Now go and find someone to carry these things," she said, waving a finger over the luggage. The driver stamped off in search of a porter and Granny Jacob buried the soft folds of her chin into the warmth of her collar.

At first, it was only the shape of the head that brought a glimmer of hope – the old woman's eyes were too weak and she could not properly distinguish her from the other passers-by. But, as she drew nearer, her face came into focus and Granny Jacob's heart soared with relief.

Anna had seen Granny Jacob first and she smiled nervously as the old woman caught sight of her and waved her purse in the air.

"You're coming?"

Anna nodded tensely.

"Good, because that stupid driver will never find a porter. Here," she pointed to the heavier trunk, "you take that and I'll take the other one."

The air was filled with the shrill cry of gulls as they wheeled through the steely grey sky overhead and for a few moments Anna did not move. She stood in the same spot staring down at the luggage as if the sight of it reminded her of why she had come.

"Well, come along, we don't have all day, the boat

sails in half an hour."

The two women took hold of the trunks and hauled them down the sloped path towards the boat that was waiting to take Anna Barry to another life.

*   *   *

Anna sailed for England in July 1922. The crossing was rough and she was sick from the moment the boat left Dun Laoghaire. The endless swell of the English Channel made her wish that she had never set foot out of Ireland. Anna had never been on a boat before and, as she watched the last piece of land disappear, the sickness worsened. Granny Jacob insisted that she sip brandy from the silver hip flask she produced from her handbag, but it only succeeded in making Anna retch.

"Go and walk around on deck," she told Anna. "The fresh air will make you feel better."

Outside, the seagulls screeched and circled above Anna's head as she clenched the boat railings and tried to control her breathing – but her mouth filled with acrid saliva and she vomited all over her shoes. By the time they reached Holyhead, Anna was barely able to put one foot in front of the other. Granny Jacob took her by the arm and steered her down the gangway, towards the waiting car that had been sent from Leeds to collect them. Once inside the car, Anna leaned her head against the window and slept for the entire journey.

The house in Leeds was called Bradley Hall and was bigger by far than any house Anna had ever seen before. She woke with a start, just as they turned into the sweeping avenue that led up to the house. Between the oak trees that lined the drive-way, Anna could make out the shape of the vast ivy-clad mansion.

"Well," Granny Jacob shouted over the noisy engine, "do you like my home?"

But Anna was too weak to say anything. She stared ahead blankly at the enormous house as it came into view.

A maid dressed in a black and white uniform showed Anna to her bedroom at the top of the house. When Anna was left alone, she fell onto the bed fully clothed and slept again until the following day.

Granny Jacob let Anna have a few days to find her feet and gather her strength before introducing her to the staff at the factory. All traces of bruising had at last disappeared from her face, and Anna felt both nervous and excited as she entered the noisy factory floor. It was like a visit from the queen herself and Anna saw the fear the old woman instilled in each employee. As they climbed the stairs to the office, Anna could feel her heart thumping as she was about to meet Peter Jacob, Daniel's older brother, who no doubt had heard all about her.

Peter was sitting at his desk and stood to attention as they walked in to meet him. He went over to his grandmother and kissed her cheek obediently.

"Say hello to Anna," Granny Jacob said, pulling Anna over towards the two of them. "You two will be working alongside each other from now on."

Peter's face flushed. He reached out and shook Anna's hand, squeezing her fingers together tightly.

Anna looked up and him and smiled meekly. He looked nothing like Daniel. He did not have the fair skin or delicate features of his younger brother. Peter was portly and slightly ruddy of complexion, and certainly did not possess the self-assurance that had come so naturally to Daniel. Anna could see tiny beads of sweat on his forehead as the three of them stood there in awkward silence.

"Well, what are you standing about for?" Granny Jacob shouted over the noise of the factory machinery. "Show Anna where her desk is and help her to get settled in."

Peter nodded and pointed to the desk in the corner that had been brought up for her that morning.

Anna turned to Granny Jacob with a look of bewilderment. "I'm starting now?"

Granny Jacob had led her to believe that this visit was only an introduction and she was not at all prepared to begin a day's work.

Granny Jacob tilted her head to one side. "Well, of course you start now. Why else did we come?"

"If you follow me, Anna. I'll show you where everything is," Peter stuttered.

"I'll be off then," Granny said, and with a sweep of her skirt she was gone.

Epilogue

Leeds, 2006

The scene is set and Bradley Hall looks magnificent. We have planned for this party all year and have been rewarded with a perfect evening. Glass lanterns hang from the oak trees that line the driveway, giving the impression of a giant glow-worm in the dusky twilight. The sides of the marquee billow in the gentle summer breeze. Through the open bedroom window, I can hear the excited laughter of the catering staff as they lay out the food and drink.

Ben, my oldest son, has arrived and together with his father is helping the band to set up the music in the orchard. His wife Maria and my two granddaughters are in the room across the hall, fussing over what to wear. My younger son, Nigel, is late – as he is for everything. But he phoned earlier and assured me that he was on the road and would be with us no later than seven.

There is a time to celebrate, and tonight our time has come. The idea came to my husband one evening last winter while we were sitting by the fire just before bedtime.

"Do you realise that this year will mark the hundredth year that Jacob's has been in production?" Bernard stated proudly.

I marked the line in my book with a finger and smiled over at him.

"Why don't we do something next summer to celebrate?" he said. "Have a big party."

No sooner had I agreed that it might be a nice thing to do, than Bernard was fumbling through a drawer for a notepad and pen to start compiling the guest list.

He has talked about nothing else but the party since that night last January, and now that the day has arrived he can barely contain his excitement. Bernard came to manage the factory almost forty-seven years ago, when Father's health was failing. I was working in Jacob's as a bookkeeper at the time, and it was pretty much love at first sight.

Outside my window I hear the giddy laughs of my granddaughters Hannah and Kim. I look out to see them negotiating the pathway down to the marquee. They wear strappy gold sandals that are so high – I wonder how on earth they are going to survive the night without twisting an ankle. The breeze blows Kim's flimsy skirt upwards, she shrieks hysterically as she puts a hand behind her to pull it back down. They are the epitome of youth – both smiling and beautiful in rapturous anticipation of what the evening might bring. Mind you, if Rebecca arrives, she will no doubt have something to say about the length of their skirts!

Rebecca phoned yesterday to say that her arthritis is bad this week and that she may not come tonight. I told her that I understood completely but I was silently devastated. Without her, the evening's celebrations will seem incomplete. But what could I say? She is eighty-three years of age and does not *do* parties as a general rule – she never did.

Even when I rang her six months ago to tell her we were having the party, she found the idea wholly unpleasing. Rebecca's husband, now deceased, was a Scottish Presbyterian minister and her life has been one of measured frugality.

"What an odd notion!" were her very words.

Downstairs in the hall, Bernard has organised a

display of memorabilia from the factory. Tools and machines from the earliest days, before technology gradually took over. He has also covered the entire back wall with photographs, one which dates back to the opening day in 1905. The photograph is slightly out of focus, but standing by the factory gates are my great-grandparents, standing in line with the factory workers.

The clearest photograph on display is one of my great-grandmother, known to everyone as Granny Jacob. This must have been taken professionally after the birth of her first child. In it she sits stoically clutching her newborn son, my grandfather, Ben Jacob.

Another photograph shows two young men standing under a huge tree. They have their arms thrown carelessly around each other, their faces set in eternal happiness as they smile into the camera. The man on the left is my father, Peter Jacob. The man on the right is Rebecca's father, Daniel – it is the only photograph we have of him.

My mother, Anna Barry, came to Leeds to live with Granny Jacob, not knowing that she was carrying the child of her dead lover, Daniel Jacob. Her sickness from the boat journey continued for weeks after her arrival, and it soon became apparent that her condition was of a more serious nature. My mother thought of returning to Ireland, but Granny Jacob wouldn't hear of it. After Rebecca arrived, my mother returned to work in the factory, and Granny assumed the role of childminder. I have no memory of Granny Jacob as I was only five when she passed away suddenly one morning, while making her weekly inspection of the factory. But Rebecca was twelve years old, and Granny's death was a terrible blow to her – she still talks about her to this day.

Five years after my mother came to Leeds, she converted to Judaism and married Peter Jacob. I arrived two years after that. I am Ruth Jacob.

We were both brought up as the daughters of Peter Jacob and it wasn't until mother was terminally ill with ovarian cancer that she told us about Rebecca's father and how he had died. I was forty, and Rebecca forty-seven, but we were nonetheless bowled over by her revelation. By that time, father had passed away and poor Rebecca was terribly upset that she never had the chance to talk to him about it. It was a very odd thing to have to deal with, and Rebecca never talks about it anymore. As far as she is concerned, her father will always be Peter Jacob.

When mother died, I couldn't get her story out of my head. No matter how hard I tried to forget about it, it just kept coming back to haunt me. What had happened to the people that had been such a huge part of her life? Her father, her brother. I knew I couldn't rest until I found out. I asked Rebecca's permission, and she agreed that I could go ahead and investigate, as long as I didn't discuss my findings with her. I have written everything down in a journal which will probably never be read, but it was something I had to do. Sometimes I felt my mother was behind me, urging me to find out what happened so she could finally rest in peace.

My grandfather Ben Jacob finally passed away the year after his son Daniel was killed. Irene Jacob left Ireland shortly after her husband's death and went to live in London. Her relationship with her mother-in-law deteriorated further when she discovered that Granny Jacob had brought Anna to live with her in Leeds. Irene married again and went to live in France with her second husband. When Peter informed her of his intention to marry Anna, she refused to attend the wedding and broke off all contact with her son.

Seán Barry went on the run after he escaped from the Four Courts. He hid out in Wexford for a few weeks, then moved to County Kerry where he continued his work as a volunteer for the Republican Army. Four months after he left Dublin, Seán returned to see his father and stayed in a safe house in Dun Laoghaire. However, the city was in the throes of civil war and informers were rampant. The safe house was surrounded by the Free State Army one night as Seán returned from seeing his father. He managed to run to the end of the street – and made it halfway over a garden wall before they opened fire. He was shot seven times and died immediately. My mother was informed of his death in a letter from Joe Maguire which was posted from Cobh, County Cork just before he boarded a ship to America.

She did not travel home for the funeral.

She never saw her father again.

Joe Maguire emigrated to America and joined the New York Police Department where he worked until his retirement. A few years after his arrival in America, Joe met and married a girl from Belfast. They settled in New Jersey and had three sons. He never returned to Ireland and never spoke to anyone about his involvement with the Irish Republican Army. It was only after his death in 1981 that his family became aware of what had happened to Joe. Behind a drawer in his desk they found an old notebook in which he had kept an account of his life in Dublin. Stuck inside the yellowed pages were two photographs. One of his family, taken shortly before his brother's death. The other was of a young woman; on the back was an inscription that simply read, *Anna Barry*.

★ ★ ★

The guests have started to arrive. Factory workers, suppliers, sales reps all mingle on the lawn as their children jump on the bouncing castles hired for the occasion. I put the lid back on my lipstick and gaze at the old woman that looks back from the mirror. When did I turn into this old person? Where did the years go? How I wish I were young again, just for tonight! I would dance till dawn and drink too much champagne – and not feel in the least bit tired when I hear the birds begin to sing at first light

A car winds it way up the driveway and I go to the window to see who it might be. All cars were told to park in the field adjoining the orchard, to avoid any congestion when the party is over. A green Jaguar slows outside the front door, and my heart skips a beat when I see that the figure in the back seat is Rebecca. My nephew, Max, gets out of the car and opens the door for his mother. Slowly, she emerges from the car looking slightly bewildered by the crowds of people who brush by her, oblivious to the importance of her arrival. She leans heavily on her walking stick, and, as if I had called down to her, she turns around and looks straight up at my window. I wave to her but she gives no indication as to whether she has seen me or not. Max takes a blue pashmina from the back seat of the car and fixes it around his mother's shoulders, before helping her into the house.

Rebecca is entering the hallway when I reach the end of the stairs and we both quicken our pace and embrace each other. As I put my arms around her, I am looking over at the last photograph taken of Granny Jacob before her death. I stand back and look into Rebecca's face and realise that they are the same person. And I know that whether it is recorded in a journal, or locked away in our souls – the past will always stay with us.

I slip my arm through hers and we walk outside to join the party.

The End

Published by Poolbeg.com

A Life Left Untold

GER GALLAGHER

"My eyes filled with tears and all the conflicting emotions I had for her somersaulted through my head. I loved her. I hated her. I resented her. And now, looking at her lying on the dirty crumpled sheets, I mostly pitied her."

Iris Fortune never questions why her alcoholic mother Grace seems to have no love for her, while her grandmother Lily has enough obsessive love for two parents. Just who is Iris's father, how can she overcome the die that fate cast for her mother, and would she recognise happiness if it fell in her lap?

When Lily dies and her lifelong friend Sarah reveals some hidden details about the past, Iris has to decide whether to protect her mother or reveal the truth. Keeping secrets can be dangerous, and when they work their way to the surface all hell can break loose.

A novel about three generations of women whose lives have been dramatically shaped by a secret from the past.

ISBN 1-84223-252-5

Direct to your home!

If you enjoyed this book why not
visit our website:

www.poolbeg.com

and get another book delivered straight to
your home or to a friend's home!

www.poolbeg.com

All orders are despatched within 24 hours.